T0129212

Well-bred, well-dressed, and well-read, Henrietta, Harriet, and Hero are best friends who have bonded over good books since their schooldays. Now these cultured ladies are ready to make their own happy endings—each in her own way . . .

Lady Henrietta Parker, daughter of the Earl of Blakemoor, has turned down many a suitor for fear that the ton's bachelors are only interested in her wealth. But despite the warnings of her dearest friends, Harriet and Hero, she can't resist the challenge rudely posed by her half sister: transform an ordinary London dockworker into a society gentleman suitable for the "marriage mart." Only after a handshake seals the deal does Retta fear she may have gone too far . . .

When Jake Bolton is swept from the grime of the seaport into the elegance of Blakemoor House, he appears every inch the rough, cockney working man who is to undergo Retta's training in etiquette, wardrobe, and elocution. But Jake himself is a master of deception—with much more at stake than a drawing room wager.

But will his clandestine mission take second place to his irresistible tutor, her intriguing proposal . . . and true love?

Visit us at www.kensingtonbooks.com

Books by Wilma Counts

An Earl Like No Other
The Memory of Your Kiss
My Fair Lord

Published by Kensington Publishing Corporation

My Fair Lord

Wilma Counts

LYRICAL PRESS
Kensington Publishing Corp.
www.kensingtonbooks.com

Lyrical Press books are published by
Kensington Publishing Corp. 119 West 40th Street New York, NY 10018

All Kensington titles, imprints, and distributed lines are available at special quantity discounts for bulk purchases for sales promotion, premiums, fundraising, and educational or institutional use.

To the extent that the image or images on the cover of this book depict a person or persons, such person or persons are merely models, and are not intended to portray any character or characters featured in the book.

Special book excerpts or customized printings can also be created to fit specific needs. For details, write or phone the office of the Kensington Special Sales Manager:
Kensington Publishing Corp.
119 West 40th Street
New York, NY 10018
Attn. Special Sales Department. Phone: 1-800-221-2647.

First Electronic Edition: October 2017
eISBN-13: 978-1-60183-907-7
eISBN-10: 1-60183-907-3

First Print Edition: October 2017
ISBN-13: 978-1-60183-908-4
ISBN-10: 1-60183-908-1

Printed in the United States of America

This book is dedicated
to the memory of my friend,
MARILEE SWIRCZEK
who lost her battle with depression
in July, 2016.
What she once wrote about someone else
is a fitting tribute to Marilee:

"She truly used her art to teach,
To comfort, to witness.
There's a hole in the soul
Of the universe."

Chapter 1

London

Late September, 1814

Henrietta Georgiana Parker, *Lady Henrietta* to members of the *ton,* that highest echelon of London society, was simply Retta to her intimate friends, to her father, and to her siblings—her younger half-brothers and half-sisters. Her father's siblings, Uncle Alfred and Aunt Georgiana, also affectionately called her Retta. Her stepmother, Countess of Blakemoor, on the other hand, deplored the vulgarity of having one's name shortened thus. Retta did not mind it at all.

One sunny day in early autumn, Retta was hosting visitors in the drawing room of her father's elegant London town house.

One might wonder why the eldest daughter of the Earl of Blakemoor was hostess on this occasion, for everyone knew the countess would never tolerate a lesser being usurping her position—and a stepdaughter was certainly a lesser being.

The explanation: the earl and his countess were not in residence.

Only the children were, along with the earl's brother, the aforementioned Uncle Alfred, and the countess's rather aged and somewhat dotty but lovable Cousin Amabelle, whose presence was intended to lend propriety to the temporarily parentless household that included two single young women. Society would, of course, have considered the newly married Lady Lenninger as far too young to be an appropriate chaperon for her sisters.

To say that only the "children" were in residence was misleading. Lady Henrietta and her twin half-brothers, Gerald and Richard, had all reached the age of majority—and more—and the younger sisters, Rebecca and Melinda, were nineteen and eighteen. Rebecca had recently married a properly titled young man, Baron Lenninger, and Melinda had danced her way through her second season.

Retta was fonder of her twin brothers than of her sisters, perhaps because they were closer to her in age, there being less than three years between them. She often recalled with pleasure hours in the nursery reading to the little boys as soon as she had herself mastered that skill. Even then, she had sensed that Gerald, Lord Heaton, would grow up to be the more responsible and scholarly of the two, and that Richard would always be easily distracted by sport and any scheme offering adventure.

In their nursery days, she had earnestly tried to be as fond of the girls too, but found she shared very few of their interests. Besides, Rebecca and Melinda had, in those early days, spent much time in their mother's company—a circle in which Retta rarely felt truly welcomed. Playing with dolls and dressing up to pretend to be ladies of fashion had never interested Retta, whom her stepmother often scolded for having her nose in a book or riding her pony far too fast. "You will never get a husband if you continue to behave in such an unladylike manner, Henrietta."

The absent Earl of Blakemoor and his countess, along with many of the rest of London's governing ministers and social elites, were traveling via Paris to Vienna, Austria, where the earl was to fulfill a minor role in the Congress of Vienna, set to open at the beginning of November. The countess, Retta knew, would try mightily to fulfill a self-declared role as one of the leaders of the sparkling social whirl intended to alleviate the tedium of the serious business of the Congress: dividing up the imperial spoils of the recently deposed Emperor of France.

Napoleon, of course, was not to be present in Vienna. After his defeat at the Battle of Nations at Leipzig, and his subsequent abdication, he had been consigned to the island of Elba where he presumably licked his wounds and regretted his folly. Retta was aware that not everyone shared that prevailing view of the former dictator's current activities. Even as England had all that summer of 1814 engaged in giddy celebration of the emperor's defeat, there were some—voices in the wilderness—warning that the intrepid Napoleon Bonaparte might have more up his sleeve than his heretofore powerful arm.

Her last casual guests, having stayed the obligatory quarter hour for a "morning" call, had departed, and Cousin Amabelle had excused herself for her customary afternoon nap, so Retta was enjoying a "comfortable coze" with her two best friends—the Honorable Harriet Mayfield and Miss Hero Whitby. The three of them had been thrown together at the age of fifteen in Miss Penelope Pringle's Academy for Young Ladies of Quality. All three girls had been essentially motherless, though Retta did have a stepmother. Both Harriet and Retta had lost their mothers early on—Retta in infancy, and Harriet as a child of seven. Hero's mother, whose love of classical myth showed in the girl's name, had died when her daughter was in her teens, and, on arriving at the Academy, Hero was still feeling her loss keenly. Retta recalled that Hero's father, a wealthy country squire and a doctor, had lovingly insisted that his daughter have the kind of education his wife, only child of a knight, would have wanted for her. Retta and Harriet, on the other hand, had found refuge at the Academy from their rather indifferent families.

Today, seated in the drawing room that the Countess of Blakemoor had recently redecorated in the popular Egyptian style with its vivid colors and a good deal of gold leaf and gold paint, the three friends looked exactly what they were: young women of fashion enjoying each other's company. With her reddish brown hair and hazel eyes, Hero was dressed in her favorite soft green. Retta loved that Hero had long ago got over her embarrassment at her profusion of freckles. Harriet, in half-mourning for her sister and brother-in-law, wore a mauve day dress trimmed with black grosgrain ribbons that complemented her almost-black hair. Retta herself wore a dress of soft gray, simply because she liked the color. It was trimmed with touches of green velvet at the scooped neckline. The colors reflected the color of her eyes, which were essentially gray, but often showed a hint of green, depending on her clothing or mood. Her maid had dressed her brown hair in the popular "Greek" fashion: piled loosely on her head with soft tendrils before each ear.

As schoolgirls, the three had shared many interests. Each had taken supreme delight in escaping to faraway times and places through the medium of books. This fact alone would have earned them the label of "bluestockings" and relegated them to the sidelines in the society of their peers, but they also shared a passion for "doing good deeds," though they might not have expressed it in precisely those terms. In fact, they had earned the sobriquet by which they were known in school for one of those causes. The "Ha'penny Hs" had campaigned—successfully, it turned out—for every girl in the school to give up at least a halfpenny of her allowance each week to provide relief to poor children in a nearby workhouse.

Now, a few years later, while each still held many of those interests and concerns, only Retta followed through on them with any degree of regularity, for the other two had busy lives in the country, Hero in assisting her father in his medical practice and Harriet in caring for her young nieces and nephews who had lost their parents in a horrible carriage accident. Harriet was determined that those children never feel as lonely and rejected as she once had.

"I do appreciate your helping with the Fairfax House charity during your visit," Retta said, refreshing their cups from a covered teapot on a tray before her on a low table. "I hate that you are both returning to the country tomorrow. If only you could be in town more, just think what we might accomplish!"

"Fairfax House is a most worthy cause," Hero said. "What the Fairfax sisters do for abused and abandoned women and children is simply amazing. But I must not desert Papa and his work any longer. That spell he suffered in the spring weakened him far more than he will admit."

"I regret missing the next meeting of your literary group," Harriet added. "I so enjoyed that last one. Imagine being able to talk with Maria Edgeworth herself after all these years of reading her novels! And I envy your having heard Lord Byron read his own work. What a treat that must have been."

"You cannot stay for even a few days more?" Retta wheedled. "I shall be at sixes and sevens once you've left me on this desert island."

Harriet exchanged a skeptical look with Hero and swept her hand in an inclusive gesture at their surroundings. "Such a desert island! A bit like an Arabian seraglio, is it not? At least I think that is the term for a Turkish harem."

Retta shared an amused glance with them. "Yes. It *is* the right term—as you well know. The countess is quite taken with modern fashion."

Retta rarely referred to her stepmother as anything but "the countess" and limited her direct addresses to the woman to "ma'am" or "my lady." She respected her stepmother's position in the household, but Retta had never quite forgiven the countess for persuading her husband to send his eldest daughter away to boarding school when the twins—as was wholly customary for boys—left home for school. The countess's own daughters had been allowed to continue their education at home with a succession of governesses, art teachers, and music masters.

Of course, as she looked back on it, Retta realized that Miss Pringle's Academy was the best thing to happen in her young life, but at the time she had felt lost and rejected and resentful, especially toward the countess who had engineered the change, but also toward her father. Although he had always been aloof with the "nursery set," she had thought he cared about her enough to regret not having her near. She had felt betrayed. Just last week her feelings of resentment and abandonment had resurfaced.

"What is it, Retta?" asked Hero, always one to be in tune with the emotions of those around her. "We lost you there for a moment."

Retta shrugged. "Oh, I was just thinking how wonderful it would be to be in Vienna where such important matters are to be decided—things that will affect all Europe for decades to come, and not just England and France. Wouldn't you love to be there?"

"Of course," Hero said. "Meeting all those important people would be an experience to remember in one's dotage."

Harriet leaned forward from her chair to set her cup down. "Hero, neither you nor I has the connections that would give us entrée to such exalted company."

"But Retta does."

Both her friends looked at her with eyebrows raised in question. "I wanted to go," she said. "Oh, how I wanted to go. I thought I had convinced Papa to allow me to accompany him and the countess, but then he informed me that it was no place for a young woman. As though I were some green school girl!"

"Your stepmother talked him out of it." Fiercely loyal, Hero was always quick to get to the heart of a matter. "I would wager she did not want an adult daughter to show her up. How very selfish."

"Certainly unfair," Harriet said.

Just then they heard laughter and chatter coming from the entrance below. It grew near as five young people climbed the stairs and burst into the drawing room enthusiastically discussing a curricle race they had witnessed. They exchanged greetings with Retta and her friends, whom they had all met previously, and returned to the excitement of the day.

"You should have seen it, Retta," Richard said. "Bingham and Willitson neck and neck on Park Lane."

"Good heavens!" Retta sat up straighter. "It is a wonder someone was not injured. *Willitson* was party to this?"

"Yes. Willitson," Rebecca said with a sly look at her older sister as the newcomers arrayed themselves on chairs and settees. The door opened and Jeffries, the butler, entered carrying another, heavier tea tray. "I ordered more refreshments," Rebecca added.

In the silence that ensued while the tea things were arranged and distributed, Retta surveyed the new arrivals. The girls were, of course, attired in the latest fashion of walking dresses with perky little bonnets to match: Rebecca in a vibrant blue to set off her silvery blond hair; Melinda, whose hair was a darker blond, in soft pink. Gerald, Viscount Heaton, always seemed aware of his position as heir to the earldom—having beat his brother to that status by a mere twelve minutes. Thus he was outfitted in a dark green coat, a gray silk waistcoat, and tan pantaloons; his neckcloth was tidy, but rather conservative—as was the cut of his light brown hair.

Baron Lenninger, Rebecca's new husband, was dressed more flamboyantly in a blue coat, dark pantaloons, and a canary yellow waistcoat; his neckcloth was tied in an intricate pattern that must have taken his valet an age to achieve and his shirt points were so high Retta thought it must be difficult to turn his head. Lenninger obviously fancied himself a member of the dandy set.

Richard, the other man of the group, wore a tidy new scarlet uniform signifying his membership in His Majesty's Army; he had his brother's coloring—brown hair and brown eyes—but a very different disposition. Whereas Gerald was thoughtful and bookish, Richard was fun-loving, teasing, and restless. Often during the recent summer celebrations, Retta had heard Richard lament that "Boney" had been captured and incarcerated before many a deserving young officer such as himself had had a chance to win honor and glory on the field of battle.

When the butler had retreated, taking the earlier tray with him, Rebecca reached for a biscuit from a tiered serving dish. She nibbled at it daintily, then spoke again. "Is it true, Retta, that you refused Willitson's offer? I simply could not believe it when his sister relayed that bit of news to me! He is handsome and titled. What more could a woman wish for, especially one who has been on the marriage mart for a goodly length of time?"

"It is not as though *you* must hold out for a fortune," Melinda said.

Retta felt chagrin and annoyance spreading warmth across her cheeks. She glanced at the painting on the ceiling, a scene of cherubs frolicking in white clouds, and wished herself anywhere but right there, right then. Finally, she brought her gaze back to the group where she sensed sympathy from her friends and curiosity from her family members.

"Viscount Willitson's sister has no cause to be airing her brother's private business," she said to Rebecca, hoping she would see the obvious parallel. She turned to Melinda, who sat next to her on a settee, and added, "Moreover, this is hardly the place to discuss financial affairs—mine or anyone else's."

"So it *is* true." Rebecca ignored Retta's less than subtle admonishment and made a show of examining her nails. "Well, I suppose that means that as an elder—*spinster*—sister, you really should have danced barefoot at my wedding."

"Old wives' tales notwithstanding, I believe my behavior that day was proper for any guest at an elegant *ton* wedding," Retta said primly. As she returned the teapot to its place on the tray, she silently berated herself for allowing Rebecca and Melinda to annoy her so.

Gerald rose to stand next to the unlit fireplace and leaned his arm along the mantel. "So, Retta, now that Willitson's sister has made the matter public fodder, would you care to share with us just why you did refuse the fellow?"

"May we just dismiss the subject with a simple statement that I did not think we would suit?"

He nodded. "As you wish, my dear."

"But that is ridiculous!" Rebecca insisted. "Willitson is not some doddering old man seeking only to get an heir on a young wife before he departs this world. Willitson is not yet thirty. He is heir to an earl. And . . . he is known to be of the Prince Regent's set."

"Viscount Willitson has much to recommend him," said Harriet who could always be counted on to lend a calming influence. "No doubt he will find a suitable bride in due time."

Hero nodded her agreement and tried to divert the topic, if only slightly. "You know . . . in some circles, being of the Prince Regent's set is not exactly high praise. Princess Caroline enjoys a remarkable degree of support in her efforts to force her husband to recognize her rightful place as the future queen of England. One can only feel sorry for the poor woman."

Retta smiled her appreciation to her two friends who sat together on a gold and teal striped settee opposite the one she and Melinda occupied. However, she was not surprised when her sisters refused to drop a subject that would cause her discomfort.

"So why—or how—did you not 'suit'? It seemed a perfect match to everyone. Did it not, my darling?" Rebecca cocked her silver blond head to send a simpering look up at her husband, who had risen to stand near her chair.

"That it did." He patted her shoulder in a show of possession.

"Come on. Tell us, Retta. Do." Melinda bent her darker blond head toward Retta in a conspiratorial manner and placed her hand on Retta's arm. "I mean, after all, we are all practically family here."

"Perhaps Retta is waiting for a knight in shining armor to storm in and sweep the princess off her feet," Richard said with a saucy grin. He leaned back in his chair, crossed his legs, and laced his fingers across his chest.

Tactfully disengaging Melinda's grip on her arm, Retta rose and began pacing the room. She released a brief sigh of resignation. "Nothing of the sort. I just happen to think there should be a certain meeting of the minds—

shared interests, if you will—between a husband and wife. There should be more than just position and—and—whatever . . ." Her voice trailed off.

"I think Retta makes a very good point," Harriet said, twisting to catch Retta's gaze.

"So do I," Hero said.

"Well, you two would, would you not?" Melinda's tart tone bordered on rudeness, and she ignored Retta's glare of reprimand. "My friend Rosemary said that when she went to Miss Pringle's school just last year, the three of you were still famous as a trio of bluestockings who took no interest in society and were held in contempt by the girls who did. And just look at you—not one of you is married yet."

Retta was embarrassed, more by her sister's lack of manners than by the hurtful things she was saying. But rather than becoming overtly angry and making a scene, she merely said, "Perhaps one would do well not to listen to idle gossip."

"Besides, those tales are somewhat exaggerated," Harriet said. "We liked society well enough. Much of it, at any rate. And we loved music and dancing. Still do."

Retta said in her best "reasonable" tone, "We liked books. We *enjoyed* learning. Still do. But in certain circles—"

Hero broke in. "After Retta was so audacious as to criticize members of the Four Horse Club as reckless fools whose racing on public highways was endangering the lives of others and was an abuse of horseflesh as well, Lady Frances Pennworthy gave us the cut direct. Her friends followed her lead. And—not that it matters a great deal—they are merely civil even now, years later. Her brother was one of the leaders of the Four Horse Club, you see."

"The man is still a great horseman," said Richard.

"After that—" Harriet threw up her hands. "Some members of the *ton* have long, if not wholly accurate, memories. And young girls can be very . . . well, adamant in the lines they draw. But you must not think for a moment that we had no other friends—that we cried ourselves to sleep every night out of pathetic loneliness."

"Good heavens, no," Hero said. "Remember the time Miss Pringle herself caught a number of us girls in Retta's room having a gab session—"

"At two in the morning!" Harriet said.

Hero deepened her voice to sound stern. "'You girls stop making so much noise and the rest of you go to your rooms this instant. Disgraceful. Utterly disgraceful.' We have such memories, have we not?"

A murmur of nervous laughter followed as everyone seemed to find refuge in a teacup or a biscuit.

Then Rebecca, setting her cup and saucer on a table near her chair, again returned to the topic she had introduced. "But why, Retta? You have refused at least five offers since your debut. Whatever do you find so objectionable in England's eligible men? The rest of us find them quite unexceptional. Some are quite adorable." A coy glance at Lenninger accompanied this declaration. "You even refused the heir to the Marquis of Dorset, though he comes of excellent family and Mama thought him an eminently suitable match for you."

Retta fought her rising temper. Why on earth was Rebecca pressing her so? "Yes. The countess made her view very clear. But she would not be the one to marry the Dorset heir, to sit across from him at the breakfast table every day, would she? And, yes, he is a very handsome man. A very pretty face. And I doubt there are even two worthwhile ideas floating around in his well-groomed head. Beyond his horses and hounds, that is."

"Oh, I say—" protested Lenninger.

Too late Retta remembered that Lenninger had close ties to Dorset's family. But by now she had become decidedly provoked. She refused to back down. Nor had she quit pacing; she paused in front of Rebecca.

"Look, Rebecca. Your views and your interests have always been very different from mine. I am sorry to say that I have found the marriage mart sadly lacking in possible partners. For me, that is. It is true that I had offers, but most were extended because I am—as Melinda unnecessarily pointed out, and thanks to my maternal grandmother—very rich. What is more, on my birthday in February, I shall have sole control of my affairs. Why would I turn all that over to some fortune hunter?"

Rebecca sniffed. "You cannot appear in company on the arm of your fortune."

Richard gave a low whistle. "Egad, Retta, you underestimate yourself. And you don't think much of men, do you?"

She took an empty chair near him and patted his arm. "I like you well enough, little brother. But I am heartily tired of being seen in terms of all those pounds sterling that I will have one day. I daresay one could take any worker off the London docks, dress him appropriately, teach him to talk without a cockney or country accent, limit his discussions to horses, hounds, and gaming, and you'd have a splendid specimen of your typical gentleman of the *ton*."

"Oh, ho! Did you hear that?" Lenninger asked of no one in particular.

"You do not really mean that, do you, Retta?" Gerald cautioned from where he still stood near the fireplace.

She lifted her chin. "Yes, I think I do."

"You may be right," Harriet said, "but it is a hypothetical proposition that cannot be proved."

"Why not?" Rebecca challenged. "I should like to see you put that theory to the test, oh sister mine."

"As would I," her husband echoed.

"Hear! Hear!" Richard said with a grin.

Melinda squealed and clasped her hands together. "A wager!"

"Oh, Retta," Hero and Harriet said in unison, shaking their heads.

"This is preposterous," Gerald said, straightening his stance. "All of you, do stop teasing Retta and discuss something else. Ladies do not make wagers."

"Spoilsport." Melinda directed a small moue at him.

"She was the one who said it could be done," Rebecca said. "Let us see if she can follow through on such a bizarre claim."

"What would be the terms of such an arrangement?" Richard asked.

They were all silent for a moment: Gerald, Harriet, and Hero apprehensive; the sisters, Lenninger, and Richard clearly considering the possible terms of such a wager. Retta mentally kicked herself for allowing the matter to get out of hand, but she would certainly not back down now!

"I have it," Rebecca announced. "If Lady Henrietta fails to transform her dockworker into a gentleman by her birthday, she will forfeit to me that black mare Papa gave her on her last birthday."

Retta gritted her teeth. All her life, it seemed, she had endured Rebecca's envy and covetousness. The countess had once forced Henrietta to give up her favorite doll to the pouting Rebecca. "Rebecca is just a little girl and you—" Later, it had been a ball gown that Retta had bespoken with a modiste. Nothing would do but that Rebecca should have one exactly like it, though in a different color, thus making Retta's gown less special. Retta remembered the vicious whispers. "Oh, look, another set of Blakemoor twins. Are they not just too sweet?" And now Rebecca wanted her precious Moonstar? No. It could not happen.

But she found herself snapping, "And if I win?"

Rebecca laughed. "I doubt you would want my first born son. No, really—how about my emerald necklace and earbobs? They are worth far more than a horse."

"I cannot believe any of you are taking this idea seriously," Gerald protested. "If Father were here, he would forbid it. Neither Mother nor Uncle Alfred would consider it quite proper, either."

"But they are not here, are they?" Rebecca said. She gestured at Retta. "If *her ladyship* truly thinks so little of English gentlemen that she can pass a commoner off as one of us, let her just try to do so. Perhaps she could present him at an assembly at Almack's."

"Almack's!" Melinda hooted. "Oh, how delicious. Foisting some shabby man off on the patronesses of the *ton's* most exclusive club! If you were found out, Retta, you would be barred from society forever."

"Oh, Retta," Harriet implored, "do not do this. You know how much you love that mare."

"It is an improbable if not impossible task, my friend," Hero warned.

"Well, if she wants to renege, we must allow her to do so," Lenninger said slyly.

"Of course." His bride smirked.

Retta was silent for a moment, wondering just how it was that she had underestimated all these years the full extent of Rebecca's animosity towards her. Then she said, "All right. I shall do it. If nothing else, it should prove to be an interesting social experiment. Your emeralds against my mare.

She rose and extended her hand to the still seated Rebecca. They shook on it just as men might have done in Brooks's or White's or any other of London's gentlemen's clubs.

Chapter 2

There was long moment of silence as the seriousness of this whole idea sank in, then Richard said, "So just how do you intend to select the subject of this, uh, experiment?" His view of the situation seemed to have sobered as he rose to stand next to his brother, his hands clasped behind his back. "What kind of man would you choose? And how will you know who won?"

"He must be reasonably young," Retta said, "and in good physical shape. Intelligent enough to play his part convincingly. If he fools any of the patronesses and other members of the *ton* for an entire evening, I will have won."

"We shall simply go down to the docks tomorrow morning and find someone," Rebecca said.

"The docks are no place for ladies," Gerald said.

"We need not get out of the carriage," Rebecca said, "and with you stalwart men to protect us, surely no harm could come to us."

"I get final choice," Retta said, asserting herself that much at least.

"Oh, no. You will be too persnickety," Rebecca objected.

Richard offered the compromise. "How about this: We visit the docks. We choose, say, three possible candidates. Then Rebecca has final choice from among our three. Gerald and Retta will then interview the man. If Retta accepts him, the wager is set. If she rejects him, we choose another three for Rebecca's choice."

Rebecca folded her arms across her chest. "How many times must we do this before she is required to forfeit?"

"Until *you* select a suitable specimen," Retta retorted.

"I should think no more than three times would be needed," Gerald said.

"Well . . . all right then," Rebecca said grudgingly.

"The point is," Richard emphasized, "the choice will be *yours*, Rebecca. You cannot come back, when all is said and done, and cry 'foul' for any reason."

Rebecca glared at her brothers. "You two always take her side."

Richard rolled his eyes.

Retta said in a more subdued tone now, "Fine. I accept those terms."

Gerald looked around the room. "If you insist on doing this, it must be done in utmost secrecy. No one outside this room can know of it. That condition must extend to Uncle Alfred and all the servants," he warned.

"Right." Richard appeared to be rather cautious now. "Must avoid scandal and ostracism. You know it would extend to all of us. It must eventually be seen as a *fait accompli*. Are we agreed?"

His listeners all murmured acquiescence, but Richard turned to his sisters. "Rebecca? Melinda? No coy hints to your friends or your maids about a secret you just can't share yet."

"We know." The girls spoke simultaneously and with the same note of childish impatience.

"Well, should either of you forget, and let slip even a hint, Retta will have immediately won. Is that clear?" Gerald warned.

The two grumbled at being singled out for the repeated warning, but they did agree.

Then Gerald added, "We cannot all go parading down to the docks in elegant carriages. It will be tight squeeze, but six of us could fit into one of the vehicles Papa left us."

Quickly Hero and Harriet, both of whom clearly had reservations about this scheme, explained that they were returning to the country the next day.

Already Retta was regretting the sheer foolishness of this project—this possible debacle. *How on earth did I allow things to get so out of control?*

* * * *

After a nearly sleepless night spent berating herself for allowing others to goad her into such a scrape, Retta gave up and went down to breakfast early the next morning. She was surprised to find Gerald there before her.

He waited for her to get her food from the sideboard, then said quietly, "You know, Retta, no one whose opinion counts will think the less of you if you wish to, uh, forego that wager."

"And surely you know, Gerald, that I cannot renege now."

He sighed. "I was afraid you would say that."

"I do regret keeping it from Uncle Alfred, though," she said as she stirred cream into her coffee.

Lord Alfred Parker, their father's younger brother, had always been a fixture at Blakemoor House. As a child and even as a young woman, Retta had confided in him, taking to her dear Uncle Alfred her troubles and triumphs. He had invariably listened, offering opinion when it was asked for, offering sympathy when it was called for. It felt strange to withhold anything from him.

Gerald nodded his understanding. "'Twould be impossible, though. He would never condone this. Keeping him unaware is not going to be easy."

"I know."

Two hours later she sat with her sisters on the forward-facing seat in the earl's plainest traveling carriage. Her brothers and Lenninger sat opposite them. It had suited her mood to dress in a walking dress and pelisse of subdued gray that emphasized the gray rather than the green of her eyes. She had tucked her dark brown hair under a rather non-descript straw bonnet. The others were all dressed in their usual finery for, say, a stroll in the park.

She caught expressions of quiet sympathy from Gerald, and from Richard too, but the other three seemed in high spirits at the prospect of a break in routine that promised an adventure, if only vicariously.

As the carriage rumbled near the docks, Retta, seated at an open window, caught the smell of rotting fish, sour mud, and a plethora of other malodorous things. She conjectured that the tide, which reached this far up the Thames, was at its lowest ebb. At least the weather offered a cloudless, sunny sky. Several tall ships rocked gently near the docks. She felt the magical attraction of travel to faraway places, places she had only read about in books.

For a moment she allowed herself a foolish daydream of stowing away on a ship and sailing off to some exotic location. Then harsh voices intruded. She heard not only the shouted orders and advice of dockworkers to each other, but also a few of their comments clearly aimed at persons perceived to be intruders;

"What cause the quality got down here?"

"Ain't no ship takin' passengers today as I know of."

"Bloody hell. They's jus' gonna be in the way."

"Or cause trouble."

Rebecca, seated near the other window, leaned to point across Melinda and Retta. "There. How about that man in the black felt hat?"

"Good lord, Rebecca, that fellow is sixty, if he's a day!" Richard said.

"Well, there is a more likely one," Melinda said, also pointing. "See? That one with a red neckerchief of some sort. He looks young."

Retta saw that the man was young, all right. He was also small and wiry looking and, when he gazed directly at the carriage, there was a vacant look to his stare. She thought he might be somewhat dimwitted. They continued in this manner as the coachman drove very slowly along the road paralleling the docks. She could see that they were attracting some annoyed attention and a few catcalls.

"Yes! That fellow there." Rebecca gestured beyond another man Melinda had pointed out. "That one with dirty leather breeches and a sweaty shirt. See? He is wearing a black cap. He looks a likely candidate. I choose him. We need not look further."

The man was tall with broad shoulders and slim hips. Retta could not discern the color of his hair, but she conjectured that it was dark. He looked toward the carriage full of people he must have viewed as idle sightseers, and Retta felt as though he was looking right at her and possibly through her. But of course, at this distance, that was a ridiculous notion. Suddenly, his attention was diverted by a shout. Still, in that instant, she felt something had somehow passed between them, though she was not ready to acknowledge such an utterly preposterous idea.

"You need not decide so immediately, my dear," Lenninger was saying to his bride.

"Are you sure about this one, Rebecca? There are plenty of others to consider," Gerald said. "We have not traversed but half the dock area."

"You *are* given to changing your mind," Retta reminded her. "Perhaps you would do well to look some more."

"No. I am sure. I choose that one. He looks repulsively rustic and dirty. 'Twill be a daunting task, indeed, to make a gentleman of *him*! Besides, I am ready to faint from the foul odors here."

"Oh, my dear girl," Lenninger said sympathetically, and Retta tried not to roll her eyes.

She looked at the man again. Rebecca was right about his appearance. His breeches had a long dark smear along one leg and his shirt showed large sweat stains. She had been sure Rebecca would deliberately choose what she thought to be a least likely candidate. Her own misgivings and apprehension gnawing at her, Retta watched as Gerald and Richard clambered out of the carriage and approached the man. He was too far away for her to see clearly the expression on his face or hear the discussion, but she saw him lift his cap, wipe his sweaty face on his shirt sleeve, and pause as her brothers approached him; then she saw his disbelief and perhaps a touch of contempt, though she could hear none of what was said. He turned away in what seemed a dismissive manner, but when Gerald and Richard persisted, he nodded abruptly, waved a hand, and went back to his work.

Her brothers returned to the carriage. "His name's Bolton. He agreed to meet with us during his midday break at a pub called The White Horse," Gerald announced. "He says it has a private room in the back."

"I want to be there," Rebecca whined.

"We cannot all go traipsing into a local workingmen's hostelry," Gerald said flatly. "Retta needs to interview him. You do not. It is enough that you know if Retta accepts the choice you made. You will simply have to trust us."

"He's right, my love," her husband cajoled. "We shall drive around for half an hour or so—get some fresh air—and come back for Lord Heaton and Lady Henrietta. We shall hear all about it then."

Retta thought Rebecca was not best pleased, but she appeared to be mollified.

If only Retta could control her own apprehension.

* * * *

Jake Bolton, as he was known on the docks, knew immediately who the two men in fancy dress were as they approached him. After all, the Blakemoor town house, along with certain other homes and establishments frequented by persons found to be of interest, had been under discreet surveillance for several weeks. Even before so many government leaders had departed London for the journey to Vienna, the Foreign Office had learned of efforts to undermine England's position, first at the ongoing discussions in Paris, then at the Congress of Vienna, by leaking information to other participants. The whole thing was a rather delicate matter, for it possibly involved some very prominent people. Besides the Earl of Blakemoor, there were the Marquis of Trentham, the Earl of Hitchens, and Baron de Richfield, all of whom—like Blakemoor, his son and his brother—had varying degrees of access to sensitive information. Moreover, as was the case with many a member of England's aristocracy, these all had strong ties of family or property in France.

"I leave it up to you and Fenton, then, Bodwyn." Lord Castlereagh, the Foreign Secretary, had said in his last meeting with his chief agents before setting off for Paris from which he would continue to Vienna. "I cannot have my hands tied by that wily Austrian knowing what we are planning at every turn. Not to mention that infernal Frenchman!"

Jake knew Castlereagh referred to Austria's representative, Prince Metternich, and France's Prince de Talleyrand. In recent diplomatic communiques and in negotiations in occupied Paris, these two had often seemed able to counter England's proposals even before they were offered. The explanation was clear: a dangerous leak.

Lord Jacob Theodore Bodwyn, third son of the Duke of Holbrook, had not been pleased when the Duke of Wellington, his commanding officer in the Peninsula, then the military leader of occupation forces in Paris, had informed him that he was to be seconded to the Foreign Office in London.

"But, sir," Jake had protested. "I've not been in England for ten years."

"That is the point, Major. We need someone who can slip into position incognito."

"Incognito? In England? Let's not forget that I attended school at Winchester with some rather well-known sorts, and during my years at Oxford, I was hardly what one would call a faceless wallflower."

"I know all about your proclivities for fast horses and fast women, but in India and on the Peninsula too, you proved able to slip into any number of disguises and God knows how many native speakers you managed to fool with your talent for languages and dialects."

"But, sir, that was not in England."

"Castlereagh and I feel sure you will manage it at home too. Look, Bodwyn, you are no longer that fresh-faced ensign—a mere boy—who showed up in my command in India in 1802. That scar alone has effected a change in your appearance and you've probably added a couple of inches as well as a stone or two of flesh on those bones. People see what they want to see—or what you tell them they are seeing."

In a characteristic gesture, Jake ran a finger along the scar that ran from the hairline at his right temple to his chin, a souvenir of the first battle of Badajoz. It occurred to him that a broken nose, another souvenir—this one from an altercation with some partisans—had also altered his appearance a bit, along with the added height and weight. He nodded his reluctant acceptance of the assignment. "Yes, sir."

That conversation had taken place in Paris in late May when Major Lord Jacob Bodwyn had been summoned to the palatial dwelling the Duke of Wellington had occupied on his triumphant entrance into the city. Now, three months later, Jake "Bolton" was indeed back in England after more than a decade abroad, but unable to make himself known to any of his family or friends. So far, he and the team had followed dozens of tips and leads, with little success in ferreting out even one spy, let alone what might be an elaborate network of them. What little progress they had made suggested that the purloined information was almost surely being transferred via shipping activities that had resumed between England and France almost before the ink was dry on Napoleon's abdication document.

Hence, Major Lord Jacob Bodwyn's presence on an English dock in the guise of an ordinary dockworker.

Now he watched with a blend of curiosity and annoyance as the two younger males of the Blakemoor household approached.

"Might we have a moment of your time?" one of them said.

Jake paused and lowered a heavy bundle to rest at his feet; he lifted his cap briefly and wiped his brow with his shirtsleeve, then and stood with hands on his hips. "Sir?"

"I am Viscount Heaton, Blakemoor's son," the same man said. "This is my brother, Lord Richard Parker."

Jake removed his cap and bowed his head briefly. "Your lordships." He put the cap back on and looked the speaker directly in the eye. "Somethin' you need?"

"We should like to discuss a rather delicate proposition with you," Gerald said.

"What kind o' 'proposition'?"

"Perhaps a matter of different employment for you," Gerald said.

"Something better than hauling goods on a dock," the other one said.

Jake hesitated, trying to think what they might have in mind. Were they recruiting more spies? If so, this was rather a crude approach. "I kinda like this job," he said. "Ain't bin here verra long. Jus' makin' me way."

"May we at least discuss our offer?" the viscount said.

"We gits uh half hour fer the midday meal. The White Horse has a backroom." Jake gestured away from the docks.

"Bolton!" An imperious voice called.

Jake picked up the heavy bundle, perched it on his shoulder, and muttered, "Ye're gonna cost me my job."

"The White Horse at midday," the viscount said.

Jake returned to his work puzzled about this meeting and the one that would follow. What did these two have in mind? What might their appearance have to do with his own search for spies? Certainly it was highly unusual that a member of an earl's family should appear on the docks at all. The sudden appearance of two members of a family that was possibly connected to his investigation could hardly be dismissed as mere coincidence. And why had they come to the docks accompanied by women? He dumped his burden on a barge near the pier and turned for the next load. He shrugged, refusing to waste any more energy on the matter now.

At noon, he entered the backroom of The White Horse, bending his head at the low doorway. A long wooden plank table in the room would have easily seated twelve, but there were only two people on the bench at one side, the viscount, and, to Jake's surprise, one of the women. They had half-empty glasses of ale in front of them.

"I took the liberty of ordering your meal and a tankard," the viscount said. "May I introduce my sister, Lady Henrietta."

Jake removed his cap and bowed his head briefly in acknowledgement of the introduction. He slid onto the opposite bench and laid the cap on the table next to a wooden bowl of stew and a hunk of crusty bread. "Ma'am. I'm Jake Bolton."

"Please. Have your lunch as we talk, Mr. Bolton," she said. "We know your time is limited." Her voice was soft, but firm; he thought he detected a note of nervousness, but no hint of haughtiness. An earl's daughter nervous around a working man? Perhaps it was the strangeness of the situation. Her gray-green eyes seemed both compassionate and alert, and wisps of brown hair had escaped a plain straw bonnet. *"Nice,"* he thought, wishing her cloak were not so effective at covering what might be very interesting other aspects of her person.

Careful to keep to the character of the man of lower rank he was pretending to be, he broke off a chunk of the bread, dipped it in the stew, and shoved it into his mouth. He took a long swallow of the ale, wiped his mouth with his shirtsleeve, then asked, "Well, now, Guv, what's this all about?"

To his surprise, it was the woman who answered.

* * * *

Unable to quell her nervousness, Retta had fidgeted at the table as she and Gerald waited for the man. Once he sat across from her, though, she began to think, *Well, yes, this just might work.* Despite a day or two's growth of dark beard, he seemed to be clean. True, there was that streak of mud on his breeches and sweat stains on his shirt, but the man was a dockworker! He was tall and he carried himself with confidence, but with no sign of arrogance. The dark hair and unkempt beard contrasted to a pair of clear blue eyes that gave the impression of seeing more than others might like them to see. She was glad that she and Gerald had decided to explain frankly what they were about, so she said, "We are here to offer you a chance at a better kind of life than you probably have as a dockworker."

He grunted. "I likes me life well enough."

"But might you be interested in something else if you could be trained for it?"

"Like what?"

"Oh, I don't know. Perhaps an indoor servant in a great house? A clerk of some sort? It would depend on your talents, your ability to learn. If you qualify, I am quite sure I can help you to such a position."

"Qualify? What's that mean?"

"That you meet certain conditions."

"Such as?"

"That you are currently free of family obligations and you are willing to work hard at matters that may be totally foreign to you."

"Got no wife or young'uns," he said.

"Good. It is not necessary, but it would help immensely if you are literate," she said.

"Literate?" he repeated.

"Can you read and write?" Gerald asked.

"Some." He picked up his spoon, gripping it much as she had seen farm lads do in the country. He now had the spoon in one hand, a chunk of bread in the other, and he talked around a mouthful of food. "Why?"

"Why what?"

"Why you here? Suggestin' such?"

Retta held his gaze as she spoke. "To be perfectly honest, to win a bet. But also as a sort of social experiment, if you will."

Having finished his meal, he sat back slightly, reached for the ale with one hand and gestured with his other hand for her to continue. Suddenly, it seemed that *he* was in charge of this interview.

She explained the terms of the bet.

He looked at her skeptically. "Don't know as I'd like ta be party ta this here bet. Sounds kinda silly ta me. An' what'cha mean by 'experiment' anyways?"

Retta shoved her own glass aside and leaned forward to speak more persuasively. "I believe, and I should like to prove, that often it is merely education and circumstances—happenstance—that account for differences between people of one class or another."

The man looked at Gerald. "Is she serious?"

Gerald nodded. "She is."

"You win a bet. But what's in it fer me?"

"You will be amply compensated for your time. And presumably you will, in five months, be qualified for something more lucrative than dock work."

He rose. "Ye won't mind if I think this over some? Right now, I gotta get back ta work."

Retta took a card from her reticule and handed it to him. "I hope you will take advantage of this opportunity. Come around by midday the day after tomorrow if you are inclined to accept our offer."

Chapter 3

For the rest of that day and into the evening, Jake thought of little else but Lady Henrietta and her strange proposal. Even as he willed himself to sleep in a shabby room he shared with two other already snoring workers, the matter continued to dominate his musings. To start with, he was intrigued by the idea of a woman's actually negotiating the issue herself. A good-looking woman at that. Not that Jake underestimated what women were capable of doing. On the Iberian Peninsula, some of the smartest and fiercest partisan fighters he had known were women. But to find a lady of the *ton* presuming to present her argument so forcefully in a male environment was unique in his experience, though he did note that her brother's accompanying her had lent a modicum of propriety.

So she wanted to train a duke's son in the ways of society, eh? He grinned at that thought. *This could prove to be very entertaining . . .* He quickly sobered. The whole scheme was ridiculous.

However, the next evening when he informed his immediate superior in the Foreign Office of his meeting with the Blakemoor siblings, Colonel Lord Peter Fenton did not think it so ridiculous at all. The two met once a week at some facility—usually a pub—situated far away from both the docks and establishments likely to be patronized by members of the *ton*. To preserve Jake's anonymity and blend in, both were dressed in the manner of common workers, though in considerably cleaner attire than most of that rank.

Located in "the city," that oldest section of London, this particular pub catered to a motley clientele: day workers, some clerks or scriveners in law offices, a few dustmen, and a chimney sweep or two—as well as two prostitutes plying their trade. These last had seen Jake and his companion as likely targets, but the two men had laughed them off with a vague "Maybe later." A group in a far corner sat around a man with a concertina loudly singing ballads—off key and off-color—the lyrics eliciting loud hoots of laughter. The sawdust on the floor emitted the faint odor of spilled ale and wine. Light from several candles failed to permeate the dark entirely. Jake and Peter Fenton sat at a small table in a dark corner in the rear; a short candle in pewter dish splashed feeble light between them.

Like Jake, Fenton was a younger son—of a marquis rather than a duke. The two men had gone to school and then university together, and they had both served first in India and then in the Peninsula, Fenton as one of Wellington's staff officers, Jake as a "corresponding" officer gathering information among the locals or spying behind enemy lines. In any but the most formal military situations, the two conversed as the long-standing friends that they were. Fenton, as commander of the current investigation, was the only person in England who knew of Jake's undercover work now that Wellington had returned to Paris and the secretary himself was on his way to Vienna.

Fenton laughed heartily as Jake finished his report. "She wants to make you a gentleman? *You*? Impossible. Your tutors could not do it. The masters at Winchester tried. So did the dons at Oxford. Even your housemates there failed, though we did our collective best."

"Go ahead. Laugh if you will," Jake said in mock umbrage. "As I recall, it was *your* idea to put that goat in the headmaster's office."

Fenton grinned, then his expression sobered. "I know Lady Henrietta. Danced with her at Almack's once and at the Messington ball two weeks ago. Pretty, but a bit aloof. Inherits a bundle one day. Said to be something of a bluestocking."

"Yet she entered into this ludicrous bet," Jake said.

"That does not quite fit the picture, does it? But she may be offering us an opportunity we cannot pass up."

"How?"

"If you were to be lodged in Blakemoor House, it would give us more access to persons that we find rather interesting. You know, along with Richter's being a footman in Trentham's London residence, which is in the same neighborhood, by the way."

"Richter was a footman before he joined the Guards," Jake protested. "You are suggesting I pretend to be a dockworker pretending to learn the manners and speech of a gentleman! I have already slipped a time or two on the dock, though no one noticed."

"I have confidence in your ability to charm your way past any mistakes."

"And if this plan fails?"

Fenton sat at an angle to the table and idly twirled his empty wine glass. "We cannot think in those terms. The allies have been meeting in Paris since the abdication. Dispatches from Castlereagh and the duke are filled with their frustration at having Talleyrand and Metternich outmaneuver them." Jake knew "the duke" referred to Wellington and that Fenton was one of fewer than ten people in England who read those dispatches. "The Congress opens the first of November, and it is likely to last for several weeks, if not months. We must get hold of this situation now!" Frustration marked Fenton's tone.

Jake drained his glass and signaled the barmaid to bring them another round. When she had completed that task and returned to her business, he said, "I cannot believe the French and the Austrians have combined forces on English soil."

Fenton shrugged. "We don't know that they have, but strange things happen when politicians get together. The messages we have intercepted thus far—we now have agents in every port from Dover to Bristol—do not indicate collusion. Yet."

Jake ran a hand through his hair. "So. We truly are dealing with two networks."

"Seems so."

They were both quiet for a moment, then Fenton shifted in his chair and crossed his arms on the table. "Blakemoor's heir, Viscount Heaton, is only twenty-four, but he is, like his father, active in the Foreign Office. Not the highest echelons, but he does have access to sensitive information. But so do Trentham, Hitchens, and de Richfield."

"Is Heaton trustworthy?" Jake asked.

"We have no cause to distrust any of these men, but, like so many upper class English people, they all have French ties of one degree or another. Blakemoor's family, especially. The previous earl's mother was the daughter of the Duc de Jean-Marc of Lyon. In the matter of access to sensitive information, Blakemoor's younger brother, Colonel Lord Alfred Parker, is another consideration. He is a member of the House of Commons and is not only an assistant to the Duke of York, the army's Commander-in-Chief, but the two are very close friends."

Jake shook his head in wonder. "The Foreign Office *and* the army? The same family? An unusual degree of nepotism, is it not?"

"Perhaps . . . Lord Alfred is an interesting man, though. Two years younger than the earl. I'm told that in their youth, the brothers were inseparable. As a younger son, Alfred opted for the army. Sound familiar?"

Fenton raised an eyebrow then went on. "He served in India and then Canada where he was severely wounded. Still walks with difficulty."

"At least he survived." Jake leaned back in his chair, only mildly interested in this turn of the conversation.

"Lord Alfred was a renowned scholar as a university student. Surprised everyone when he chose an army career over a professor's chair. Even now, Lord Alfred Parker maintains on-going friendships with some of the greatest minds in England—and on the continent. He is one of the sharpest tools in York's domain."

"Interesting, but why is all this important to me?"

"For three reasons. One, he is very close to the Duke of York—stood by his friend through all that scandal York was involved in a few years ago. Lord Alfred knows where all our troops are at any given time. Two, he continues to live at Blakemoor House where he has his own suite and he mostly works at home, with his secretary acting as a courier to the office of the Commander-in-Chief."

Jake sat straighter. "And? Unless my instincts are steering me completely off course, there is more."

Fenton nodded. "Lord Alfred's secretary is a distant cousin, one Henry Morrow who was born Henri Moreau. Moreau was a mere child at the time, but he narrowly escaped Madame Guillotine. During the Terror, Moreau, with his sister and her child, fled to England. He anglicized his name, but they still have ties to the newly reinstalled Bourbons." Fenton paused. "I think you can see that it might prove very useful to have one of our people on the scene so to speak."

Jake sighed. "And you want me to be the sacrificial lamb."

"Well, yes. A bit melodramatic, but you might put it that way." Fenton reached into his coat to retrieve a packet of letters. "Here's your mail." Because Jake's family and friends thought him to be in France with the army of occupation, his mail was sent to France then diverted back to England—prolonging its final delivery. Fenton grinned. "One of these still has a faint odor of perfume."

"Do not let your imagination stray. Probably my younger sister, Charlotte. She fancies herself a charmer—and the rest of the family confirms that she probably is. She is to make her debut this next season. She was only eight when I last saw her." Jake tried to hide the sudden surge of emotion he often felt in thinking of his family. He slipped the missives into his own coat.

* * * *

Following that initial meeting with Mr. Bolton, Retta had spent the next day and a half engaged in a great deal of troubled musing: *Will he or will he not?* If he did not show up, would she have to go through that distasteful search again? She shuddered at the idea of considering human beings as one would animals at a cattle sale. And if he *did* show himself, how on earth were they to incorporate him into the household? It would not be like hiding that kitten in the nursery when she was nine!

She shared this concern with Gerald, who, when Cousin Amabelle had gone off to her usual afternoon nap, called the others together to bring it up with them. Retta suspected that Gerald was really looking for a way out of this whole situation and she admitted to herself that she would welcome a way out. With Uncle Alfred conveniently absent that day, they had the library to themselves as Gerald and Retta sought to discuss this new issue and to reemphasize the need for secrecy and discretion.

"Is this just an excuse to renege on the wager?" Rebecca demanded from the brown leather couch she shared with her husband.

The others were spread about in a mishmash of comfortable chairs. Retta was glad her father and Uncle Alfred had objected to the countess's desire to change this room in her zeal to modernize. Despite almost daily airings, the room smelled faintly of tobacco smoke, an odor Retta found comforting, for she remembered it from when Uncle Alfred hugged a distraught young girl being sent off to boarding school.

"No, it is not," Retta said. "None of us considered this originally. It all sounded so easy then, did it not?"

"True," Richard said. "And if word gets out, someone is sure to tell Uncle Alfred or write Father—or, worse, it will end up in one of the scandal sheets."

"We must not allow that to happen," Gerald said from his favorite position, which was leaning against a fireplace mantel.

"Right," Richard said. "So the problem is: How do we incorporate this man into the household without stirring up undue interest in his presence?"

"Could he be added to the staff in the stables?" Melinda asked. "What was his name? I have forgot."

"Bolton. Jake Bolton," Retta said.

"Probably Jacob," Rebecca commented.

"Probably," Retta said, visualizing again Mr. Bolton's commanding demeanor, his sky-blue eyes, and the way his shoulders stretched the fabric of a cotton shirt. *Really. Did he have to be quite so attractive an example of the male half of the species?*

Gerald's voice brought her back to the issue at hand. "No, Melinda. Retta will have to spend a good deal of time with him. She cannot do that in the stables."

"A footman, then," Rebecca suggested.

"Possibly…" Gerald drew the word out, obviously considering this proposal.

"Any addition to the staff would have to be explained to Jeffries, who hires and supervises staff members," Retta pointed out.

"Perhaps he could be a cousin come to visit," Melinda said.

"Oh, yes. By all means," Richard said sarcastically. "Jeffries has been with the family only since Noah's flood and knows so few of our relatives. Not to mention what Uncle Alfred knows of the family tree."

"Well, it was just an idea."

"Not a good one," he jibed.

A glum silence ensued.

Surprisingly to Retta, it was Lenninger who came up with the most acceptable solution. "What if we were to put it about that the earl, traveling in France, had received word that Lady Henrietta's life had been threatened because of her charity work and he insisted that someone be hired to protect her?"

"Yes!" Richard chimed in. "Someone from Bow Street."

"That way we can have the man be a house guest." Rebecca sounded triumphant. "Oh, Conrad, my love! Such a brilliant idea."

"Perhaps not 'brilliant,'" Retta said, "but it might work. What do you think, Gerald?"

"It seems a little shaky, but if no one probes too deeply, it should do. "Of course," he added with a direct look at Rebecca, "if it is revealed too soon—regardless of how—the bet is off, you know."

"Yes, I do know. You need not think *I* will make a slip." She gave Retta spiteful look. "I want that mare."

Annoyed, Retta rose to leave the room, but turned at the door to say, "Nevertheless, she currently belongs to me."

She paused at the door when she heard Rebecca add, "You forget that Melinda and Conrad and I will not even be here! We, along with Cousin Amabelle, have been invited to Lady Bertrand's house party all next month. After that, we are to go to Grandmother Howe for the rest of the winter. We shall not even return to town until the end of January. So you may disabuse yourselves of the idea that any of *us* will endanger the scheme."

Retta had herself declined to share those invitations and had temporarily overlooked her own need for a chaperon if Cousin Amabelle were not present. Drat. Well, she would deal with that issue later.

* * * *

The next day, Retta and Gerald met in that same room with Jake Bolton, who had arrived to give them his response. Retta was slightly miffed when the man nodded his approval of the plan for him to appear to be a Bow Street Runner just as though his opinion were truly pertinent to the matter. *Well, maybe it is,* she conceded in an afterthought and reminded herself that she was grateful that he had shown up and was willing "to get on with this here project."

Gerald had taken his customary position near the fireplace and Retta occupied a wing chair nearby. Bolton sat gingerly on the edge of the seat of a barrel chair facing her and twisting his cap, which he had refused to surrender to a footman, but hastily removed in the presence of a lady. He was dressed just as he had been two days earlier, though he had added an open sleeveless jerkin over the shirt. The streak of mud on his breeches had dried and been brushed off, but its stain was still visible.

"Our first consideration will be to see that you are properly attired," she said when the preliminaries of his agreement had been established. "Perhaps as a clerk or a man of business. I have no idea how a Bow Street Runner dresses. My brother will see to that this afternoon. By the way, do you ride?"

"Yes, milady. Me folks is farmers. I learnt early on how ta sit a horse."

"Farmers? I am guessing Yorkshire, but your accent is not so *very* pronounced," she said.

"Yes, milady. Yorkshire. I ain't bin back there in some yars now."

"Riding in a London park is not quite the same as riding a draft animal on a farm, but I assume you are familiar with the basics, at least."

"Yes, milady."

He bent his head and Retta wondered if he might be hiding a grin.

* * * *

That night, Jake lay on a bed staring at the ceiling in what he assumed was a second-best guest chamber in the very large and richly appointed Blakemoor town house. Second best or not, it was the most luxurious accommodation Jake had enjoyed in many months. The room was done in shades of blue with a large, comfortable bed and a thick, figured carpet. An alcove contained an armoire and a marble-topped chest on which was a large porcelain basin and ewer. A deep-cushioned armchair and table were placed near the window. Two gas lamps provided light. He conjectured that at least a mile of convoluted hallway and stairs separated him from any of the family rooms on a different floor. Well, never mind. He would learn his way around soon enough.

Viscount Heaton had introduced Jake to the butler, Jeffries, and informed the man of a threat directed at Lady Henrietta and that Mr. Bolton had been hired to see to her protection.

"Very good, my lord," the butler had said, but Jake was aware of the man's subtle scrutiny. He was also aware that two footmen had been assigned to patrol this floor, albeit unobtrusively. Jake fully approved of Heaton's or Jeffries's taking precautions with a stranger in the household.

The excursion to procure "proper attire" had proved less of a problem than Lady Henrietta might have anticipated, for a Bow Street Runner might easily pass for a clerk or merchant on a London street. Back at the house, Jake was shown to his room and, since the rest of the residents were engaged for the evening, a footman had delivered Jake's supper on a tray. He was pleased to see that someone—he suspected it was Jeffries—had thought to include a newspaper on that tray. The supper was excellent—a fine white fish in a lemony sauce, then lamb chops cooked perfectly. Blakemoor had obviously left his French chef at home. *Yet another tie to France?*

Jake congratulated himself on having passed the first hurdle—getting established in the household. As a soldier in winter quarters, he had once known a former actor who explained in answer to Jake's question, "Getting into character is easier if you can forget *you* and just *be* this other person as you 'strut and fret your hour upon the stage' as the bard put it." That advice had served Jake well more than once. The Yorkshire accent came smoothly enough; he *was* from Yorkshire. He had grown up hearing the speech of country folk—and his family *were* farmers—of a sort. The dukedom consisted of thousands of acres of farmland in Yorkshire and thousands more in Derbyshire, not to mention odd pieces of arable land in Hampshire and Kent. It was a family truism that Dukes of Holbrook never gave up any of the property achieved in several generations of marriage settlements. Moreover, from his maternal grandfather, Jake himself had inherited a vast estate comprised of several farms that had long been managed for the absent soldier by a capable steward.

A twinge of nostalgia prompted him to reread the letters Fenton had delivered to him. He usually tried not to think of being in England all these months, unable to visit his own land, to see to its proper working, to feel the soil, pat the backs of his animals. But most of all, being on English soil again brought home to him how much he missed his family despite a serious rift in the past. His three brothers and two sisters—even his father—had been faithful about writing him while he was abroad, especially Elizabeth, the sister nearest him in age. Only seventeen when he'd last seen her, she was married now—happily so, according to her letters—with three children whom he longed to meet. Elizabeth had assured him that her older children, eight and six, were anxious to meet their war hero Uncle Jake and that neither they nor she understood why he was still in France with the war over and so many other soldiers coming home. His other sister, the oldest of the siblings, was also married—to a plantation owner in the Far East. Jake seldom heard from her.

Letters from his brothers were less frequent than those from Elizabeth and usually shorter, but they gave him glimpses into the life of wealthy young men about town. As a schoolboy and then university student, Jake, who had always felt quite close to his brothers, had been surprised by the jealousy and antipathy with which some of his classmates regarded their siblings. Yes, there had been an abundance of sibling rivalry among the children of the Duke of Holbrook, but the brothers always closed ranks against even the merest criticism from outside.

But that idyllic picture of familial accord had ended when Jake had been sent down from university during his third year for becoming involved in a public brawl defending the virtues of a female who had very few. It was the last straw for the Duke of Holbrook. Jake recalled vividly the dressing down he had received in the Holbrook library.

"You are too old for me to take a strap to you and a public flogging is out of the question, though I swear that is precisely what you deserve." His father's barely controlled fury and disgust had been indication enough to the youthful Jake that this time he had gone too far. The squealing pig let loose during the bishop's boring sermon and a horse race that upset venders' tables during a town festival had elicited stern rebukes, but nothing like this. "You will not bring another iota of shame to this family's name. You are not welcome in this house—in any of my houses—until you have learned at least a shred of proper behavior. Henceforth, you will receive not one penny of allowance. I am purchasing a commission for you. See how you fair as a subaltern in the army. Perhaps the army will succeed where I have failed in teaching you any sense of proper decorum for one of your station."

His mother and his sisters had cried and his brothers had tried to intercede, but the duke was not to be deterred in his solution to the problem of this younger son. In the end, Jake had gone off to serve with the army in India. His older brother, Herald, Marquis of Burwell and heir to the dukedom, had managed from time to time to supplement the meager earnings of an ensign and, later, of a lieutenant. Jake had often wondered if his father knew of this subterfuge. Jake had been a captain when, with his maternal grandfather's death, he had become rich enough in his own right to sell out and live as a gentleman farmer and man-about-town. By then, however, that life held little attraction; he was firmly entrenched in the military life, which, between bouts of sheer boredom, offered excitement and a sense of purpose. Burwell had overseen the absent captain's, then major's interests.

Since his return to England, Jake had, in fact, seen his older brother, but only from a distance as the marquis rode in an open carriage as part of one of the impromptu parades during the summer festivities honoring the Russian Czar and the King of Prussia. Jake had sought permission to visit his family, but both Castlereagh and Wellington refused "until we have a handle on this spy business." Now, as the weeks wore on, Jake deeply regretted all those times in earlier years when his pride had kept him from taking leaves when he could have done so. He had even hovered around the Holbrook town house, hoping to catch a glimpse any of his family members. He knew precisely when the family had returned to the country.

Seeing the camaraderie that seemed to exist between Lady Henrietta and her brother had renewed his desire to try to make amends with his father and spend time with the rest of his family.

His thoughts focused on Lady Henrietta. No green girl, the woman looked to be in her mid-twenties. And she was damned attractive. For a moment, he allowed himself to think of an idle dalliance, but then reminded himself he was on an official job. Still, should the lady be willing . . .

An unmarried, attractive woman from a prominent family and, according to Fenton, an heiress of some means—why had she not been snatched up on the marriage mart? In an era when most women panicked at not having a husband by nineteen or twenty, he had the impression that Lady Henrietta's single status bothered her not at all. She did not seem to be lacking in wits, but she had allowed herself to become embroiled in what seemed to him a patently silly scheme. She treated her brother with respect, but showed no excessive deference. Jake liked the easy rapport he observed between the two of them. He wondered if that extended to the rest of the family. Surely he would find out soon enough.

He laid his letters aside and turned his attention to the newspaper.

Chapter 4

The next morning Jake answered a knock at his door to find a footman standing there with a bucket of hot water.

"Good morning, sir. Lady Henrietta will be happy to have you join her for breakfast in the morning room. I am to show you there when you are ready," the young man recited.

"Thank you, uh—"

"Baker, sir."

"I'll be a few minutes." Jake quickly completed his morning ablutions and shrugged into a tan jacket which complemented his black trousers and a pair of new black boots that he hoped would mold to his feet sooner rather than later.

"Her ladyship's an early riser, eh?" he commented as he strode down the hall and stairs beside the liveried servant.

"Yes, sir. She's always the first to come down—'bout two hours afore the rest does. Usually she heads directly to the stable for her morning ride, though."

"Does she now?" Jake murmured, thinking his "lessons" were beginning already and hoping he did not make some silly mistake in his masquerade.

"Here we are." The footman knocked, and at a clear "Come," opened the door. "Mr. Bolton, milady."

"Thank you, Baker," she said. "Leave the door ajar, please."

So. She is not willing to flout convention by being totally alone with a man to whom she is not related, Jake thought.

The room was small and cheerful with yellow flowered wallpaper above light oak wainscoting. White wicker furniture dominated the room—a round glass-topped table with four padded chairs, along with an oak sideboard, and a few other chairs with colorful cushions. Early morning sunlight flooded in from French doors that led to a small patio and a well-tended garden beyond. A profusion of potted plants gave the impression of extending the garden to the interior. Lady Henrietta sat at the main table with an elaborate silver service in front of her; he noted fragile china plates and cups at two place settings. All the table items were embellished with the earl's coat of arms.

He had noted the room and its furnishings, but it was the woman who truly commanded his attention. Her muslin dress was light forest green embroidered with tiny blue and white flowers. A square neckline revealed just a hint of the cleavage of what promised to be a tantalizing bosom. Elbow-length sleeves ended in a narrow fringe of white cotton lace. Her lower arms and hands were bare. Dalliance crossed his mind again.

She lifted her head and smiled. "Good morning, Mr. Bolton." The smile was devastating, showing a well-shaped mouth and white teeth that were not exactly perfect in their symmetry. Her eyes, a smoky green today—they had been more gray than green on those two previous occasions—reflected only a friendly but business-like expression.

"G' mornin' ta ye, milady."

"Please. Have a seat, Mr. Bolton." She gestured to the other place that had been set. When he was seated, she asked, "Would you like coffee or tea?"

It had been ages since he had had breakfast–or any meal, for that matter—with a pretty woman in such an intimate surrounding. "Coffee, please," he managed, having observed that it was what she was drinking. He willed himself to remember who and what he was supposed to be. "That is, milady, I'd kinder like the coffee, though truth ta tell, I'm more used ta tea in the mornin'."

"I am more accustomed to tea," she said.

"Ye are? Why ye drinkin' coffee, then?" He tried to keep his expression impassive, for he had recognized her correction for what it was.

She suppressed a moue of annoyance. "So which will you have today?"

"Coffee, please, milady."

"You misunderstood," she said, pouring his coffee. "I was attempting to tell you how to express that idea in polite society."

"Oh. I 'spect ye gots lotsa work to do wit' me."

She sighed. "It would appear that I do. So let us begin. This table setting is very simple. Ordinarily, we shall have breakfast in the dining room, serving ourselves from the sideboard, but I thought you might be more comfortable in here today." She proceeded to explain and demonstrate the correct use of items on the table—how to hold the silver, which knife for this, which spoon for that, to use the tongs rather than fingers for small lumps of sugar, and so on. When she had finished, she rose to tug at the bell pull, which signaled a footman to bring a tray with covered plates already filled with buttered eggs, sausages, and ham, along with plates of toast and muffins.

When the covers were removed, Jake noted that his plate was considerably fuller than hers. He looked up with a raised eyebrow, but she shrugged and said, "We did not know what sort of appetite you might have."

"Oh." He tucked in, trying to keep in mind the instructions she had given earlier—and his supposed ignorance. It occurred to him that she had deliberately arranged this morning's tutorial out of deference for what might have been an ordinary dockworker's feeling out of place in such an environment as an earl's London dining room with a number of other people present. He wondered how many *ton* misses would have had such foresight and empathy.

During the meal, she kept up a flow of small talk, explaining that they would work on diction and language, manners and deportment, and, well, whatever might come to mind. She encouraged him to ask questions, any question, no matter how foolish or unimportant he might think it. Jake thought she seemed nervous, but he also noted that she had apparently put a great deal of thought into this endeavor. As they were finishing, the door opened wide and Lady Henrietta's younger brother, Richard, sauntered in. He was dressed in his Guards uniform and did not take a seat, but leaned across the table to snatch a muffin.

"Morning, Retta. Bolton. I trust everything is proceeding apace," he said with this mouth full. He pulled a face. "I am off for some early morning training. Marching. Though why a cavalry officer needs *marching* practice, I know not." With that, he was gone.

She returned to her "tutorial" tone. "Ignore my brother. His manners are abominable. Generally at any meal if you just take it slowly and watch what others are doing at table, you will probably get along without incident."

"Yes, ma'am."

* * * *

Retta had been nervous as she waited for Mr. Bolton to appear in the morning room, for she had been remembering the conversation she and Gerald had with Uncle Alfred the previous night. At their instruction, a footman had informed Lord Alfred when he returned for the evening that Lord Heaton and Lady Henrietta wished to speak with him in the young ladies' sitting room. Meanwhile, Gerald and Retta played piquet as they waited in the sitting room that Retta still shared with Melinda; in the absence of the earl and his wife, Rebecca and her husband had been invited to use the master suite after returning from their wedding journey. Prior to Rebecca's marriage, all three young women had had bedchambers off this room. As Retta and Gerald sat playing cards, Rebecca popped in, wearing her go-to-the-ball finery, to collect Melinda. Retta complimented her on a gown of blue silk with a net overskirt of the same color.

"Very nice." Retta said. "The gown exactly matches your eyes as we thought it would."

Rebecca twirled around, then glanced at a clock on the mantle. "Yes. It turned out very well. I do wish Melinda could be more prompt. I do not want to sit and crush my skirt any more than necessary before the ball."

"Melinda went down ten minutes ago," Gerald said.

"She did? Well, then, I suppose Lenninger has waited long enough for me." She stepped toward the door and added, "By the way, Retta, I heard you two in the library with your Mr. Bolton this afternoon. I think I chose very well." She giggled and left with a parting shot, "Very well, indeed."

Retta grimaced. "Which means she thinks she has all but won already."

"For what it's worth, my money is on you," Gerald replied and handed her the cards. "Your deal."

A short while later, Retta found Uncle Alfred's reaction to be exactly what she and Gerald had expected.

"Wha-at?!" he asked in surprise as he took one of the empty chairs at their card table and Gerald told him not only that a threat had been made against Retta's life, but that a Bow Street Runner was now in residence to see to her protection. "And I am only now hearing of this? Your father said nothing of this in his last communication with *me*."

"I think he was wary of putting the message in the dispatch papers that usually contain his letters to you. This arrived by special courier this morning after you had left for the day. Seems to have been written rather hastily." Gerald handed over a missive he and Retta had spent the better part of an hour composing.

"Hmm." Uncle Alfred read it through twice, then said in a worried tone, "I am not sure one man from Bow Street will be up to such a task."

"I must admit that I was somewhat doubtful about that myself," Gerald said, "but I discussed it with two of Castlereagh's men in the Foreign Office, and they assured me that they would also keep eyes and ears attuned to unusual activities directed our way. And the Bow Street magistrate tells me we have his best man on the job, though he stressed that we must be very discreet about Bow Street's involvement. *Very* discreet."

Retta was mildly surprised by the aplomb with which Gerald carried off blatant lies.

Uncle Alfred scratched his head of snow-white hair and turned his dark eyes on each of them in turn. "Hmm. Well, if Sir William Hendrickson is satisfied with Bow Street's involvement, I shall not question it, though I do wonder why you did not inform me sooner. The army might have supplied a suitable body guard."

"We wanted to do so," Retta said. It took little effort to feign regret, for she really *was* sorry to be deceiving one of her favorite people in all the world. "But you had already gone, and Papa's letter was quite explicit, you see."

She felt relieved when Uncle Alfred rose to take his leave, kissed her on the forehead, and said, "He probably feared you would be off to some charity work in an unsavory part of town—or something of that sort—before he could put protection in place."

* * * *

Now, as she dealt with Mr. Bolton for the first time—really dealt with him, one on one—she was happy to let good manners carry the day. In the back of her mind, she remembered Miss Pringle's admonishing all her pupils, "A lady always seeks to put others at ease no matter differences in rank."

Mr. Bolton proved to be an amiable companion once her brother dashed away. Seeing this as an opportunity to assess the strengths and weaknesses of her "pupil," she allowed herself only an occasional correction of grammar or pronunciation as they discussed the weather that promised a sunny day and then how subdued the city seemed now that the frenetic victory celebrations of the summer were over. They had both seen some of the street parades of nobility and could share impressions of the Czar of Russia, the King of Prussia, and the popular generals, Blücher and Wellington. They agreed that having Napoleon tucked away on the island of Elba was itself cause for England's general mood of self-satisfaction.

"Don't know as how I'd trust that feller even on an island, though. I heard he was allowed 'bout a thousand people to go with him," Jake said.

"Really? So many?" she responded. "Well, perhaps they will keep him occupied enough that he will not even dream of trying to repeat his offenses against the world."

"Mebbe . . ."

This morning, Mr. Bolton was clean-shaven, so the scars on his face were less noticeable than they had been as white streaks through a two- or three-day growth of dark beard. His firm jaw was more pronounced too, but his blue eyes were just as intense as they had been across that plank table in The White Horse.

One could lose oneself in those eyes, she thought, then immediately chastised herself for such an unacceptable thought about someone so unsuitable. A proper lady should never find a near-servant so personally attractive. Lady Henrietta was not especially prim and proper, but she was aware of obligations to her family whose position in society and government entailed certain responsibilities. Nevertheless, she also noted the way the fabric of Mr. Bolton's coat stretched across broad shoulders and that his hands, long-fingered and, like his face, deeply tanned, looked strong but not necessarily rough. That his nails were clean and trimmed struck her as unusual in a common laborer, but she shrugged off that observation. How had he become so tanned on the docks of a city so often enshrouded in cloud as London was?

He gave her a quizzical look, which, along with a half-smile and a raised eyebrow, suggested that he knew exactly where her thoughts had drifted. *Arrogant man. He is probably used to having women fall all over themselves for him.*

She sensed him gazing at her with a questioning look at her hands, and she realized that she had so lost herself in the ease of conversation with him that she was sitting casually with both elbows on the table, her coffee cup suspended between her hands. She replaced the cup in its saucer with a clatter and spoke in a business-like tone that changed the relaxed atmosphere.

"I must attend to some errands this morning, and I should like you to accompany me."

"Yes, milady."

"My brother and I have discussed the matter, and we feel that, initially at least, when you and I appear in public, it would be better for you to seem to be a member of the Blakemoor staff. Jeffries has, I think, laid out proper livery in your room. You and Annie shall accompany me."

"Annie?"

"I do apologize, Mr. Bolton. Annie is my maid. I gather you have not yet met her."

He looked thoughtful for a moment. She wondered if he might object to appearing to be a servant, but then he said quietly, "No, ma'am, I ain't met 'er, but I'll do as ye tell me ta do."

The most important of her objectives this day was to call upon her aunt, Lady Georgiana Mickelson. Since she intended the visit to be a short one, she instructed Mr. Bolton and Annie to wait for her on a bench in the Mickelson entrance hall.

Lady Georgiana, widow of a very successful man of business, was her father's sister and her godmother. Retta had always been fond of her "Auntie Georgie," who had been a fiercely independent woman even before she lost her husband at a relatively young age and was thus forced to cope alone with much that life had tossed at her. Retta knew that Lady Georgiana had held out against family censure to marry a man with whom she was truly in love even though he was engaged in trade.

"William and I were ready to fly off to Gretna Green," she had once confided to her goddaughter, "but the family—even your stepmother—finally gave in, and the wedding took place at St. Martin's in the Field."

That her husband had left her a huge fortune—along with a comfortable home in the Bloomsbury district—had, of course, made her independence more palatable to nay-sayers. An ever-critical society that had long since learned to tolerate Lady Georgiana's eccentricities and her tendency to speak her mind.

With Cousin Amabelle planning to accompany Rebecca and Melinda into the country, Retta needed a chaperon. Who better than her beloved Auntie Georgie—if she could be persuaded to perform that task?

Lady Georgiana received her niece in her drawing room and the two of them sat together on one of two couches upholstered in deep gold. "Oh, my dear girl, what sort of scrape have you got yourself into now?" her aunt asked rhetorically when Retta, after first swearing her aunt to secrecy, had explained not only that she needed a chaperon, but also the particulars of the wager with Rebecca. Retta had always confided in her aunt, who had been far more of a mother than the countess had proved to be. "I suppose if I refused, you would be required to give up the scheme and join your sisters in the country."

"Possibly . . ." Retta conceded. "I had thought of having Miss Pringle suggest someone, but I am sure you recognize the delicacy of this matter and the need for utmost discretion."

"Yes, I do." She gripped her niece's hand briefly. "And I am glad to see that *you* recognize that need too. This could well blow up in your face, my dear, but, frankly, I should like to see you succeed. It promises to be very entertaining—and just the sort of come-uppance some of those society cats have coming to them. And your sisters could use a life lesson or two as well."

"You will do it then? Remove to Blakemoor House?"

"You must give me a few days to arrange matters, but yes, when Amabelle and the girls leave, I will remove to Blakemoor House and try to lend some semblance of propriety to your residing in that mausoleum with only your brothers and Alfred and some strange man."

"I assume Madame Laurent will accompany you," Retta said. "With Rebecca and Melinda both in the country, you may have their rooms next to mine." Madame Laurent, also a widow and a cousin to the earl of Blakemoor and his sister, had been Lady Georgiana's companion for several years.

Lady Georgiana nodded. "But of course. Celeste is away at the moment, attending to some business with her son. That young scamp is something of a trial to his mother. She does not talk about it much, but I gather that he is not exactly happy as a country curate. She will be sorry to have missed you."

"Please do give her my regards. And, thank you, Auntie, for rescuing me from a fate not to be contemplated—the censure of the *ton's* leading tabbies. Thank you so very, very much!" Retta impulsively hugged her aunt and kissed her cheek. "Mr. Bolton is waiting below. Would you like to meet him?"

"Of course."

Lady Georgiana dispatched a servant to bring Mr. Bolton to the drawing room. When Retta introduced them, he bowed and stood patiently as her aunt looked him over thoroughly, but seemed to withhold her judgment for now.

"You remind me of someone I know—or once knew," Aunt Georgiana said in a thoughtful tone. "But never mind that now, I assume you are fully aware of what is involved in this rather unorthodox scheme?"

"Yes, ma'am. Leastways, much as a body can be, I ken."

"And you have agreed to it freely?"

"Yes, ma'am."

"Well, then . . ." Lady Georgiana shook her head in reluctant acquiescence. "I do hope nothing untoward comes of this for either of you."

Mr. Bolton bowed again and Retta hugged her aunt again as they took their leave. They retrieved Annie and set out for the rest of Lady Henrietta's errands of the day. As they approached the carriage, which had been left standing in the roadway in front of her aunt's house, a smart curricle pulled up in front of the Blakemoor carriage. A stylish young couple alit and immediately called greetings.

"Oh, Lady Henrietta, do tell me we have not missed you," the young woman said with a pout.

The man lifted his hat and bowed, "Lady Henrietta, how nice to see you."

"Lord Ralston. Lady Ralston. I wish I could stay to visit with you, but I fear I must get on with an important errand this morning." She gestured at Annie to enter the carriage as Jake held the door, and she paused to exchange a bit of small talk with her friends concerning the weather and her promise to visit the newest addition to the Ralston nursery.

Retta sensed a rigidity in Mr. Bolton that she had not noticed before, and she noted that his hat was rather low on his forehead as he stood stiffly and seemed to gaze beyond the small group.

She took her leave and stepped into the carriage, Mr. Bolton handing her in ever so correctly.

* * * *

Jake had accepted the idea of his seeming in public to be a servant in Blakemoor House as yet another layer of disguise. He just hoped he could keep all these roles straight—and that in performing such duties he might never encounter anyone he had known in his youth. As he and Annie waited for Lady Henrietta, he had learned more about her ladyship and about the dynamics of the family of the Earl of Blakemoor. Annie was a pretty blond girl who seemed to Jake to be rather young for her position as lady's maid to an earl's daughter; he guessed she had no more than sixteen or seventeen years. She was fiercely loyal to her mistress who was a favorite in the servants' hall.

"She ain't like them other two. Or the countess. Lady Henrietta has heart," Annie said fervently. "Always lookin' out for those women and children at Fairfax House."

"Fairfax House?" he asked with mild interest.

"A charity house in Spitalfields run by the Fairfax sisters. They takes care o' women what's been beaten or left without, and orphans too."

"Spitalfields?" This had piqued Jake's interest. "Are ye tellin' me her ladyship goes to sich a rough part o' London?"

"Ya. She does. Takes them clothing and other things. What'd ya think we put them bundles and that basket in the boot fer?"

"'Twasn't my place to wonder none." But in fact he *had* wondered. "She goes to Spitalfields alone?"

"Well, with me an' the coachman an' at least one footman usually. You, today. Sometimes they's one or two other ladies goes with us. Sometimes not."

Before Jake could pursue this discussion, he had been called to meet Lady Georgiana. Later Annie's prattle had been overshadowed by that near miss he had endured outside Lady Georgiana's house.

When he heard Lady Henrietta greet Lord and Lady Ralston by name, he drew in a long breath and willed himself to be but part of the scenery. Years ago Ralston had been a fellow student at Winchester, though two years behind Lord Jacob Bodwyn and Lord Peter Fenton. Still, they had then spent a good deal of time in each other's company, engaging in the usual schoolboy pranks. Now, if Ralston recognized him, all was lost.

Jake deliberately turned himself at an angle to the Ralstons as he held the door for Annie and her ladyship, then jumped in behind them and closed the door. He breathed an inward sigh of relief.

Wellington was right: people see what they want to see or what they expect to see.

Chapter 5

The next morning, at her request, Jake, dressed as a groom in leather breeches and a short black jacket, met Lady Henrietta at the stables. She, in a fashionable medium blue riding habit, was accompanied by an older gentleman in gray trousers and a black coat. Jake immediately—and accurately—surmised that this was Lord Alfred, and, recalling what Fenton has said of the man, cautioned himself yet again to be careful. Introductions over, the three of them turned to their mounts. Lady Henrietta patted the neck of a sleek black mare, murmured to the animal, and fed her an apple. Jake assumed this was the horse her ladyship stood to lose if she lost that wager. He could see why she would mourn the loss of such a fine horse.

A groom assisted Lady Henrietta in mounting, and Lord Alfred, with some stiff-legged awkwardness, mounted a sturdy roan, then looked from Jake to the horse that had been equipped for him. Jake, too, looked with dismay at the animal and thought longingly of his faithful Pegasus being stabled now with Fenton's cattle.

"I say, Retta," Lord Alfred said. "You cannot expect this man to ride an animal that is almost as old as he is! 'Tis a mystery why your father even keeps that nag!"

Lady Henrietta seemed embarrassed as she actually looked at the animal in question. "Mr. Bolton informed me he is used to riding draft animals. I thought it best not to challenge his skills too much."

Lord Alfred snorted. "Even so, the bay will not do. At least try him on that gray. What say you, Bolton?"

"This'n do seem a mite wore out," Jake said.

"Very well. Take old Sailor back and saddle Storm Cloud," she ordered the groom. "It is on you, Uncle Alfred, if there is any problem," she added with a smile.

"We shall see," Lord Alfred replied.

They waited quietly as the exchange was made. The new animal was not in the same class as his Pegasus, but Jake could see it was a tremendous improvement over the bay. Perhaps later he would be allowed to examine Blakemoor's stock to find a mount more suited to his own skills, though, for now at least, he needed to keep up the image of the bumpkin Lady Henrietta thought him to be. Army officers were generally skilled horsemen; even those commanding infantry units were mounted, for officers had to be visible in battle by the men they directed.

Because traffic forced them to ride single file, the three of them did not talk much until they reached the park. Then Jake fell behind the other two. He could hear snatches here and there of their conversation and occasional laughter. It occurred to him that these two not only loved each other, but they seemed to *like* and respect each other. Even as he was aware of his companions—especially the trim female figure of one of them—he set himself to just looking around, enjoying this sojourn in a small world of nature offered in the center of the city. Dew still sparkled on the grass and the sun had not yet aroused the usual town smells. Birds twittered in the trees and shrubbery. They had almost all of Rotten Row, the riding path, to themselves. Lady Henrietta frequently looked back to see how well he was faring. When she seemed satisfied he was not going to take a spill, she put her own mount to a gallop and shot ahead. Now Jake understood why Lady Henrietta chose to ride so early in the morning: she would never have been able to indulge in that breakneck pace later when the park would be full of slower traffic.

Jake moved up to ride next to Lord Alfred who said, "Retta does love to let that mare show off. You are doing very well, Bolton. I think you must have been bamming my niece."

"Mebbe some," Jake admitted, reminding himself to be cautious around this sharp-eyed old man. He tried subtly to hold his horse back, though what he wanted to do was take off after her ladyship. Working on the docks, he had missed the freedom, the exhilaration of riding.

After the near miss with Ralston, Jake had been apprehensive about riding in Hyde Park, a gathering spot for the *ton's* elite. However, he conjectured—rightly, it seemed—that at this early hour, few of that element of society would be up and about yet. He relaxed his vigilance and concentrated on not only keeping his horse at a pace with Lord Alfred's, but also on his mission of gathering information.

"I weren't 'specially listenin' to you talkin' wit' her ladyship, my lord, but Lady Henrietta seems ta know a good bit 'bout yer army work," Jake said.

"She understands it well enough," Lord Alfred replied. "Had she been born a boy, she would have made a fine officer."

"But wouldn't she uh bin the heir then?"

Lord Alfred chuckled. "Right you are, lad. She would have performed very well there too. Smart lass, that one. When I first returned to England, I was all but absolutely finished. Bed bound. Unable to do much of anything but feel sorry for myself. Retta was just a little girl then, but she would climb on the edge of my bed and tell me what was going in the household—even some things she was not supposed to know about." He chuckled again at the reminiscence. "Then she would entertain me with fairy tales and stories for children and tell me how those 'silly stories' *should* have turned out."

"A talker, eh?"

"Well, to some degree. But a listener too. Used to pester me for stories of my 'ventures' in foreign places. Of course I felt I had to edit those for the ears of a young girl. But as she got older, she was having none of that. 'Tell me *all* of it' she would demand. So I did. Well, mostly, at least."

They rode in silence for a moment, then Lord Alfred added in a soft tone, "That young lady very likely saved my life. Made me want to live again. If there is anything—anything at all—I can do to help you protect her, you let me know. In the Commander-in-Chief's office, we always have soldiers who need something to do—especially now that Boney if off to Elba."

"I will, sir. I sure will."

As Lady Henrietta rejoined them, she was not alone. Two men accompanied her. One was a tall blond whom she introduced as Viscount Willitson; the other was Sir Michael Hamilton.

"You know my uncle, of course," she said, "but allow to introduce Mr. Bolton, the man I mentioned to you earlier."

Jake touched his hat and bowed his head to each in turn. "My lord. Sir."

"Bolton." Both men nodded their acknowledgements, but each was clearly more interested in furthering his pursuit of the lovely woman in their midst as they vied with each other in flirtatiously begging dances at an upcoming ball.

"The opening dance, my lady," Hamilton pleaded. A handsome, dark-haired man dressed conservatively, but in the first stare of fashion, Hamilton seemed of an age with her ladyship.

"The first waltz is mine, however," Willitson said in a rather firm tone, but he flashed white teeth in a charming smile. The viscount was perhaps thirty, and sat his horse—a fine specimen of horseflesh—very well.

Just the sort a woman would find attractive, Jake thought with an unexpected twinge of sourness.

Back at Blakemoor House, they changed out of riding gear and reported to the dining room for breakfast. Jake waited at the door for her appearance, for he thought that was what a Yorkshire farmer-cum-dockworker might do.

"I am sorry if I kept you waiting," she said. She wore a pale yellow day dress with splashes of white flowers and green leaves. She looked young—and delectable.

"Ye didn't. I jus' got here."

He reached for the door, but she put a hand on his arm and flashed that devastating smile. "Do not be nervous now, Mr. Bolton. You will do very well. If anyone says anything—or even looks untoward—I shall glare them down and change the subject."

He grinned and opened the door, trying, none too forcefully and none too successfully, to quell a purely physical response to her touch and her smile.

The meal passed without incident.

Jake was introduced to Cousin Amabelle, Baron and Lady Lenninger, and Lady Melinda. He knew the younger women were Lady Henrietta's sisters, and he knew from Fenton's briefing that the sisters and the twin brothers were progeny of the earl's second marriage; Lady Henrietta was the only child of the first marriage. The cousin was a relative of the current countess, and like Lady Blakemoor, belonged to the Howes, a prominent family in Sussex.

Cousin Amabelle looked at him through a near-sighted squint. "Goodness. My father never set such a handsome fellow to look out for *me*!"

"Cousin Amabelle, you were married at fifteen," Lady Lenninger said with what she must have fancied to be an attractive tinkle of a laugh. "Your *husband* would have been responsible for your protection."

"And I was widowed at nineteen," Cousin Amabelle said to Jake. "Never remarried. Oh, I had offers enough, mind you—just like Retta here. But never found anyone to measure up to my Bertie. He was so handsome in his regimentals. Oh, you should have seen him. As handsome as our Richard, even. Other girls were so very envious of me!"

Seeing both Lady Lenninger and Lady Melinda roll their eyes at this, and the men at the table taking decided interest in their food, Jake surmised this was a too-familiar tale to the family. Lady Henrietta forestalled any continuation of it.

"Mr. Bolton and I must have some breakfast." She steered him to the sideboard and said softly, "If you will hold the plates, I will dish up the food. Just tell me if there is something you dislike."

"Looks right good to me," he said, aware that he was still the focus of interest in the room. "Ridin' sure stirs a body's appetite, don't it?" *Even the sedate pace I kept this morning,* he added silently. "Oh! No. None o' them kippers, milady. Never could abide 'em. Too salty by half!"

"You need not take them if you do not prefer them," she said and he grinned inwardly at the subtle correction. He realized there had been a pause in conversations behind them and, turning, he saw Lady Lenninger direct a not-so-subtle smirk at Lady Henrietta as she and he took empty seats at the table.

A footman, holding two pots, automatically filled Lady Henrietta's cup from one and cast a quizzical glance at Jake who said, "I think I should prefer coffee this morning." Lady Henrietta favored him with a smile of approval, and it was almost as though the two of them shared a secret.

In a short while the others scattered to various activities for the day, leaving Jake and Lady Henrietta dawdling over second cups of coffee.

"I think we should start to work on your language skills," she said. "I shall never be able to pass you off as a gentleman if you continue to employ your native accent and diction."

"Aye, milady."

"As it is a nice day—and we have so few of them left—let us go into the garden and work on proper speaking."

"Aye, milady," he said again, thinking of all those hours he and his brothers and sisters had endured in the Holbrook nursery as a nanny or a governess, and later a succession of tutors, had tried to instill proper use of language on several young Bodwyns. Those hours had paid off, though, for they had given him an appreciation of the nuances of language—any language—so that now Major Lord Jacob Bodwyn was fluent in not only his native English, but also in French, Spanish, Portuguese, Basque, and at least one Hindi dialect, all of which he had learned "on the job" so to speak during his army years. He had as well a working knowledge of Latin and Greek from his university days. His concern now was to feign learning to speak "properly" without revealing himself. Curious as to how her ladyship intended to proceed in this task, he followed her into the garden where they occupied a stone bench that was visible from any of a number of windows. It was a small garden sporting only two trees that in summer would provide ample shade, but at this time of the year were shedding their leaves and appearing rather skeletal. A few roses were still trying their best, but gardeners had already prepared most of the flowerbeds for their winter sleep.

"Perhaps later we can read a book or a newspaper together to work on proper pronunciation, but for now let us just chat," she said, fidgeting with her skirt. Was she nervous, then?

"What'll we talk 'bout?"

"Oh, anything that interests us. Tell me about your family. Are your parents still living? Do you have brothers and sisters?"

"Ya. Me da cares fer the land in Yorkshire. Me mum died 'bout seven yars past when I was in—after I'd already left home."

"'Yes. My father has a farm in Yorkshire.' Say it that way."

He repeated it as she instructed.

"I am sorry for the loss of your mother," she said. "Were you and she close, then?"

"I 'spect she got on better wit' d' girls than wit' us boys," he said, remembering his mother as a rather austere, but very correct woman, so conscious of her position and duties as a duchess that she often seemed very remote to her children, especially to her sons.

"Perhaps she felt she shared more interests with her daughters than with her sons," Lady Henrietta said. "Could you rephrase that as I have?"

"Hmm. 'I believe me mum had more in common with her daughters than with her sons.'"

"'My mother' not 'me mum,'"

He nodded and repeated it, more interested in the way a tendril of her brown hair had worked itself from what appeared to be a hasty arrangement after her morning ride. She sat half facing him and her gray-green eyes reflected friendly concern as well as her determination to make these "lessons" successful. She held his gaze for a long moment, then seemed to collect herself and returned to her "teaching." He also found himself distracted by a subdued tangy floral scent that was *not* emanating from those rose bushes nearby. He felt a mischievous desire to tease her and prolong the sense of intimacy, but he had decided earlier that he would cooperate in these lessons fully, and with a degree of formality, so that he could perhaps revert to his customary manner of speaking sooner. Helping her to her goal would leave him in a position to pursue his own mission more efficiently.

"Where were you when you lost your mother?" she asked. He looked at her questioningly. "You said you were away from home when your mother passed."

"Oh. Aye. I were." He had almost slipped there, then inspiration took him. "When I left—uh—the farm, I signed on wit' a merchant ship out o' Liverpool. Didn't get the news 'bout Mum 'til months after it happened when we come back ta home port."

"How sad. You have brothers and sisters, though?"

"Aye. Three brothers and three sisters. Ain't seen much o' me famly in recent yars . . ." He let his voice trail off, hoping she would not pursue this line of the discussion too intensely.

She repeated his information as it might be related in a London drawing room and bade him repeat it after her. They continued in this manner for about an hour, then she called a halt to the lesson by announcing that she would be going out that afternoon.

"Ye want me to go along as a footman again?"

"No, I think not," she said. "We must not raise too much speculation about your presence in servants' quarters other than our own."

"Ye ain't agoin' out to Spitalfields again, air ye?"

"Not today," she said. "Why do you ask?"

"That there's a kinda rough part o' the city, ye ken."

"Yes, I do know it is a dangerous district of London," she said in the precise tones of the "lesson." Then she added, "When I go there again, I shall be sure to have you accompany me, though perhaps not as a footman."

"However ye wish, milady."

He let the matter drop. With her not making demands on his time, perhaps he could finally really explore the household, and, if the servants were as talkative as servants often were, he could learn more about outsiders who frequented the home of the Earl of Blakemoor as well as gain more detailed information about the family itself.

* * * *

Retta's outing that afternoon was to attend the monthly meeting of the London Literary League. Founded to promote literature in all its forms, the League had expanded its interests to include politics and science. Each gathering featured a formal speech on a topical matter, followed by refreshments and informal mingling of participants. Retta loved the League, for it rarely failed to energize her with new ideas. Ordinarily Uncle Alfred would have accompanied her, but he had begged off this day.

"I had dinner at White's last week with Stephenson," he had explained, naming today's speaker. "He is very persuasive on his favorite subject of steam locomotives and rail traffic as the coming thing. Don't know as I need to hear it again."

Meetings were held in members' homes and as today's meeting was to be in the home of a neighbor residing less than half a mile from Blakemoor House, Retta chose to walk, accompanied only by Annie. The hostess today was one of the League's founders, Lady Gertrude Hermiston, who was, in fact, a contemporary of and friends with both Uncle Alfred and Aunt Georgiana.

"Oh, my dear girl." Lady Hermiston greeted Retta with outstretched hands as soon as the butler had announced her entrance to the already crowded drawing room. "Never tell me you walked here today!"

"Why ever not? Annie, my maid, came with me."

"Oh, but we have all heard of the threat against your person. We were just discussing how we applaud your papa's efforts to protect you."

Retta waved her hand dismissively. "Pish-tosh. I doubt I need fear in the middle of the afternoon in my own neighborhood."

"You never know, Lady Henrietta," a male bystander said. "Just last week two homes were burglarized in Russell Square." Retta recognized the speaker as a man whose contributions to most League conversations were either negative or worrisome.

"Homes whose owners had taken the door knockers off and left only caretaker staff as they themselves removed to the country for the winter—or joined all those English folk flooding into Paris these days." This caustic bit of information came from a pretentious matron who prided herself on being "in the know" on virtually everything.

Retta only half-listened to this and other preliminary chitchat. It occurred to her that her friends Harriet and Hero would have loved this—the flow of ideas, the chance to hear a first-hand account of something as new and potentially significant as rail travel. But later, seated next to her Aunt Georgiana, she found her attention drifting as Mr. Stephenson assured his audience that yes, indeed, rail traffic was the wave of the future and likely to make horse and carriage transportation obsolete, though perhaps not exactly tomorrow. The subject was one in which Retta truly was interested, but her mind kept drifting no matter how many times she jerked herself back to the here and now.

What really annoyed her, of course, was to what—or, rather, to whom— her minded drifted: Jake Bolton. She had not been so foolish as to think this project would be easy, but she certainly had not foreseen that it would involve so much deception, which, in turn, caused her to engage in an unusual degree of soul-searching.

When she had so glibly agreed to that ridiculous wager with Rebecca, she had given no thought to having to deceive so many others. Particularly Uncle Alfred. He who had been a confidant all her life. And now she was forced to realize that the deceit extended even to casual acquaintances like Lady Hermiston. Thank goodness she had been totally frank with Aunt Georgiana. But to what extent might she have forced her aunt into deceiving others also? She glanced at the woman sitting beside her. She had no doubt that "Auntie Georgie" would keep her confidence, but might that wonderful lady have to compromise some of her own scruples to do so?

And then there was Mr. Bolton. What right had she and her siblings to play games with another's life? Yes, Mr. Bolton had entered into the scheme willingly. And, yes, her brothers and sisters shared in any guilt that might ensue, but she could not absolve herself of the greater share of the blame. *She* was the one who had made that initial brash statement. And *she* was the one who had allowed herself to be goaded into that truly stupid wager. She supposed she might just call a meeting and declare the bet to be "off." No. That would never do. She could not give up when she had barely begun. Her pride simply would not allow her to make such a humiliating concession. Not to Rebecca! She had no interest in acquiring Rebecca's emeralds, but so long as there was the slightest chance of her winning, she would have to see this through. She simply could not face the thought of giving up her beloved Moonstar.

And what of Mr. Bolton? she asked herself again. The more she saw of him, the more intriguing he became. She liked him. He was bright and willing to learn. He had an amiable disposition and a good sense of humor. She recognized her physical attraction to the man for what it was—as an adolescent she had suffered through a schoolgirl crush or two. But this man stirred her senses as none of her would-be suitors had in recent years. Even now, sitting in this crowded room with a number of near strangers, she recalled what she was sure was a shared feeling of intimacy as they sat on that cold bench in the garden working on his speech. She had been aware of the warmth of his body so near hers and a scent that must have been the soap he used—along with whatever his own essence added to that. She felt herself frowning. That scent. It had reminded her of the sandalwood scent that Uncle Alfred used. Uncle Alfred had once explained that he had acquired his taste for that scent during his years in India. Unlikely that a London dockworker would even know of such, let alone be able to afford it. . . .

Above all, there was the way her whole body seemed more alive, more attuned to the dockworker's presence. A chance touch or a direct gaze aroused feelings that an earl's daughter had best try to ignore. Perhaps it was just as well she had agreed to Viscount Willitson's taking her riding in his new curricle tomorrow. She just hoped Willitson would not try to renew his suit.

The audience's applause brought an end to her musings and she chastised herself for having heard so little of the speaker's message. How would she ever be able to discuss rail traffic intelligently with Uncle Alfred later?

Chapter 6

In the afternoon, Jake went to the mews—stables shared in the city by several houses whose properties backed up to one another. In the mews, each family stored their "town" vehicles and stabled both carriage and riding stock. Grooms and coachmen to tend them had quarters above the stalls and tack rooms. Jake was on a mission: to find, if possible, a more suitable mount for himself. He was generally impressed with the quality of horseflesh owned by the Blakemoor household—with the exception of the bay Lady Henrietta had tried to foist on him.

Finding Viscount Heaton in the stable yard checking on a new acquisition as well as showing it off to two grooms, Jake commented, "Ye've got some fine lookin' mounts here. 'Specially that one."

"He does look good," Heaton agreed, holding tight to a bridle on the horse. "He's a little skittish yet. I just bought him this morning at Tattersall's. They usually have only quality stock there, you know."

Jake nodded. Yes, he knew well enough, but it would not do to reveal just how much he did know.

"Uncle Alfred told me you acquitted yourself quite well out there on Rotten Row this morning."

"I jus' tried ta keep up," Jake said.

"Well, you impressed my uncle—and he is not easily impressed. I expect you will be riding quite often with my sister in the next few weeks."

Again Jake nodded. "She mentioned me doin' so."

Heaton patted the neck of the new horse, a chestnut with white stockings on all four legs. "With this fine fellow, I now have two saddle horses of my own. Come, look at my Blaze."

Heaton handed the chestnut's reins to a groom and led Jake into the stable where he pointed out a buckskin gelding with a blaze of white from its ears to its nose.

"Oh, ya. He looks fine too," Jake murmured.

"He is," Heaton said, "but the thing is, I simply have not the time to exercise both of them properly, and we are currently rather shorthanded in the stable, so you would be doing me a favor if you would take some of the pressure off the staff by riding Blaze here when you go out with Retta."

"Ye sure 'bout this, milord?"

"Uncle Alfred thinks it is worth trying. I suppose that the worst that could come of it is you could take a spill."

Jake hardly knew what to say. Heaton was giving him access to one of the finest mounts in this stable. "I'll do me best, milord. Leastways, I swear I won't hurt 'im none."

He and Heaton entered the stall and, with Heaton watching carefully, Jake made himself properly known to the horse, which seemed a bit standoffish at first, stamping his feet and backing away. When Jake made sure the animal was able to smell him, and then patted his neck and crooned to him softly, the animal came around to accepting this new friend.

"I'll tell the stable hands to saddle Blaze for you when you ride in the mornings," Heaton said.

"Thank ye, milord."

A short while later, Jake enlisted the aid of the housekeeper, Mrs. Browning, in his effort to become more familiar with the house. A kind and open woman of some fifty years or so, she willingly showed him around and opened the "public" rooms to him. She proudly showed him two of the more elegant and currently unused guest rooms. As he had hoped, she turned out to be something of a chatterbox.

"This here's the main drawing room," she said, showing him a large and elegantly furnished room on the first floor. "Lady Blakemoor had it and her private chambers redecorated this past year. Just beyond is the dining room, which you've already seen. The previous countess didn't like for her guests to have go up and down flights of stairs when she entertained."

She went on down the hall to a large double door that opened onto a room that took up fully half the entire floor. "This is the ballroom. You know, many fine town houses have no ballroom, but this one does. See the dais for the musicians? That little balcony overlooking everything is where the children used to watch from. We keep the drapes closed most of the time, but that whole wall has two sets of sliding French doors to let in fresh air during a ball."

"Ver' nice," Jake murmured, noting that the wall opposite the draped doors had two tapestries flanked and separated by tall mirrors. The ceiling had carved walnut panels and displayed two huge chandeliers.

She then took him to the ground floor to the library, which he had previously seen, of course, but now he had time to examine the room more closely. Unlike the drawing room above, this room was clearly geared to comfort rather than fashion. The furniture showed that someone had a liking for leather and wood and, in the plush pillows and lap robes scattered about, for colors from nature—variations of brown and green. There were two huge oak desks in the room and a long map table, as well as the requisite shelves loaded with books on three walls. There were also books scattered about the room on smaller tables and on a chair or two. Jake thought the earl's collection might rival the Holbrook library in Yorkshire. French doors on one wall opened onto the garden in which he and Lady Henrietta had sat earlier.

"The earl needs two desks, does he?" Jake asked.

Mrs. Browning chuckled and pointed at one of them. "Oh, no. That one is Lord Alfred's. Some days he works in here for hours with his secretary seated at his lordship's desk. Not today, though—they're at Whitehall today."

Jake wondered how difficult it would be to get into either of those desks to see if they held anything of interest to him and Fenton. He banished that idea as he strolled about the room, noting titles here and there. One caught his eye and he could not stop himself from reaching for the book and glancing at a page or two. "Do ye think I might borrow this'n?" he asked.

Mrs. Browning regarded him with some interest. "I think it would be all right. The family encourages the staff to read if they want to. Now, if it was out here on a desk or table or a chair or such, I'd say best not, but none of the family would object if you took a book to your room."

"I thank ye." He ran his hand over the rich leather binding.

"Now, this room," she said, bustling herself and him across the entrance hall outside the library, "is the music room. The harp belongs to Lady Rebecca—Lady Lenninger, that is—though she don't play much these days. Actually, never did, but she will probably take it with her when she and Lord Lenninger move into the baron's town house in the spring. Lady Rebecca likes things her way. She insisted her husband have his house completely redone for her. Meanwhile, since Lord Blakemoor is out o' town, the countess said the newlyweds could have use of the master's chambers."

"Who plays the piano?" Jake asked, noting a highly polished instrument positioned so that light from a window would show on the music. That window and another had cushioned seats and there were a number of chairs and small tables about the room. A music stand was placed not far from the piano.

"Lady Henrietta, mostly," the housekeeper answered. "Lord Alfred plays too, but not so often as she does. Lady Melinda had lessons, but I don't think she fancies it any more. Lord Heaton plays the violin."

Jake strolled over to the piano and struck a few keys. The instrument was definitely in tune.

"Do you play?" Mrs. Browning again seemed mildly surprised.

Jake quickly caught himself. "Nay. But I likes ta listen, ye ken?" He wanted to bite his tongue at the lie. The Duchess of Holbrook had required that each of her children master at least one instrument. Jake's had been the piano. His fingers fairly itched to try out this instrument.

"The other rooms in the back on this floor, besides the morning room, which ye've seen, are upper servant's quarters and some service rooms. Kitchen, the servant's dining hall, and footmen's quarters are in the basement. Maids have rooms in the attic."

Her tone suggested that she had shown him as much as she could, so he thanked her and returned to his own room where he changed into his most nondescript street wear. The terms of his "agreement" with Lady Henrietta allowed him one afternoon and evening a week free. Jake knew it was standard among the *ton* to allow servants such time off and he had insisted on it for himself—largely to facilitate his meetings with Fenton.

Early on, he and Fenton had decided it would not be wise to meet always at the same location. After walking some distance from Blakemoor House, Jake flagged a hackney cab. He was not surprised when the driver made a common worker prove he had the fare before taking him up. This time the meeting was at a coaching inn that served a varied clientele of local laborers and coach travelers. Typical of his and Fenton's meeting places, this one was dimly lit, making it difficult to discern the faces of patrons at neighboring tables. Candles on each table helped, but only just.

"Well, has the lovely Lady H made you a gentleman yet?" Fenton asked when they had finished ordering a meal and a mug of ale each from a comely barmaid.

Jake grinned. "She is trying. Taught me table manners so far and she is working at ridding me of the farmer's accent."

"Mind you don't learn too quickly. I still think you might be in a position to learn some valuable information there. Try to get closer to the servants—Blakemoor's and others. Hitchens and Trentham both live in that neighborhood, too, you know. Servants always know more than anyone wants them to, and they share gossip from house to house."

"Right," Jake said. "So far all I've learned is that Blakemoor's offspring are mostly quite ordinary."

"A peer's family is hardly 'ordinary'—as you well know."

"'Ordinary' for who they are. Lady Henrietta does not fit the mold, but her sisters seem to be the usual self-centered, spoiled misses you so often find on the marriage mart. Hard to see them as serious agents."

"You never know. Remember that sweet Spanish girl in Toledo? A general's daughter too!" Fenton finished his meal, pushed his plate aside, and leaned forward. "Anyway, we've had a bit of luck in Devon this week."

Jake merely lifted an eyebrow as he reached for his mug.

"The militia arrested a smuggler near Plymouth who carried documents naming assistants to our negotiators in Paris and Vienna."

"Hmm. Assistants, eh? Trying to find possibilities for bribery or blackmail?"

"You always were a bright lad, Bodwyn," Fenton said. "That was our immediate assumption too."

"This smuggler. Did he know what he was doing, or was he just a courier? Can he be turned?"

"We are working on that angle." Fenton drew a folded piece of paper from inside his coat. "Take this and see if you can figure out later what the devil it is all about."

"What is it?" Jake asked as he took it and slid it into an inside pocket in his own coat.

"A copy of something Richter found on the blotter on a desk in Lord Trentham's place. You do remember that Richter is passing as a Trentham footman?"

Jake nodded and Fenton went on. "It is from the blotter, so was rather smudged and fragmented, but Richter copied it exactly as it appeared. If you look at with a mirror, you can make out what appear to be words and numbers, but none of it makes any sense."

"Code?"

"Very likely. But nothing we've seen before. And no clue as to who left it. Trentham has had a number of guests in recent weeks; some were holdovers from all those victory celebrations this summer. Trentham himself has been laid up with a serious attack of gout—hence an unusual number of callers as well as his physician who comes every day. Anyway, you were always good at decoding messages, so I thought to give you a go at it."

"Thanks. I think."

Fenton rose, paid his tab, and left. Jake ordered another mug of ale and sat nursing it for the next half hour, and then he too left. Back at Blakemoor house—after going through the same ritual with a hackney driver regarding his ability to pay—Jake briefly studied the paper Fenton had given him, but gave it up after a while, and settled into the leather-bound volume he had borrowed from the earl's library.

* * * *

For Retta, the next two weeks were fairly ordinary—on the surface at least. She went out three times with David, Viscount Willitson, in his new curricle, and was grateful that he did not renew his suit in earnest, though he did say on one occasion that he "hoped to win her regard on a deeper level than he had achieved heretofore." Retta put him off with a laugh and suggested that they concentrate on establishing a firm friendship before taking on anything more serious. His agreement seemed reluctant, but he *had* agreed, and the outing proceeded quite pleasantly. Retta was aware of the fact that these excursions took place in Hyde Park during the hours in which London's elites sought to see and be seen, and that her appearance with Willitson was likely to renew gossip in that quarter. She was not surprised when two hostesses saw fit to make the viscount her dinner partner.

Despite the gossip that had followed his sister's disclosure to Rebecca—and thus to the world at large: that the Viscount Willitson had proposed marriage to her—the two of them managed to reestablish a comfortable, though far from intimate relationship, and both managed to deflect presumptuous hints of "an interesting announcement" to come. Such hints, usually from pretentious dowagers, became private sources of amusement between them. Willitson was not much of a reader and his knowledge of current affairs was largely a knowledge of who was having an affair with whom among the *ton*, but he was discreet in relating such *on dits* to her, and the information made seeing these notables in the park or at evening soirees rather interesting at times. As Rebecca had reminded everyone at the time of that infamous bet, Willitson was a member of the Prince Regent's crowd and his insights into the machinations of this or that member of the government added spice to what was reported in the newspapers.

She could not help comparing her discussions with Willitson to those she had with Mr. Bolton. Sensing that he did not really want to discuss his family and youth in any detail, Retta had sought other means of dealing with his diction and vocabulary. When weather permitted, they would sit in the garden; on other occasions—more frequent now that winter was clearly in the offing—they would utilize the morning room. When it was just the two of them on morning rides—as it often was—they would discuss "safer" topics of reports in the newspapers: progress in the Paris discussions, labor unrest in the Midlands, calls for parliamentary reform, and so on. Retta found these discussions far more stimulating than those with Willitson, but she meticulously refused to examine too closely just why she did so.

Their sessions began to assume a pattern. She would either read a passage from a newspaper or bring up a topic she had read about earlier, and then they would share their views on it. At first, he surprised her in that he had frequently read the same item, but later she simply accepted that he might well have some familiarity with a given topic, for, after all, the man had never made a secret of the fact that he was literate. However, his being able to *read* something was distinctly different from his being able to *discuss* it in the sophisticated manner expected of a true gentleman.

On one occasion, she had read a report from the *Times* of the Irish Secretary's plan to set up a Royal Irish Constabulary in the city of Dublin.

"What do you think of Sir Robert Peel's plan?" she asked.

"I dunno. Mebbe them Irishers needs policin'."

"'I do not know. Perhaps the Irish need a police force,'" she corrected.

"Aye." He repeated it as she had phrased it, then added, "But I misdoubt Dublin needs one any more'n London does."

"Just say 'doubt,' not 'misdoubt.' And try not to slur your words together: 'more than' not 'more'n.'"

"Aye, milady. I mean, 'Yes, ma'am.'"

"Good. You really are improving, Mr. Bolton. And I must admit that you are doing so far more rapidly than I had thought you would."

"I am tryin'."

She made no attempt to suppress her smile. "'I am trying.' Try not to drop the *g*."

"Yes, ma'am."

His answering grin sent one of those familiar tinges of warmth, which she told herself to ignore, but not before enjoying it and offering him a smile. "Back to the point: Do you see a need for a police force in the rest of Britain?"

"Aye. I mean, yes, I think I does—do. In cities, anyways. London, Glasgow, Manchester, 'n' so on. Local magistrates can't handle all the different crimes, ye ken. The militia should be called on only fer matters pertainin' to the whole nation—smugglers, an' major unrest—that sort o' thing."

"Hmm. I had not considered it quite that way," she said, not bothering to correct his diction. "Certainly, the present system, with wealthy folk hiring their own protection—often in the form of additional service staff—is neither very consistent nor very efficient."

"Right."

Occasionally, she would bring up such topics during the morning rides when Uncle Alfred accompanied them. After all, this was a mode of discourse she and her uncle had shared ever since she had reached an age approaching adulthood. She noted that Mr. Bolton and the older man often shared political views and vigorously discussed the nuances of this or that issue. She intentionally did not correct Mr. Bolton's use of language on these occasions, but she was glad to see him sometimes correct himself—and she noted that he made far fewer errors with her uncle than with just herself. She thought perhaps he was trying to show her that her efforts were not being wasted.

She brought this up to him at one of their sessions in the morning room. "Is it my imagination, or is your speech distinctly better in some instances than in others?"

He looked thoughtful for a moment, then he grinned and said, "I'm a learnin', milady."

"Yes, you are." She handed him one of two books she had brought to this session. "But you will need to know how to address people properly in social situations and perhaps follow their discussions of others too. This should help. Please read this and absorb as much of it as you can."

"What is it?"

"Debrett's. *The Correct Peerage of England, Scotland and Ireland.*"

"Thick as it is, this Debrett fellow must not of left anyone out." He hefted the book which fell open; Jake glanced at an entry. "Hmm. Don't leave out much about anyone, either. Names their children, even."

"I believe he did try to be thorough, but this was published more than ten years ago, so it may be somewhat out of date. Uncle Alfred has made occasional corrections in the margins. However, it truly may help you to place people and names you may encounter."

He grinned. "Homework, eh?"

"You might put it that way." She stacked the second book on the first. "Here is another you will find useful: *A Gentleman's Handbook: The Complete Guide to Proper Behavior in Social Situations.* This author chose to remain anonymous, but some suspect he may be one of Beau Brummel's crowd."

"More homework? You sure the author is a man? Seems to me them are topics more innerestin' to women than men."

"'Those topics are more interesting,'" she corrected. "You may be right. The countess bought the book for my brothers."

"Well, 'tis only a guess, but I'd say them two learned more from observing Lord Alfred and probly their father than from any book."

"'Those two' and *probably* you are right again, but if one has not had the advantage of such models, one might find the book of some use."

Jake wanted to laugh out loud. His mother had once pressed exactly such reading material on her sons—particularly when one or more of them had committed a social *faux pas*—like shoving past a sister to be first at something or other. "Sit there and read for an hour," she would say. He wanted to share the joke with his Lady Henrietta, but he would have to be satisfied with sharing it with Fenton.

* * * *

Blakemoor House was at sixes and sevens these days as the two younger women of the house, plus the husband of one of them, prepared to leave the city for the winter. Retta tried to avoid the chaos as much as possible, ignoring the trunks spilling over from the bedchambers Rebecca and Melinda had used for years to the sitting room they shared with her. There were also flurries of activity between this area of the house and the master's chambers that Rebecca and Lenninger occupied temporarily. Retta chose to just stay out of the way by accepting invitations she might otherwise have ignored or by subjecting her pupil to additional lessons.

It happened that one afternoon, the five Blakemoor siblings, along with Rebecca's husband, were gathered after lunch in the drawing room. Gerald had thought it prudent for the six of them to meet before the younger women and Lenninger departed for the country.

Rebecca was the last to arrive. She made a show of looking around. "So. Where is your pupil?" she said to Retta. "Should he not be here too?"

"We did not think it necessary," Gerald answered from his usual standing position of authority near the fireplace. The others were scattered about the nearest grouping of seats.

"And the lessons? Are they going well?" Rebecca's tone was a blend of derision and curiosity.

Retta lifted her chin. "Well enough. He is an apt student."

"Hmm. Judging by his manners and discourse at lunch today, I would venture to say you have much to do yet. I think my emeralds are safe."

Retta felt her jaw tighten, but she merely schooled her voice to a false sweetness. "You have not won the bet yet, my dear. We shall see what transpires when you return." The truth was that the idea of winning Rebecca's emeralds, though they were worth a fortune, did not appeal much to Retta, but the idea of losing her beloved Moonstar was nothing short of heart wrenching.

"I think Bolton's a great gun," Richard observed. "He seems to be trying his best."

"Yes, he is," Retta agreed.

"He certainly *looks* better than he did on that dock," Melinda said. "He will cut a fine figure in evening wear. You may be sorry for your choice after all, Rebecca."

"Just remember: handsome is as handsome does, and he must be accepted in the best circles of the *ton*." Rebecca's voice had an edge to it.

Gerald shifted his stance and looked at his younger sisters in turn. "And you just remember that while you are gone, there must be no whisper of this affair. After all, even in the country, you will be socializing with some of London's finest. Any whisper of scandal will extend far beyond the six of us. Mama would be furious. No doubt the Dowager Lady Lenninger would react the same way. You must be very careful."

Her husband shifted uneasily in his seat and Rebecca said, "I do wish you would stop assuming that Melinda, Lenninger, and I are incapable of keeping a secret."

"I merely wanted to reinforce the gravity of the situation," Gerald said.

"Well, now you have." Rebecca rose abruptly and gestured to her husband. "We must get on with our preparations for leaving early in the morning."

* * * *

The Lenningers, Melinda, and Cousin Amabelle—amidst a flurry of last-minute reminders to other family members and servants—were finally on their way the next morning. Baron Lenninger and his baroness rode in style in his crested traveling carriage. Melinda and Cousin Amabelle occupied a hired carriage with servants and luggage in yet another rented carriage. All three vehicles were accompanied by armed outriders and Lenninger footmen riding with the coachmen.

Retta heaved a sigh as the entourage pulled out. Then she and Mrs. Browning spent the next few hours supervising footmen and maids in moving furniture around and preparing rooms for the arrival of Lady Georgiana and Madame Laurent.

Chapter 7

Jake welcomed the departure of those four members of the household. He found Lenninger and his wife to be fashionable fribbles and Lady Melinda seemed determined to emulate the baroness. Cousin Amabelle was simply pathetic, operating as she did within her own confused understanding of reality. He felt sure he could safely eliminate these four as being of any real interest in terms of his primary mission.

As he came to know the residents of Blakemoor House better, he was inclined to dismiss the idea that *any* of them could be directly involved in purloining information for foreign elements. Lord Alfred, the member of the family with regular access to truly sensitive information, seemed very much old-school English, absolutely devoted to king and country. The younger ones were more Whig than Tory, but Gerald, Viscount Heaton, whose position in the Foreign Office might have afforded him some remote opportunity for espionage, just did not seem the type. *But remember the girl in Toledo*, he reminded himself. Richard, the low-ranking Guards officer, did not have the sort of access necessary for a concerted spy. And besides that, Richard's army unit was being deployed to Cornwall to supplement the local militia in its attempt to control coastal smugglers.

And then there was Lady Henrietta. He shied away from any real consideration of her as a conduit for information. Yes, she was bright and concerned with the sorts of things that might interest a spy—or, more particularly in her case, things that might arouse the enthusiasm of domestic reformers. But, so far, he had seen nothing of that sort, either—though she had decided views about the less fortunate beings in the body politic. What was more, she chose to act on her opinions within the bounds of legality and propriety—though she might stretch the latter a bit. He smiled himself at that. The lady had spirit!

He recalled his second trip to Spitalfields with her and Annie just last week. Once again he was attired as a Blakemoor footman, for he had agreed with Lady Henrietta that he would be less conspicuous in that role than in any other. And once again the carriage was loaded with bags and baskets containing food and clothing, but also he noted the inclusion of writing materials, paint boxes, and children's books. The vehicle was so loaded with these items that Jake was forced to ride above with Charley, the coachman.

When they arrived, having driven through a cold rain, Jake and Annie, with the help of the Fairfax butler and a young man of perhaps thirteen or fourteen, were left to do the unloading as Lady Henrietta was ushered upstairs to the drawing room. Jake conjectured that the butler, a man in his forties who was missing one arm, was one of hundreds, perhaps thousands, of ex-military men who had been turned loose on England with the end of the wars on the continent. Jake allowed himself a moment to wonder silently how in the world England would cope with another influx of demobilized soldiers, now that the ill-advised war with the United States had also come to an end.

Jake and Annie were invited to wait for Lady Henrietta in the warmth of the kitchen in the basement where the scent of spices and yeast added to the comfort being offered. Annie introduced the butler and his wife, the cook-housekeeper, as Samuel and Maggie Boskins. The young boy had been sent with a heavily laden tea tray to serve the ladies in the drawing room.

"Jus' the three o' ye, then?" Jake asked to make conversation.

"Oh, no. They's others—prob'ly 'bout ten or twelve, total. Maggie's always got the maids cleanin' to beat all. The two of us—we're sort o' permanent," Samuel Boskins said. "The rest comes and goes."

His wife, a plump motherly sort, placed mugs of hot cider in front of her husband and Jake and Annie who were now seated at the long work table that dominated the center of the kitchen. "Here ye go. This should warm ye up some." She then returned to her tub of bread dough at the other end of the table and picked up the thread of her husband's conversation. "Soon as they gets 'em proper trained, Miss Fairfax or Miss Penelope finds 'em places elsewhere. They mostly does quite well too. Ain't that right, Annie?"

Annie, looking somewhat embarrassed, merely nodded and sipped at her mug.

Jake gestured at Boskins' crippled arm. "Army?"

"Aye. Talavera—'09. Talavera made Wellington a viscount, but me 'n' Maggie had a real tough time of it fer a good many months. Nobody wants ta hire a one-armed man, don't ye know."

"Don't know what we'd a done if the Fairfax ladies hadn't a come along," his wife said. "They was a godsend, that's fer sure."

"Were ye in the Peninsula too?" Boskins asked Jake.

"Nay. Not me." Jake lied for Annie's sake.

"Hmm. Thought you had the look of a soldier," Boskins said.

"Nay. Jus' London docks." Jake drank from his mug grateful for the warm liquid sliding down his throat. "I have ta tell ye, I'm real curious 'bout this place," he said to change the subject. "Bein' in Spitalfields, an' all."

"Ain't much to tell," Boskins said. "The Fairfax ladies inherited this house and a small fortune from their father who had a silk factory here fer many a year. When the silk business died, so did he, an' they decided to set up this house as a sort of refuge for women and children needin' a place ta stay."

"The flotsam and jetsam of the streets, ye might say," his wife said, pounding away at her bread dough. "That's what we was too."

"But in Spitalfields?" Jake asked. "Most folks tend to avoid Spitalfields even in daylight hours."

"Guess this be the place where the most need is," she replied, brushing a strand of graying hair off her face and leaving a streak of flour on her cheek. "Folks here needs a hand up."

"And the Misses Fairfax supply that, eh?"

"Well, they does have help. Lady Henrietta and some other ladies brings much needed goods—an' they often help find places—especially for young folks ready to move on."

Jake glanced at Annie who seemed quieter than usual. "'Tis true. They all does good work," Annie said. "Not like some of the swells, you know."

Just then the young boy came in to announce that Lady Henrietta was ready to leave. Jake and Annie said their goodbyes. Jake was grateful to have a seat inside the carriage for the return journey, for it continued to rain. The excursion had given him new insight to Lady Henrietta. And he now understood better Annie's fierce loyalty to her mistress.

* * * *

Both before and after the trip to Spitalfields, Jake struggled with that slip of paper Fenton had given him. The message Richter had faithfully copied from the blotter was a reverse image. Jake transposed it so it would read as the original must have appeared, but it was still a fragment and it was still puzzling. He had what appeared to be nine rows of alternating words and numbers, all of them in a code that Jake had never encountered.

Furthermore, some of the letters in the "words" seemed to be numbers and in the rows of numbers, there was an occasional letter. Also, there were two symbols off to the side, just below—or at the top—of the others that resembled a hasty *C*, or half a zero, and either a *4*,or maybe an *L*? Initials, perhaps?

He conjectured that the words were the names of geographical locations. He tried matching just the number of letters in the words to locations in both France and England, but he came up with too many matches to make that approach practical. He also thought they might be names of people. He filled page after page in his notebook with possibilities, but still had nothing to report to Fenton.

If only he had more than just a fragment . . .

"Has Richter found anything else?" he asked Lord Peter Fenton when they met at yet another pub.

"No, but Richter did send me a message a few days ago that he had something. Unfortunately, he did not show up at the rendezvous he himself had suggested."

"That's strange."

"Yes." Fenton sighed. "And it becomes more so. I sent someone to Trentham House to do a discreet inquiry. The butler said Richter had been let go without a reference for pilfering."

"Pilfering? Richter?"

"A guest accused him of going through a bag or a valise and demanded that Richter be dismissed on the spot. The butler complied."

"Do we know if Trentham approved?" Jake asked. "Do we know who the guest was? Male or female?"

"No. No. And no." Peter's white-knuckled fist on the table showed his frustration. "The butler refused to explain and other members of Trentham's staff are simply not talking—yet. Richter has family up north—in Durham—but I cannot believe he would just leave like that."

"Nor can I," Jake said. "Meanwhile, I'll keep working on this message."

"Your little charade may be annoying for you at times, but there is still a chance you may come up with something useful. Our sources in English ports report that activity has picked up now that the Congress has finally and actually convened."

"But nothing solid, eh?"

"Nothing solid."

November had brought chilling cold, but during intermittent spells of dry weather, Lady Henrietta insisted on sticking to her schedule of morning rides. Jake thoroughly enjoyed these excursions with her ladyship and, often, with Lord Alfred as well. Now that he had a decent mount in Blaze, he was able to keep up with her when she insisted on something other than the sedate pace that was considered proper for ladies riding in the park. He loved the color that rose to her cheeks and the sparkle in her eyes that the hard riding engendered. He did not love it when he felt he had to lag behind, either alone or with Lord Alfred, because she had encountered on the bridle path some gentleman of her acquaintance. He suspected that at least two of these fellows were rarely chance encounters—especially when he noted that one of them was the same Viscount Willitson he had met earlier. According to the gossip below stairs at Blakemoor House, the viscount's name was often linked with Lady Henrietta's. Jake recognized insipient jealousy for what it was, and tried to brush it off—only to have it recur the next time.

Activity in the park had considerably lessened as a good portion of London's fashionables had left the city for their country estates to wait out the most inclement months of the year. Of course many of that set were frolicking on the continent, now that Napoleon was incarcerated and Europe was free of war and blockades for the first time in years. Jake was glad that Lady Henrietta chose to ride whenever the weather permitted—and that she was not intimidated by a soft drizzle of rain now and then.

The departure of Lady Henrietta's sisters and the other two, and then of her brother Richard, was followed by the arrival of Lady Georgiana and Madame Laurent. Jake found conversation at the dinner table and in the drawing room much more interesting than it had been previously. But he also found himself much more aware of who and what he was supposed to be. At dinner, he would occasionally hesitate at which piece of flatware he should be using and he would look to Lady Henrietta for a slight nod or shake of her head to direct him. The Yorkshire dialect was of course very familiar to him, but remembering to use it among people who were, after all, truly his peers, was not always easy. The longer he and Lady Henrietta worked at his "elocution lessons," the more he was able to revert to his own manner of speaking. He had to be careful, though, not to abandon the dialect too easily. To this end, he often slipped a word or phrase into his discourse, then made a point of "correcting" himself.

"I just cannot believe how wonderfully well you are doing with your speech," Lady Henrietta remarked one day. She leaned back in her chair set next to his at the table in the morning room where they had been reading the daily paper together. "Aunt Georgiana is very impressed too. We were talking about it just last evening."

He twisted to look at her directly. "Other folks's talk has always come easy ta me, ye ken." He deliberately exaggerated his country tone. "You meets up wit so many diff'rent types on board ships, ye ken. What I mean to say is: sailors meet with people from many parts of the world. I have always been quite adept at imitating the speech patterns of other people."

"Have you now?" she asked, holding his gaze for a long thoughtful moment, and Jake suddenly felt panicky. Had he gone too far?

"I truly do be a workin' on it, milady," he said, trying to retrieve the ease of the lesson.

"Yes. Well. Back to our 'workin' on it'," she said brusquely and leaned forward again to tap at the newspaper item they had been discussing. "What do you make of this writer's story about the so-called Luddites?"

"I'm a thinkin'—that is—I think that writer is trying to take a very simple approach to a complicated problem. An' he's got no sympathy for workin' folk."

"'Has little sympathy for working people.' Remember your gs," she cautioned.

"Right. 'Tis just that workers gets lost in these matters. Mill owners and mine owners forget the folks what are puttin'—who are putting—all that money in their pockets. An' them folks are facin' 'nother problem too."

"What problem do they face?" Her precise speech, he knew, was intended to show him how to put these matters correctly without interrupting the flow of discussion too much. He thought she enjoyed their verbal fencing as much as he did.

"All these soldiers comin' home. They needs jobs and some is so desperate that they be willin' to work for less than the fourteen or fifteen shillings a day other folks bin gettin'—have been getting."

"Fourteen shillings?" She sounded genuinely shocked.

He nodded. "Think about that. And trying to feed a family."

"And this General Ludd? You believe he has the answer—destroying looms and threatening strikes?"

"Well, now, milady, as to that, no one seems to know fer sure that there even is a General Ludd. Might a bin someone o' that name in years gone by—twenty years ago--but it ain't fer sure now."

"Nevertheless, the tactics are the same now as then—smashing the very machinery needed to maintain their livelihood. It simply makes no sense."

"Gets attention, don't it?"

"Yes, it certainly *does* get attention. But is it the right kind of attention?"

Later he reflected on this last session. He thought perhaps his adherence to country speech was more pronounced when it was just the two of them conversing—that he truly enjoyed having her correct him. In more normal situations—with others at dinner or in the drawing room, or with Lord Alfred on their rides—he found he dropped those speech patterns more readily. For the hundredth time, he wished this farce were finished; he wished there was not this social divide between him and the lady. He often found himself distracted by the contour of her cheek, the swell of her breast against the fabric of her dress, or the way her eyes changed from gray to green, reflecting her emotions at any given time. There was also the fact that he simply enjoyed her company, that he felt a sense of loss when she declared a session finished for the day. He was forced to remind himself on more than one occasion that he was on a job.

* * * *

Now, several weeks into what she thought of as "the project," Retta was finding the whole situation more and more frustrating—and on more than one level. Keeping the truth from Uncle Alfred was not only difficult, but she felt guilty about doing so, especially now that his sister, Aunt Georgiana, who *did* know the truth, had joined the household.

Also, there was Madame Laurent who had accompanied Lady Georgiana to Blakemoor House and added unforeseen complications. The two older women, now occupying the rooms next her own that had heretofore held Rebecca and Melinda, made liberal use of the sitting room connected to those three bed chambers. In general, Retta enjoyed the company of both the older women, but she did not feel totally free in her conversation when Madame Laurent joined her and her aunt. Aunt Georgiana had agreed early on that it would be better not to share the truth of Mr. Bolton's presence in Blakemoor House with Madame Laurent, for that lady, charming and agreeable as she was, might be inclined to let things slip during dinner conversations, with visitors in the drawing room, or when she visited other drawing rooms. Besides, she might well discuss it with her son, Charles, who was something of a hanger-on with London's dandy crowd when he was in town and often saw casual gossip as a way of ingratiating himself with that group.

There was also the matter of the servants. Blakemoor servants were far too well trained and too loyal to openly question the actions of the family they served, but who knew what was said below stairs? Or communicated abroad on days off. They must have noted that she spent an inordinate amount of time in the company of Mr. Bolton, and surely they too could see the improvement in speech and even his demeanor. This thought startled her. Yes, it was true: his demeanor had taken on a degree of confidence and ease she had not seen in that dockworker twisting his cap in the library some weeks ago. It was almost as though like Hamlet he had been "to the manner born."

What if he had been? She indulged herself in that fantasy briefly, but only very briefly. One afternoon when Madame Laurent had gone driving with a friend, Retta and her aunt sat in padded chairs at a small table in the sitting room, enjoying cups of tea.

"As I told you earlier," Aunt Georgiana said, "your Mr. Bolton seems to be progressing very well in modifying his speech patterns."

"Yes, he does," Retta agreed absently. "And he gets along quite well in conversations at dinner and in the drawing room. I was initially concerned that he might bring up an inappropriate topic, but he has not done so at all."

"But—? I hear a note of worry in your tone."

"But there is only so far I can go with this. What do I really know of what men discuss over port after a formal dinner? Or in a card room or some other 'male only' discussion? How can I instruct him in such?"

"Ask your brother. Heaton can surely help with that. After all, he bears a degree of responsibility in this whole affair." Aunt Georgiana set her cup and saucer down rather firmly.

"I wish Uncle Alfred—"

"Oh, no!" her aunt interrupted. "I love him dearly, but Alfred would put a stop to this whole business immediately. He would see it as 'not quite the thing,' you know. Unfortunately, he would be right."

"But you—"

"Frankly, I see it that way too, but I do want you to come out of this unscathed. Eventually, the *ton* may see this as a great joke—but only if it is carried off with a degree of finesse. Should it become an *on dit* earlier, it could become uncomfortable for all of you. All of us."

"Oh, Auntie Georgie." Retta laughed and gripped her aunt's hand across the table. "You were ever the master of understatement."

"Yes, well." Her aunt's tone became more matter-of-fact. "Have you given any thought to Mr. Bolton's decorum in a ballroom?"

"Hmm? I—uh—"

"If you are to introduce him at a ball, you had best be sure he will conduct himself properly in that milieu."

"You mean—?"

"Dance, my dear. The man needs to know how to dance and how to manage the niceties of a ball. He may have some skill with country dances, but what about the waltz?"

"The waltz?" Retta asked dumbly.

"The waltz. And do stop speaking in monosyllables, Retta."

"Oh, my heavens. I suppose I shall have to teach him."

"*We*. We will teach him. A few sessions in the music room should suffice. I will play for you and you may teach him the steps."

"Thank you, Auntie Georgie. Once again you are coming to my rescue. I remember very well how you used to run interference for me with the countess."

The other source of frustration for Retta was one that she could *not* share with her aunt. It was the fact of her growing attraction to Mr. Bolton. She had fought it for some time, even refusing to acknowledge its existence, but to no avail. She simply could not control that frisson of awareness when their hands happened to touch, or when they brushed by each other, or sat close enough for her to feel the warmth that emanated from his body, or when she caught a whiff of his shaving soap or whatever it was. Most of all, there was that teasing twinkle in his eye when he glanced at her after a minor triumph during a meal or a drawing room discussion. Such exchanges never failed to make her catch her breath for the merest moment, or to feel that her whole body was responding to this man's presence.

She recognized the attraction she felt. But it simply would not do. Society still talked disparagingly of the daughter of a certain marquis who had run off with her father's coachman. The whole family had been ostracized for years. It was true that two decades ago Aunt Georgiana had managed to marry the man of her choice despite his being a tradesman, but Uncle Mickelson had been educated in some fine schools and was immensely wealthy. Everyone knew that eventually enough money could override other objections to any person. But Jake Bolton was a dockworker and before that, a farmer's son. She doubted he had more than a few coins in his pocket. That he was even literate was something of a surprise, though it was a boon she readily accepted since it made their training sessions far more interesting. More and more, she felt that Mr. Bolton just might pull this off for her.

Meanwhile, to fend off her growing attachment to the man himself, she threw herself into social activities that often took her away from home during afternoons and evenings. Even with much of the *ton* in the country or cavorting on the continent, London offered a full social calendar of musicales, soirees, dinners, theater outings, and even a ball now and then. Not only was she accepting more invitations than was her wont, she also encouraged would-be suitors more than she might otherwise have done. Viscount Willitson was, of course, a steady caller, though she had persuaded him to put off any serious suit for the time being at least. She engaged in idle flirtations with the Earl of Beauchamp, the Baron Mathisson, and Sir Michael Hamilton.

She credited herself with knowing precisely what she was doing: forestalling her attraction to Mr. Bolton. She enjoyed her relationships with these others with whom she had, in fact, developed sound, though light-hearted, friendships. So until Mr. Bolton could be presented to society in February and she was free of that overriding obligation, she would welcome these other engagements to keep her from even thinking the unthinkable.

Chapter 8

Jake's particular work in the search for persons leaking information to foreign powers was proving fruitless. Having virtually ruled out members of the immediate family of Blakemoor House, he turned his attention to the servants and to regular visitors.

Jeffries, the butler, seemed an unlikely candidate, for the man was uncommonly alert and protective of the family. Only in recent weeks had he reassigned the footmen alternately charged with the task of seeming to be busy in areas adjacent to Jake's room. Jake had been aware of them immediately, but the naïve Baker had let slip that he was there for more than polishing brass sconces and moving pieces of heavy furniture. Either Jeffries or a footman or Mrs. Browning had, in those first weeks, always been nearby whenever Jake was alone with Lady Henrietta, but that watchfulness had gradually lessened.

To keep to the guise of his being in the house to provide protection to the "threatened" Lady Henrietta, Jake, along with Annie, usually accompanied her ladyship on shopping excursions or when she called on friends in the afternoon. On shopping trips he dressed in ordinary attire to blend in with street traffic, but when she made calls or visited the Fairfax sisters, he wore the Blakemoor livery. Moreover, on those occasions he was armed; a pistol in a holster hung in the carriage, but Jake also had a lethal knife in his right boot. When she went to Spitalfields, Lady Henrietta herself also carried a small pistol in her reticule.

"You know how to use that thing?" he had asked when he first noticed the unusual bulge in a lady's handbag.

"Of course I do." She sounded defensive.

"Just askin'. Not many ladies does."

"Well, I do. Uncle Alfred and my brothers taught me."

"I 'magine that means ye badgered 'em into teachin' ye. Ain't that right?"
She lifted her chin. "Well—"

"Mind. I ain't criticizin'. 'Tis good for a female to be able to pertect herself."

"Oh, I am so glad you approve, Mr. Bolton."

Jake grinned at her tone, but he did not pursue the discussion. Later, over a cup of tea in the servants' hall, Annie took him to task for being "cheeky" with her mistress.

"I know that you bein' a Bow Street Runner an' all, you ain't really a servant like the rest of us, but you hadn't oughta talk to her ladyship like that."

"Those Fairfax ladies taught ye real good, didn't they?" he said.

"They done a lot more than just teach me how ta get on," she said.

"Oh?"

But she refused to explain further and he thought she welcomed a summons just then to attend her ladyship.

Jake was thankful that his bodyguard duties did not extend to accompanying Lady Henrietta when she went out driving with a gentleman friend. Those fellows were deemed sufficient to fend off any threats to her. He did occasionally accompany her and Lady Georgiana and Madame Laurent when they attended the theatre or an evening soiree, though he saw them only to the door and then reappeared with the coachman later.

When he was free to do so, he often wandered into the library or the servants' hall off the kitchen. Early on, Jake had been welcomed in the servants' hall where staff members were allowed to take breaks during the day.

"That is quite unusual, isn't it?" he asked Mrs. Browning when she joined him and two others one afternoon.

"Yes, 'tis. But so long as everyone does their work, no one complains. Mind you, Lady Blakemoor might want to have things more rigid like, but her husband and Lord Alfred leave matters of staff up to Mr. Jeffries an' me. We all been in Blakemoor House longer than she has."

"So everyone just has the run of the whole house?" Jake asked.

"Oh, no. By no means. People got particular assignments, and if they be found in other places, they better have a good reason."

"Like Baker and Wilson always outside my room, eh?"

She looked a little sheepish. "Mr. Jeffries was just being cautious, you see."

"Yes, I do see," Jake told her. And, indeed, he did. He knew that many a great house, both in town and in the country, ran smoothly largely through the efforts of retainers like Mr. Jeffries and Mrs. Browning. His father's houses, both in Yorkshire and here in London, certainly did. He hoped that was true of his own property as well . . .

Jake knew the staff mostly regarded him as "neither fish nor flesh." He was not a member of the family; he was not precisely a servant; nor was he a genuine guest, though servants had obviously been instructed to treat him as such. He welcomed his ambivalent status, for it allowed him freedoms he might not otherwise have.

On another occasion when he joined staff members taking a break, he found himself having tea with two of his favorites, Annie and Baker along with another footman and maid. It was not the first time he had seen Annie and Baker together, and he wondered if there might a bit of romance in the air there.

"Well," he said, trying to sound very casual, "I imagine the absence of the earl and countess, and now these others, has made a big difference in the work load for the staff."

"Uh, not much," Baker said. "Lord and Lady Blakemoor traveled with mostly their personal servants—his valet and her maid. John Coachman and a couple of footmen. 'Tis said they planned to hire temporary service in Paris and Vienna. They traveled with other folks too. The gentlemen hired some ex-soldiers for protection against brigands and such. It was quite a sight to see, I tell ye. Like one o' them medieval processions of royalty! Same with the young ladies, though there's not as much danger here in England, I'm thinkin'."

"That could be," Jake agreed.

"Still, the house needs taken proper care of. Mrs. Browning always sees absence of family as a time for what she calls 'deep cleaning' though it must not interfere with normal activities. There's always some extras too, you know," said the other maid, a woman in her late twenties named Bertha Morton. "Like Lady Georgiana and Madame Laurent, now." Jake thought she might have wanted to add "and you," but she did not.

"And there are always callers too," Baker added. "Almost as many as when the whole family is here. Lady Henrietta has many friends. So do the other ladies."

"An' don't forget those folks who come here regularly, but are not especially social callers," said the other footman, the one named Wilson.

"Oh, you mean that lawyer fellow. Brixton. He handles business affairs for both Lord Blakemoor and Lord Alfred," Baker explained to Jake. "But he comes only two-three times a month."

"Don't forget Mr. Morrow," Annie said. "Or the doctor."

Jake had known Morrow, Lord Alfred's secretary, but not the doctor. "Doctor?" he queried.

"Sir Cecil Lindstrom," Wilson said rolling his eyes. "God help you should you announce him as a mere mister."

"Touchy, eh?" Jake encouraged.

"Oh, yeah," Wilson said. "He attends some of the Prince's crowd and doesn't want you to forget it."

"So, who does he treat here?" Jake asked. "I've not seen him yet."

"You will," Baker said. "He used to treat Lord Alfred real regular like, but now he just comes when he feels like it. Got to be a real good friend of Lord Alfred an' I guess—to give credit where 'tis due—he really did help his lordship walk better."

"He's treating Lord Trentham's gout too," Wilson said. "Poor Lord Trentham's been laid up over a month now."

Jake wanted to ask about the missing Trentham footman, but hesitated to introduce the topic lest his curiosity be seen as extraordinary.

But then the group broke up as they returned to their assigned tasks.

* * * *

One afternoon later in the week, as the ladies entertained callers in the drawing room, and Jake knew Lord Alfred and his secretary to be out, he thought it might be the opportune time to investigate those desks in the library. Armed with his small penknife that had two tiny blades, one of which resembled an icepick more than a knife blade, and carrying the book he had borrowed earlier, Jake entered the library and looked around to be certain that he did, indeed, have the place to himself. He left the door just slightly ajar so that he might hear any activity in the entrance hall.

Using that odd blade of his knife, he quickly picked the lock of Lord Alfred's desk. He found what he might have expected to find—some unfinished correspondence with an Oxford don interested in pre-Roman Britain, and a letter outlining expenditures to be made on Blakemoor country properties in the absence of the earl, and, of course, some paperwork from his position as an assistant to the Duke of York. These pages, so far as Jake could tell, dealt with procurements and named firms from which the army would be buying uniforms, weapons, foodstuffs and other necessities to keep an army adequately supplied. But he also noted that the document dealt with the *distribution* of goods—and such information would immediately signal the locations and numbers of troops at various postings.

Jake studied these pages briefly, but hearing Lord Alfred greet the footman at the street door and the footman's response to his lordship and to Mr. Morrow, he quickly put them back in place and relocked the desk drawer. He stood, pushed the chair to its original position, grabbed up his book, and started to saunter casually across the room.

"Ah, Bolton. Were you wanting something of me?" Lord Alfred strolled toward his desk and Morrow took a seat at the other desk. Jake said a prayer of hope that he had disturbed nothing on the surface of Lord Alfred's desk, for he was sure that this old man would miss nothing in his mental inventory of the desk top.

"No, sir. I just came in to return this book I borrowed a few days ago. Mrs. Browning said as how you'd probably not mind."

"No, no. My brother and I always encourage folks to read. 'Tis the path to enlightenment, you know."

"Yes, sir."

Lord Alfred sat at his desk, pulled a small key from a pocket, and inserted it into the lock. He opened a drawer and removed a sheaf of papers and seemed about to settle into dealing with them. He looked up at Jake. "Well? Carry on, lad. Don't let me trouble you. If you cannot find what you want, just let me know."

"Thank you, sir. But I just wanted to return this book for now."

As he returned the book to its original location, he heard the shuffling of papers and Lord Alfred saying to Morrow, "Here, Henry, make a copy of this and make sure it is on York's desk by noon tomorrow."

"Yes, sir," the secretary responded, unlocking his own desk.

Breathing a sigh of relief, Jake quietly made his escape and went up to his room, but he felt distinctly frustrated in not being able to try the lock on that other desk.

Henry Morrow seemed, on the surface, to be something of a non-entity. He went about his business unobtrusively and did not linger when his work was finished of a day. In casual conversations with Lady Henrietta and Lord Alfred, but mostly with the servants, Jake had fleshed out the sketchy information he had had from Fenton. It was true that Henry Morrow had been born Henri Moreau and had himself barely escaped the not so loving touch of Madame Guillotine, for the family had had close ties to France's royal family and, as Lord Alfred had put it when he and his niece and Jake were returning from one of those morning rides, "when they got around to lesser nobility, some of the family tried to escape. Not all of them succeeded."

"But Morrow did?" Jake had asked, hoping to learn more.

"Yes. He and his sister and her small son arrived here virtually destitute. My brother provided for them and ensured both boys would be educated. They were, after all, family. Henri hated what had happened to his immediate family so much that he anglicized his name."

"They were family, you say?"

Lady Henrietta had not contributed much to this conversation, but now added, "My grandmother was related to the Moreau family. Henry and his sister, Madame Laurent, are cousins to my father and Uncle Alfred and Aunt Georgiana."

"What happened to Monsieur Laurent?" Jake asked.

"He was able to get his family out, but not himself," she said. "It is a familiar—and sad—story of those days of terror."

Jake nodded sympathetically. "So the boy Henri becomes Henry and your uncle's secretary."

Without his prompting she answered his unspoken curiosity about the other two. "And when both her brother and her son had finished school, Madame became companion to my newly widowed aunt."

"She and her son did not adapt to England as well as Moreau did," Lord Alfred said. "Charles, the son, is not truly happy in his position as a curate to a country vicar. I think they both long for some restoration of the Laurent family fortune now that the Bourbons have returned to the throne of France."

"I s'pose anything's possible," Jake said vaguely. But he had wondered about these French connections and he continued to do so. Morrow was in a perfect position to gather information from a too-trusting member of the Duke of York's staff. Jake had grown fond of Lord Alfred and did not want to think the old gentleman was at all involved, but he simply refused to allow himself to rule out the possibility.

* * * *

Retta loved to dance, so she welcomed Aunt Georgiana's suggestion that they ensure that Mr. Bolton be able to acquit himself well in a ballroom. She even permitted herself to fantasize about a ball and the romantic atmosphere of an attractive partner, one who stirred her senses as no one else ever had. To preserve his supposed position in the household, they arranged the first dance session in the music room one afternoon when both Madame Laurent and Uncle Alfred were away from home.

It went far more smoothly than Retta had thought it might. Aunt Georgiana sat at the piano and played several tunes for them. Occasionally, she called a direction or encouragement. Practicing the steps was somewhat awkward as it was just the two of them performing dances that usually included at least three couples and often as many as twenty pairs of dancers. Nevertheless, Retta explained and demonstrated the steps of country dances such as the quadrille and the "Sir Roger de Coverly." When, to make conversation, she informed her partner that the latter dance was known in North America as the "Virginia Reel," he raised an eyebrow, but made no comment. Aunt Georgiana played the accompanying tunes for each dance, and Mr. Bolton executed his share of the steps perfectly.

"I must say," Retta said, catching her breath, "you perform these dances very well. Surely, they are not new to you?"

"Not exactly," he responded with a grin. "Even in the wilds of Yorkshire we have village assemblies. I learnt most of the traditional country dances early on. Never done 'em this way with just two people, though." He flashed another grin. I do 'preciate your teachin' 'em to me again."

She tried to ignore her susceptibility to that grin. "Well. Perhaps we need not be too concerned about these more common dances. A bit of refreshing might be in order before a ball."

"That's true. Been a while since I went to a real assembly."

"What about the waltz?"

"The waltz?"

"Yes. Surely you have heard of it, though it was introduced in England only last year." She sang the rhythm of a waltz tune in nonsense syllables and then Aunt Georgiana picked up the tune with a few bars on the piano.

"Oh, yes, ma'am, I've heard of it, but it's still considered rather risqué in Yorkshire, you know. But there's a dance hall here in London where workers goes to on Saturday nights, so I has—have—done it a time or two."

"Good. Let's see if we need to practice that one," Retta said. She proceeded to demonstrate the steps and her aunt immediately played the tune Retta had sung earlier. Retta closed her eyes, losing herself in the music and the flow of waltz steps.

Suddenly she was startled as Mr. Bolton grasped her right hand and slipped an arm about her waist, his hand splayed across the small of her back. With a mastery never shown by any of her previous waltz partners, he guided her in the elegant steps. Without a single thought to the contrary, she put her left hand on his shoulder, closed her eyes, and not only gave herself up to the music again, but she positively reveled in the fluid movements of the dance. She was keenly aware of the strength and grace with which he controlled their gliding about the room. Once again, she was also aware of the warmth of his very masculine body and the faint, but now familiar smell of sandalwood soap blended with his own essence. She was scarcely aware when her aunt stopped playing.

Mr. Bolton stopped moving and leaned close to murmur in her ear, "I think we are done now."

She held his gaze for a long, mesmerizing moment, then gave herself a mental shake and tried to retrieve control of the situation by saying, "Yes, I can see that we are." But she was not at all sure she had hidden a slight quaver in her voice.

She glanced toward her aunt who gave her a questioning look, but said in a brisk tone, "You both acquitted yourselves very well with that one. It was beautiful. In a proper ball gown and evening attire, you would command the attention of an entire ballroom."

"Yes. Well. Uh . . ." Retta tried to organize her words to fit the thought she *should* be expressing rather the raw feelings that were making this difficult. "I . . . uh . . . I think we have little cause to worry about Mr. Bolton's performance in a ballroom." She turned to him. "Do you not agree, sir?"

His eyes twinkled as he held her gaze again. "Well, now, mebbe another lesson or two wouldn't hurt."

She glared at him. "Perhaps. We shall discuss it later." Dratted man. He knew exactly how that dance had affected her. How he affected her.

Later, in the solitude of her own bedchamber, she took herself to task for even allowing him to affect her so. No. She could not be falling in love someone from the London docks! And where had that ridiculous thought come from anyway?

* * * *

Retta would have been interested to know that Jake, too, had been profoundly affected by that dance. Actually, by these weeks in the Blakemoor household and his daily interaction with its members, especially one Lady Henrietta. Jake had known many women in his past, women from all walks of life: debutantes he had known before his army days, wives and daughters of army officers, sophisticated women of the upper classes in Portugal, and less sophisticated women in working with partisans in Spain. His relationships with them had run the gamut from casual friendships to sparkling, enjoyable flirtations and, occasionally, something deeper.

There had been two mistresses in the last decade, each of whom had lasted for a period of a few months. The first liaison, with a Portuguese widow slightly older than he, had ended amicably. The second had been with a Spanish aristocrat, Inez, whose father sided with those loyal to the king Napoleon had placed on the Spanish throne. Their affair had ended tragically when the father discovered that his daughter was giving information to those "other" Spanish—those deeply opposed to the puppet king—and to the despicable English who aided them. Jake knew, but had never been able to prove, that the accident in which Inez had died had been ordered by her own father. At the time, Jake had grieved profoundly over Inez and blamed himself at least in part for her death. But as time had healed that wound, he realized that there was little that he could have done to save her, and that in fact the affair might not have survived the war at all. Still he had vowed he would never again cause any friction between a woman he loved and her family.

A woman he loved? Well, that was pretty dramatic, wasn't it? He was not ready to face that idea head on, but he did find himself admiring the Lady Henrietta more and more. He even admired her determination in pursuit of winning that ridiculous bet. Actually, it was sheer stubbornness, he thought, but her genuine affection for the mare, Moonstar, was not unlike his own attachment to Pegasus. Moonstar had not seen her mistress wounded on a battlefield and stood over her protectively until help came as Pegasus had, but Jake recognized the strength of her ladyship's loyalty to the animal. He also admired her ties to her brothers, to her aunt, and to her uncle. He knew—mostly from what others had let drop here and there—that she showed patient toleration of, but was not close to her sisters and her father, and certainly not to her stepmother. However, to the other members of her family, he had sensed only fierce loyalty. Such loyalty extended to king and country, he thought, in ruling her out of his on-going search.

At first he had supposed this whole situation would be uncomfortable for him as he tried to keep up with his disguises—as a country yokel from Yorkshire, a London dockworker, a Bow Street Runner, and as a Blakemoor footman on occasion. But he had also approached the situation with a degree of amusement. Lately, however, he had allowed himself a deeper sense of involvement with the people of Blakemoor House, especially with Lady Henrietta.

He enjoyed their "lessons" and the way they often led to verbal sparring and sharing of views on various matters. Because they spent so much time in each other's company—and often more or less alone together—he became more and more aware of her as a damned attractive woman, and he became attuned to her little idiosyncrasies: she always wore the same woodsy-flowery perfume; she favored muted colors from nature in her clothing; she had a hearty laugh when she was truly amused; she toyed with a strand of hair when giving serious thought to an idea. She was usually frank and practical in her approach to ideas and people.

So how on earth had she allowed herself to become embroiled in this patently silly bet?

"Well? Have you bedded her yet?" Peter Fenton had asked at their next meeting—in yet another dark pub.

"Of course not. And if I had, I would hardly be sharing such information with you." Jake knew he sounded a bit huffy, but he could not shake his silent addendum: *not that I haven't wanted to.* "She is teaching me to waltz," he said by way of changing the subject.

"The waltz." Fenton grinned. "That must be interesting, given that the King's German Legions brought that dance to the Peninsula long before it was introduced here in England."

"It . . . uh . . . has its moments," Jake said.

"Ah, Bodwyn," Peter went on in mock sympathy, "you are letting down the male half of the species. Are you not aware that we are supposed to be lusting after anything in skirts?"

"I do not deny 'lusting,' but that is the sum of information you get on that score. So—what news have you for me on the spy front?"

Peter's expression turned grim. "Bad news, I'm afraid. Richter has been found."

"And—"

"He's dead. His body washed up in the Thames against a bridge abutment. The body was naked and in bad shape from exposure and God knows how long it was in the river, but he'd been tortured and stabbed."

"Oh, my God."

"Whoever did it probably intended the body to be washed out to sea, but that bridge just got in their way. He was a good man. Young and enthusiastic, but a good man."

"And no one at Trentham House knows anything?"

"They still aren't talking at all. But obviously Richter was onto something. And he paid dearly for it." Fenton's tone became even more serious. "So, you be careful, my friend. These people are worried about something. Worried enough to kill to protect their sources."

"I'm all right," Jake assured him, "but unfortunately, I have little to report other than the fact that Colonel Lord Alfred Parker takes his work home with him—but we knew that."

"The message—or part of one—that Richter found?"

"Nothing yet. Anyone else working on it?"

"Yes. But no one has worked it out yet."

"I'll keep at it."

"Right. And keep digging too." Fenton rose and give Jake an especially firm handshake. "But be careful! I certainly don't want to be fishing *your* body out of the Thames."

Chapter 9

As November rolled into December, Retta began to accept her current situation as routine, knowing full well it was temporary. Her father and stepmother would eventually come home, and so would Melinda and Richard. Aunt Georgiana and Madame Laurent would return to the house in Bloomsbury. Rebecca and Lenninger would be removing to his newly renovated town house.

And Jake Bolton would leave.

The sense of desolation she felt at this last thought surprised her. But, really, what *had* she expected?

Be honest, she told herself.

Her sense of loss was surprising, but it was also something of a revelation. What kind of life did she really want for herself?

Once upon a time she had shared the romantic dreams of all young girls: a home and family of her very own—the fairy tale happily-ever-after with a loving Prince Charming as the center of her universe. Gradually, those dreams had been quashed as she came to realize that she was pursued more for the fortune she would one day have than for herself alone. She had never been wholly comfortable in the role that society—and her stepmother—demanded of "proper young ladies." Early on, her effort to conform had brought more frustration than satisfaction. Assuming that role was rather like wearing a garment that did not quite fit, forcing one constantly to pull at it or smooth imaginary wrinkles.

Finding kindred spirits in Hero and Harriet at school had been liberating, especially as Miss Pringle had recognized the worth of "her girls" as individuals. The "Three Hs" had not repudiated society; they had simply pursued their own interests—and earned the pejorative label "bluestockings" in the process. They ignored the name-calling; in fact, all three took perverse pride in that and other aspersions tossed at them.

Thrust into the marriage mart, Lady Henrietta had thought to find a life partner with whom she could share ideas and goals just as she shared them with Hero and Harriet. She was quickly disabused of that foolish notion when she overheard one of her would-be suitors talking with one of his cronies.

"Don't know what you see in the Blakemoor chit," the crony had said. "She'll bore you to death with all that talk of child labor and the starving poor."

"One can tolerate a good deal of boredom if it comes with an income of several thousand pounds per annum," said the man who had professed to admire her compassion and her ever-so-delightful person.

Her disillusionment had been fortified as she saw certain of her friends and acquaintances virtually forced into marriages that usually offered sufficient social or financial status, but little in the way of real happiness—at least not the kind Lady Henrietta Georgiana Parker dreamed of.

Perhaps when she came into full control of her fortune, she would establish her own household. A paid companion, such as Aunt Georgiana had in Madame Laurent, would afford her some protection from scurrilous gossip, and she would have more freedom than she felt in her stepmother's domain.

Meanwhile, she had to deal with her growing awareness of Jake Bolton, the man. That was another thing: in her private musings, she had begun to think of him as *Jake*. And there were all those not-quite-accidental touches, shared glances of amusement in the midst of conversations with others, just knowing when he was or was not in a room. She needed to keep her distance! But she also needed be very sure that he could carry off a whole evening in the company of the most critical members of the *ton*.

Then what she thought of as her private "Jake dilemma" took on a new dimension.

One evening when Madame Laurent, pleading a headache, had retired early to her bedchamber, Retta and her aunt sat quietly enjoying glasses of sherry before retiring themselves.

Aunt Georgiana set her glass on the table between their chairs and cleared her throat. "Retta, my dear, you know that I am not one to interfere in others' private business, but there is a matter I would discuss with you."

"You think Madame Laurent's headache stems from worry about her son? I know he runs with a very fast crowd."

"No, my dear. Frankly, I am speaking of you and Mr. Bolton."

"Me? And Mr. Bolton?" Retta felt embarrassed and tried to dissemble. "I am sure I have no idea what you are talking about." She raised her own glass to her lips for the last sip of sherry.

"Cut line, my girl. You know that will not work with me. I have seen the way you look at each other. And that waltz the other day was a clear demonstration of *something* between you."

"At each other?" Retta repeated the phrase that had popped out at her, and rather clumsily set her glass on the table.

"Yes. At each other. You must be very careful, my dear, that you not let him get ideas above his station."

Retta decided a good defense would be an effective offense. "Just as you once did with Uncle Mickelson?"

Her aunt looked chagrined, but only momentarily. "My William did come from a family of tradesmen, but he was educated at the very best schools and he possessed a private fortune that, frankly, exceeded my father's."

"I know that," Retta said contritely. "I am sorry, Auntie Georgie. I should not have said that. It's just that—"

"That you needed to deflect the discussion." Her aunt was silent for a moment, then asked gently, "So what *is* happening, Retta? You know that I will always support you in whatever you do—short of your engaging in antics like those of Caroline Lamb in her pursuit of that scapegrace, Byron."

Retta gave a nervous laugh. "You need not worry on that score. Actually, I am simply not sure that—that anything is 'happening.' I find Mr. Bolton attractive, and I think he does not view me as an antidote, but rest assured, my dear Auntie Georgie, that despite the contretemps that could result from this bet with Rebecca, I will never—never—do anything to truly endanger the reputation of my family."

"That was not my worry," her aunt replied. "I simply do not want *you* to be hurt. You have been fending off fortune hunters ever since your come-out. But in the past, your own affections never seemed to be engaged."

"Nor are they now," Retta assured her, even as she wondered just how true that was.

Her aunt looked doubtful, but stood to signal an end to the discussion. "Hmm. Well, should they become so, your circumstances will allow you to follow your heart, but do be very careful, my dear."

Retta, too, stood and kissed her aunt on the cheek. "I will. Truly I will. And thank you."

"Good night, my dear."

Retta sat back down and remained there, thinking, long after the older woman had retired. She scarcely noticed the familiar sounds of an evening: horses' hooves and carriage wheels on cobblestones outside and quiet good-nights and closing doors within. If Aunt Georgiana had seen something untoward in her behavior with Mr. Bolton, how long might it be before others did? And how long before something *did* happen? A kiss, perhaps. A kiss. What would that be like with Jake? She shook her head.

No. It simply could not—must not—happen.

But then it did. The very next day.

As was her custom even on mornings when she did not ride, Retta had gone to the stable, her pockets and a basket loaded with treats for her equine friends. Entering Moonstar's stall, she was struck by her sheer thoughtlessness in risking the loss of this treasured friend. She fed the mare an apple, stroked her velvety nose, then pressed her face to the horse's neck.

"Oh, my precious, how *could* I have been so stupid?" she murmured. Moonstar shifted to nudge Retta's shoulder as though to respond, "Hmm?"

"But Jake—Mr. Bolton—will save you for me. I know he will." She patted the horse's neck again. "I hope. Oh, how I hope," she whispered.

Later, Retta had thought herself alone in the house—except for the servants who all seemed occupied somewhere out of her immediate presence. Aunt Georgiana and Madame Laurent had gone out to make calls. Uncle Alfred intended to report to the office of the Commander-in-Chief, and Gerald had accompanied him, though Gerald's destination was the Foreign Office. She thought Mr. Bolton, too, had left for his half-day off. She reveled in having the house to herself and being able to spend the afternoon just as she pleased. And what she pleased was to snuggle into one of those big overstuffed couches in the library with that new novel, *Pride and Prejudice,* reportedly by the author of *Sense and Sensibility.*

As she neared the library she heard the piano in the nearby music room. So, Aunt Georgiana had not accompanied Madame Laurent after all. She started toward the door, but stood outside just listening a few moments. It was a beautiful piece, one totally unfamiliar to Retta, but at first it conjured up feelings of nostalgia and longing, then the strains changed to surging waves of pain or anger, then changed again to quieter tones—of acceptance perhaps. When there was a pause, she pushed the door open.

It was not Aunt Georgiana at the piano, but Jake Bolton! He had tossed his coat onto a nearby chair and rolled up the sleeves of his shirt to allow freer movement in his wrists.

She gasped. "Oh, my goodness! I—I thought Aunt Georgiana—"

He quickly stood. "I . . . uh . . . I did not think anyone would mind. I thought to—that is, I thought everyone was out. I do apologize."

"Do not apologize for that music. It was simply beautiful. But where in the world did you learn to play like that? Since when do merchant ships have pianos aboard?" She was recovering from her surprise and now suspicion and confusion assailed her.

"Well, I . . . uh . . . that is—our vicar's wife was the organist in our church. And they had a piano in the vicarage, you see."

She looked at him skeptically. "A country vicar's wife taught you? She must have been a very talented lady."

"I . . . I guess maybe she were—uh—was."

"But to play as you just did—surely that took years of practice."

"The captain had a small harpsichord on the ship. When he found out I knew how to play it, he used to have me do it quite often. I played better than he did." There was no sense of arrogance in this statement.

She raised an eyebrow. "So you are telling me you play the organ, the harpsichord, *and* the piano?"

"Well, I ain't—that is—I am not very good on an organ." He started toward the chair on which he had tossed his coat. "I'll just be going now, milady."

"Come," she said imperiously. "Play some more of that for me." She moved toward the piano. "What did you do with the music?"

He followed her, reluctantly, it seemed to her, and his next words almost seemed to be uttered against his will. "I . . . uh . . . I—I was just sort of making it up as I went along."

"You—what?"

"I plays—play—mostly by ear. I hear it in my head, an' it—it just sort of comes outta my fingers."

"Can you actually read music?" she asked.

Again, he seemed reluctant as he answered. "Aye. Yes."

"Let's see," she demanded. From several pieces of music lying on a small table near the piano, she grabbed a sheet at random and set it on the piano. "Come. Play this for me."

She sat on the piano bench; he slowly sat down beside her and muttered something that sounded to her like "In for a penny, in for a pound." He glanced at the piece she had chosen. "Mozart. Aye. I can do that." He grinned at her and for the first time since she had entered the room, she felt that he relaxed.

Then he began to play and, as he had put it earlier, the music just seemed to flow from his fingers. She watched him intently, but it seemed to her that he scarcely glanced at the music sheet. Even as the music consumed her, she was conscious of the man next to her, of their thighs touching despite several layers of cloth between them. An aura of masculinity and sensitivity seemed to exude from him. She watched, fascinated, as his hands skimmed over the keys, his fingers caressing, coaxing the music from them. She sat mesmerized by the soft hair on his forearms, intrigued by a burn scar on the one nearest her. She was wholly caught up in the sensuality of the moment.

He finished and turned toward her, his gaze locked with hers. "How was that?" he asked softly.

"Beautiful," she murmured just as he put an arm around her shoulders and settled his lips on hers. At first it was a gentle, exploring kind of kiss, but when he felt her respond, he deepened it and her response surged as well. He brought his other hand up to stroke her bare neck as his lips moved on hers; his tongue seeking permission to enter and she was on the verge of welcoming its intrusion.

They came to their senses simultaneously. She pulled away and they both stood, staring into each other's eyes. She was sure he was as surprised—and moved—as she was.

"I'm sorry, milady."

"Don't be. Frankly, that was beautiful as well." Without thinking, she had responded with the first words that popped into her mind. Embarrassed, she felt herself blushing. "What I meant was I—we—should not have done that."

He turned away slightly as though allowing her to collect herself. "They do say 'music is the food of love.'"

"Well," she said tartly, "we need to avoid an excess of it then." Without thinking, she had responded to his quotation, but now she turned abruptly and asked, "*Who* says— Where did you hear that said?"

He looked at the floor and mumbled, "I dunno—just a sayin'. Mebbe from a play I saw once. Travelin' players do get up to Yorkshire sometimes."

She gave him a long look to which he returned a bland expression. Then he said again, "I'm sorry, milady. I—I overstepped."

"The fault was not yours alone, but we both know it must not happen again." Her tone was brusque, but she softened it as she added, "You are a man of many surprises, Mr. Jake Bolton." She stepped toward the door, then turned back. "Oh. And do feel free to play the piano whenever you wish."

"Thank you."

With that, she escaped to the confines of her own room, her search for that novel forgotten. Shaken to her very core, she relived that kiss again and again. She wondered if she had somehow willed it. She *had* thought about it, had she not? The urgency, the sheer need of her response, though, had astonished her. Lady Henrietta Georgiana Parker, sophisticated and experienced woman of that world of the London *ton*, had been kissed before.

But never like this. Never with such sweetness and urgency combined. This one she could not soon dismiss as she had others. Yet she must.

* * * *

Jake cursed himself for that lapse in judgment. Those lapses. He had thought himself totally alone in the house, except for the servants, and none of them were about on the ground floor when he had entered the music room. He had appreciated the tones of that instrument at his "dancing lesson" the other day and had longed to give it a try himself. It had lived up to his expectations and then he had allowed the music to simply flow out of him—releasing some of his loneliness and frustrations with a mission that kept him from seeking out his family and friends even as it every day set the tantalizing Lady Henrietta in his path.

Then he had succumbed to temptation and kissed her. He had expected it to be the sort of flirtatious "first kiss" of many another relationship. But it had stirred him far deeper than he had thought it might when he had occasionally allowed himself to dream of tasting the lips of the delectable Lady Henrietta, though he had long since given up his ideas of a dalliance. And he had quoted that line from Shakespeare. Shakespeare! What dockworker ever went around quoting Shakespeare? She was right. This must not happen again, for it would not only make a mess of his spy mission, but it would also play havoc with the emotions of Major Lord Jacob Bodwyn!

As to his spy mission, only yesterday he had managed to inspect the contents of that second desk in the library, the one used by Henry Morrow. In the bottom drawers he had found any number of papers obviously left by the Earl of Blakemoor before his departure for the continent, for they were largely inventories relating to this or that property of the earldom. But in the top drawer, Jake found a copy of the paper he had seen in Lord Alfred's desk. This puzzled him, for had he not heard his lordship tell the secretary to take those documents to the Duke of York, Commander-in-Chief of the Army? Jake lifted that sheet and studied the one beneath it. This one made no sense. Nonsense or not, it seemed somewhat familiar. Then it hit him: it resembled that fragment Fenton had had from Richter. Finding some blank stationery in another drawer, Jake quickly made copies of both sheets. He returned the originals to the drawer from which he had lifted them and relocked the desk. He congratulated himself on achieving his goal with no interference from Lord Alfred or the secretary. Nevertheless, he hastily left the room.

He spent the rest of that evening and the next studying the three bits of information he now had in his possession. He felt he was onto something. But what?

* * * *

Retta thought she had come off rather easily from that little chat with her aunt. Then two days after she discovered Jake's musical talent—and that incredible kiss which had since preoccupied her waking and sleeping moments—Uncle Alfred sent a footman after dinner to invite her and Gerald into the library. She met Gerald on the stairs and paused, her hand on the polished mahogany bannister.

"Have you any idea of what Uncle may want of us?" she asked.

"None whatsoever."

"What if he knows about the bet?"

"Guess we just own up to it if he does. But I do not see how he could know."

She was annoyed by her brother's stoicism in the face of a possibility that could mean the devastating loss of her mare. She sailed into the library ahead of him as he held the door for her.

Their uncle sat in a comfortable wing backed chair, an open book on his knee, and a snifter of cognac on a table beside him. A lamp on the table created an island of light in the massive darkness.

"You wanted to see us?" she asked. "Both of us?"

"Yes. Both of you. Please sit there where I have a clear view of your faces." He indicated a couch opposite his chair.

Retta and Gerald exchanged a glance, but said nothing as they did as they were told.

"Now I want a straight answer from you two. Who is this Mr. Bolton and why is he here?"

"But we told you—"

"Papa's letter—"

Gerald and Retta spoke simultaneously.

"Enough." Lord Alfred waved his hand dismissively. His voice was harsh. "Do not, I pray you, repeat that taradiddle you told me some weeks ago. I have little doubt the man is capable of protecting you, Retta, if it were necessary. But I do doubt such a necessity—beyond everyday sensible precautions, that is."

"May I ask just why you doubt us, sir?" Gerald asked sounding ever so calm to Retta's ears.

"I have had several communications from my brother in the last few weeks, and never once has he mentioned this grand threat against his daughter's life. Moreover, Bow Street has never heard of this fellow. Now I want to know exactly why we are hosting a virtual stranger in Blakemoor House—however amiable he may be."

Retta exchanged a glance with Gerald who sighed and nodded.

"It is all my fault," Retta said.

"I probably could have stopped it, if I had been more adamant," Gerald said.

"I want to know just what 'it' is!" their uncle demanded in an implacable tone.

So they told him.

Retta felt like a child caught in a particularly naughty scrape as she twisted her hands in her lap and let Gerald outline the basics of the situation, adding only a detail here and there to let her uncle know of her full complicity. Finally, she said, "You see, Uncle, it *is* all my fault. Mine and Rebecca's. Please do not blame Gerald or Richard."

"A bet? You invited a total stranger into this house over a bet? A man you just picked up on the docks? As part of a bet? That was not only patently foolish, but dangerous."

"It is not quite as bad as you make it sound," Gerald said. "I did instruct Jeffries to keep an eye on him and post a footman to report any untoward behavior immediately to me. We interviewed him rather thoroughly too."

Uncle Alfred snorted. "You interviewed him. A dockworker."

"Yes, sir. Twice. On the docks and then here." Gerald held his uncle's disapproving gaze. "Sir, you've spent time with the man—does he seem a dishonorable sort to you?"

"That is entirely beside the point," the older man said. "Honor has nothing to do with class. This has to stop. You will dismiss the man tomorrow morning."

"Oh, please, Uncle," Retta begged. She cursed the tears she felt welling. "It is only for a few weeks more. Please. I think Mr. Bolton will be able to win the bet for me. Please do not make me give up Moonstar. Please." She swallowed the sob that threatened as she faced the very real and immediate prospect of losing her mare. Moonstar was far more than a mere horse for her riding pleasure; she was a favorite pet. "I—I could not bear losing her."

"That should have entered your head before now," her uncle said in a flat voice.

"It—it did," she admitted, "b—but not soon enough."

"Rebecca and Melinda sort of ganged up on her," Gerald put in to defend her.

Uncle Alfred glared at Gerald. "And you, my Lord Heaton, you—heir to an earldom—you allowed this foolishness to go forward?"

"It was not his fault. It was mine," Retta insisted. "I made the bet. I knew it was a mistake almost immediately, but—"

Her uncle shook his head from side to side and gave her a sad but knowing look. "And you just could not back down, could you? Impulsiveness and intransigence. Those qualities may well bring disaster upon you one day, my girl—if, indeed, this does not do it." He was quiet for several moments, then said, "A dockworker? And you think you can make a gentleman of him?"

Retta thought she heard a note of acquiescence in his voice. "Do you mean to allow me to go on? Please? Surely you have noticed the improvement in Mr. Bolton's manners and his speech."

He sighed. "I have rarely ever been able to deny you anything—as you well know. But I have to tell you, this does try my patience. I shall say nothing of this for now. However, your 'project' does *not* have my blessing, though to answer your question, yes, I have observed improvement in Mr. Bolton's demeanor." Again he was silent for a moment, then he gave her an oblique look. "Am I wrong in assuming that Georgiana is in on this?"

"No, sir. I mean, yes, sir, she does know," Retta admitted. "But please do not blame her for not informing you. I . . . uh . . . we—" she looked at Gerald who nodded his encouragement to her. "We thought to have as few people know as possible."

"Well, at least you had that much sense," he said grudgingly. With that he dismissed them.

Outside the library door, Gerald said, "You'd damned well better win this idiotic bet! I do not want to endure another session like that."

Chapter 10

In early December all activity in London assumed a sluggish pace and, in some instances came to a creeping, unwelcomed halt. The cause of this enforced lack of animation in the capital was a phenomenon Jake had almost forgot existed: a debilitating London fog. When lamps were lit in areas of the city that had them, the fog hung thick and yellow, shrouding everything in the ambience of nightmares. Nor was the effect only visual. Dampness, amounting to a soft drizzle at times, permeated everything, and the heavy cloud forced effusions from gas pipes for lighting, tanning yards, dyers, breweries, and soap makers to hover next to the earth. Soot from coal fires was not allowed to escape into the atmosphere.

The members of the Blakemoor household, like the rest of the city, found the fog enervating, not only limiting their activities, but also limiting their desire for such. And, like the rest of the city, some members of the household were hit by respiratory problems. Of these, the hardest hit was Lord Alfred.

On the first day of the onset of the fog, when everyone assumed—hoped—that this was just an ordinary, momentary event, Lady Henrietta had insisted a bit of dampness and a little fog was not to deter her from her ride. Lord Alfred was just as determined to join her—despite his known aversion to the fog—and Jake was glad to accompany them. The temperature had dropped, but not alarmingly so. While they were still in the stable yard, Jake had noted that Lord Alfred seemed a bit pale, and mounting seemed more difficult for him than usual. That Jake had waited until his lordship was firmly seated on his horse before mounting himself, was not lost on the older man who commented ruefully.

"Rheumatism. Always attacks me in this kind of weather. Age brings a plethora of ills, my friend."

Lady Henrietta brought her horse next to her uncle's. "Are you sure you are up for this, Uncle? You are breathing all right, are you not?"

"I am fine. Let us proceed with the ride, and when we get to the park, you just scamper ahead as usual."

But both Jake and her ladyship stayed by his side, even after arriving at the park, for it was apparent that Lord Alfred was not "fine." He slowed the pace of his horse; his breathing grew steadily more labored, and he looked as though he might faint. Lady Henrietta exchanged a look of profound concern with Jake and proposed that they cut the ride short. At that moment, the old man swayed on his horse and would have fallen but for Jake's instantly dismounting and catching him.

"I am all right, I tell you," Lord Alfred said as he regained his footing on solid earth.

"No, sir, you are not. Allow me to loosen your neckcloth and see if that helps you get more air into your lungs." Without waiting for permission, Jake did just that.

"If you will give me a hand up, young fellow, we can continue our ride."

"No, Uncle Alfred, we will not continue," Lady Henrietta said. "We are returning immediately and I shall send someone for the doctor."

Jake aided the man in remounting, but Lord Alfred's grip on the reins seemed unsteady, and he began to sway precariously, his breathing even more labored than before.

"You lead my horse, my lady," Jake said, gathering up the reins he had dropped and handing them to her, "and ride ahead to send for the doctor. We may be dealing with something more than mere allergies. I shall ride with Lord Alfred."

With that, he climbed up behind his lordship, who scarcely seemed aware of what was happening, and Jake reached around the man to grip the reins with one hand, the other holding fast to the body in front of him. Somewhat to Jake's surprise, Lady Henrietta, simply did as he told her. When he and Lord Alfred finally arrived back at Blakemoor house, she had already sent for the doctor and had a footman ready to help Jake get his lordship up to his own chambers, where his valet and the footman helped him into a loose nightshirt and into bed.

As this was taking place, Jake started toward his own room, but encountered Lady Henrietta hovering in the hall outside her uncle's chambers. She was still dressed in her riding habit, though she had thrown off the heavy cloak; she looked pale and distraught. Jake simply opened his arms and, as though it were the most natural thing in the world, she moved into them, clinging to his shoulders and allowing the tears she had apparently been willing herself to hold back. She sobbed against his chest. Her hair had come loose in what must have been an energetic ride back to the stables. A soft strand played against his face. He was aware of the scent she always used, but there was also a hint of the atmosphere through which they had just ridden. He was intensely aware of the attractive woman in his arms, but beyond that he was conscious of his own feelings—his need to comfort and protect someone he truly cared for—feelings that had little to do with his one-time thought of "dalliance." He laid his cheek against her head and just held her until her sobs subsided.

Then she drew back, embarrassed, but she held his gaze. "Oh, I am so sorry. I . . . uh . . . I just—"

"Never mind, my lady. You were worried and scared. I understand." And he did understand her emotional reaction, but that hardly explained the sense of loss he had felt at her stepping away from him.

A movement down the hall diverted their attention and they drew even farther apart.

"Retta?" Viscount Heaton called. "What is going on? Is Uncle Alfred all right?" He directed a penetrating look at Jake and raised an eyebrow with his question.

Jake watched as she quickly regained total control of herself and explained to her brother that their uncle was suffering a spell of difficult breathing and that she had sent for the doctor. "Mr. Bolton was most helpful," she added. "I simply do not know what might have happened had he not been there."

On that note Jake bowed briefly and left the two of them to commiserate with each other as they waited for the doctor.

* * * *

Jake had changed from his damp clothing and was finishing his breakfast in the dining room when he was joined by Lady Georgiana and her companion who had heard of the morning's crisis. Jake was still answering their questions as best he could when they were joined by Lady Henrietta, her brother, and an older man who was introduced to Jake as Lord Alfred's doctor, Sir Cecil Lindstrom. Jake noted that, at some point, Lady Henrietta had changed into a yellow printed day dress; her appearance helped lift some of the gloom of the day. To Jake, the doctor appeared to be remarkably turned out for someone who must have been summoned before his own morning had fairly begun. With a full head of white hair, he was dressed impeccably and carried himself with an air of being conscious of his own place in the world. Obviously well known to all the others, Lindstrom barely acknowledged his introduction to Jake, which Jake took to mean that, at some point in the last few weeks, Lord Alfred had informed his friend that a Bow Street Runner was ensconced in Blakemoor house.

Lindstrom instantly became the center of attention, but Lady Georgiana waited until the doctor and her niece and nephew had filled their plates and taken seats at the table before demanding, "Well, Cecil? How is he? I assume you would have informed us immediately were there cause for alarm."

"He is resting comfortably, I hope. I extracted some blood and gave him a draught to ease his discomfort."

Lady Georgiana sniffed. "Laudanum, I suppose. The cure-all of the day."

The doctor took a swallow from his coffee cup, set it down, and said, "As a matter of fact, yes. It is my professional opinion that he needs rest."

"So it is not merely his usual breathing problems with this kind of weather?" she pressed.

"I do not think so. Or, I should say, it is not that alone. He was experiencing a very rapid heartbeat and said he felt faint during his morning ride. I suspect a problem with his heart, though not, I hope, a serious one."

"Uncle Alfred will rest for the rest of this day at least, and he will just have to give up his morning rides until this awful weather changes," Lady Henrietta said. "Also, Sir Cecil has suggested that he should forgo his trips to Whitehall for the time being."

"He will not take kindly to that idea, and you know it," her brother said.

She shrugged. "He will do it, though, if we all insist."

"And we shall insist," Lady Georgiana said firmly.

"He can certainly work from home," the doctor said. "He is, after all, quite used to doing so. I will just have a word with Morrow before I leave. I assume he has arrived by now?"

"Oh, yes. He is probably already at Father's desk in the library," Viscount Heaton said, "but do take your time in finishing your breakfast. I want to say again how much we appreciate your coming to tend my uncle on such short notice."

"As I told you, Alfred is a dear friend. Inconvenience is but one of the conditions of my profession," Lindstrom said expansively. "One learns to sleep when one can."

"I do so admire men of your dedication, Sir Cecil," Madame Laurent said, smiling flirtatiously at the doctor. It was one of the longest speeches Jake had ever heard from her. A petite woman with dark blond hair tending to gray, she usually said very little in company. And here she was, asserting herself to attract the medical man's attention.

"Why, thank you, Madame Laurent. A lovely compliment from a lovely woman."

She blushed, but did not respond.

Jake exchanged a glance with Lady Henrietta who seemed as intrigued as he at the exchange between her aunt's companion and the doctor.

Lindstrom rose, pronouncing himself already late for another appointment, but declared that he would "just have a word with Morrow about Lord Alfred's workload for the next few days."

* * * *

Secure in the knowledge that her uncle was all right, at least for the time being, Retta retreated to her own room for the rest of the morning. Now that the crisis was over, she found herself engaged in what had lately become a familiar dilemma: What to do about Mr. Bolton? More specifically, what to do about her feelings about the man. What on earth had possessed her to throw herself at him that way? True she was upset, but did she have to seek comfort in the first set of masculine arms available? Nor could she shake the feeling—which she dared not examine too closely—that she somehow belonged in those arms. *Belonged?* Where did that bit of utter nonsense come from?

A few more weeks, eight perhaps, and he would be gone—out of her life, come what may. But that thought gave her little comfort. Indeed, it brought with it a sense of despair. She'd had a vague idea that other men could help to divert her attention from such a patently unsuitable match. So she had lately accepted invitations that might not otherwise have tempted her at all. The usually circumspect Lady Henrietta had indulged herself in at least two idle flirtations, and she had tacitly allowed Viscount Willitson to renew his suit. Her feelings of guilt over her undeniable attraction to Jake Bolton were now compounded by her guilt over so cavalierly using Willitson.

It was in this state of angst that she met with her aunt later that afternoon. Aunt Georgiana had found Retta in their sitting room, a book open but unread in her lap.

"Dr. Lindstrom arrived a while ago; he and I have just checked on our patient," Aunt Georgiana said as she took a seat across from her niece. "He is still sleeping, though I do think he should have wakened by now."

"How is his breathing?" Retta asked.

"Regular. And the doctor listened to his heart and pronounced that regular too."

"He did not bleed him again, did he?" Retta could not contain her worried disapproval on that score.

"No. He said he would perhaps do so tomorrow."

"By then Uncle Alfred should be alert enough to decide that for himself."

"Honestly, Retta. I do not know why you and Alfred have such an aversion to what is, after all, an established medical practice."

"An overused one, I think. And so does Uncle Alfred. He blames all that bleeding for prolonging his recovery when he first came home from Canada. Made him weaker, he said."

"Well, that is as may be, but we will see what the doctor says for the immediate situation tomorrow. We have all seen Alfred through these spells before, have we not?"

"It is nothing more than the miasma of this awful fog," Retta said, hoping fervently that it was true.

"Yes. Well," her aunt said, obviously wanting to change the subject. "I have been thinking. When Alfred is feeling better, we might have a small entertainment for the Christmas season—dinner and maybe some music or games afterwards. What do you think?"

"Oh, yes!" Retta was immediately enthusiastic. "I have been missing the yule log and the caroling we always have in the country at this time of the year. Surely the flower sellers in Covent Garden will have greenery for sale."

"Such a gathering might also be a way to introduce your Mr. Bolton to interaction with society—in a small way, of course. He may then feel more comfortable when he actually makes his come out in February."

Retta was glad that both Aunt Georgiana and Uncle Alfred were reconciled to the "project," but she giggled at the idea of Mr. Bolton's making a "come out" like some adolescent debutante. She could not wait to share that little joke with her brother and her uncle. She enthusiastically endorsed the idea of an evening soiree to celebrate the Christmas season. It might help divert her mind from these other matters. To this end, she and Lady Georgiana spent the rest of the afternoon making up a guest list, and planning menus and entertainment.

* * * *

Jake, too, had gone to Lord Alfred's chambers to inquire about the patient only to find that gentleman still sleeping. Jake had grown quite fond of the old man whose patriotism and quiet determination to be useful to his country Jake found so admirable. Of course the parallel with his own life had not escaped Jake. As a younger son of the aristocracy and possessing a fortune of his own, Lord Alfred might well have chosen to live out his days in self-indulgence and frivolous entertainments. But he had not made that choice at all.

Now that Lord Alfred knew of his niece's bet and her efforts to win it, Jake felt more comfortable in the old man's presence. While he did not admit to it openly, he shared Lord Alfred's view that the whole thing was pretty silly. Jake knew very well that the old man would not have tolerated this scheme in anyone but Lady Henrietta.

Lady Henrietta had informed Jake of her uncle's confronting her and her brother the day after it happened. Only once had Lord Alfred referred to the situation in Jake's presence and then he had said only, "I just hope the lot of you know what you are doing." But Jake had noted with some amusement that Lord Alfred often subtly offered his support to her by making casual remarks to Jake about this or that person in public office, sharing information that might be well known among the *ton*, but that might not have made its way into public discourse in the lower orders yet. For instance, Prince George, now that he was the Regent, seemed to be turning away from embracing the Whigs as he had done in his youth, to endorsing more of the Tory views with which the King sympathized. This shift in attitude had not been well received by his erstwhile cronies. Such matters might or might not be touched on in the newspapers, but Jake appreciated that these tidbits were things Lord Alfred thought he should know.

Jake returned to his room and forced himself to study yet again the papers he had copied during his last foray in the library. He repeatedly tried various combinations of letters and numbers, trying to make sense of that second sheet and of the fragment Fenton had supplied. What if, in truth, there was no relationship at all between the two papers? But his gut kept telling him there was.

He could not have explained just what it was that finally unlocked the puzzle for him, but in an *"aha!"* moment, the coded document suddenly seemed to make sense. Numbers corresponded to letters of the alphabet to make up words, and letters actually stood for numbers. But they were not consistent. Sometimes the letter would be, say, three letters—or numbers—from the conventional symbol. So a *b* was written as an *f* or a *6*, or an *h* as a *k* or an *11*. In some instances the code approached the alphabet straightforwardly—*abcd*—and in others, in reverse—*zyxw*. Moreover, the groupings of words or numbers switched the code so that two of them would use one approach and the next three, the other. Then the pattern would shift. Jake thought it somewhat crude as codes went, but it did work—look how long it had taken him to figure it out. He could hardly wait to share this information with Fenton.

But he knew Fenton would foresee the next problem just as Jake himself did: Morrow was putting information from the office of the army's Commander-in-Chief into a code. But for whom? And that *whom* had ramifications. Someone in England was passing this information to someone on the continent for some as yet unknown purpose. *All right,* Jake thought, *we now know the* what. *We just need the whys and the whos. Still too many questions.*

By the time he was sure he had solved the mystery of the code, it was too late to contact Fenton. Jake cursed at the restrictions imposed by December's early nightfall combined with the continuing fog. The next morning Lady Henrietta chose to forego their usual lesson. She was grilling him these days on a gentleman's proper behavior in various situations as outlined in the book she had given him earlier such as which persons deserved a proper bow as opposed to those for whom a simple nod of the head would do. Instead, she sat with her uncle, who was alert and none too pleased to be confined to his bed. Under the pretext of taking a walk to stretch his legs, Jake left the house and made his way by a circuitous route to one of the busier commercial streets. He summoned a hackney cab and gave the driver a coin and a message to take to Fenton whom Jake knew to be staying with his parents at their town house. Luckily, the next day was Jake's half-day off, so he was able to navigate his way to the pub he had designated in his message while it was still daylight. Murky and foggy though it was, native Londoners like cab drivers seemed to almost *feel* their way through the beleaguered city.

"Good lord. This place is practically empty. The weather is so abominable that it manages to keep a proper Englishman from his pint! I do hope you have something pretty splendid to drag me out in this pea soup." Fenton's testiness was only half-feigned.

"I think so, your highness." They ordered and paid for drinks at the bar and took them to a corner table. "Have a look at this, Peter." Jake laid the papers before his superior officer and explained the code.

Fenton whistled. "Bless you, my son—this *is* pretty splendid. I knew having you in Blakemoor House was a good idea!"

"Yes, but what now?" Jake asked. "We have no idea who his contacts are—or to whom *they* are giving the information. I had thought of following Morrow when he finishes of a day at Blakemoor House . . ."

Fenton considered this silently for a few moments, then stroked his chin. "Hmm. No, I think it better that you stay in place—see if anyone contacts him there. I'll have him followed by someone he doesn't know at all. Henry Morrow—or Henri Moreau, if you please—will not stir from his quarters without our knowing about it." He fell quiet again, then asked, "Do you think Lord Alfred knows what is going on? Is he involved?"

"My gut says no, but it has been wrong before, you know." Jake covered his emotion by taking a long swallow from his mug.

"Are you *still* blaming yourself for that ambush at Aranza? That was— what?—two years ago? Good God, man, how often must you be told that was not your fault?"

"I trusted the wrong people," Jake said.

"Maybe. Maybe not. We never knew that for a certainty."

"Nevertheless, the battle of Pamplona—"

"Would very likely have proceeded just as it did. Let it go, my friend."

"I have—I think. But I will never make that mistake again."

"Your instincts on the Peninsula were, more often than not, right on target. I trust them now, even if you do not. Others do as well."

"Thank you for that vote of confidence." Jake knew that by "others" Fenton meant Castlereagh and Wellington.

"Now, drink up and get back to work. Keep your eyes and ears open, but, for God's sake, be careful! Richter's death is the last one any of us want in this business."

"Yes, sir." Jake gave him mock salute. They both rose and made their way back into the murky mess of the fog while they were still able to see at least a few feet in front of them.

Three days later, the fog lifted. The atmosphere was clearer—and smelled better—but the weather had turned much colder. It rained nearly every day and often there were flakes of snow mixed in the rain. The city's activities picked up, but were still curtailed by the weather.

Chapter 11

Ten days after Uncle Alfred's spell in the park, a freak break in the weather allowed Londoners to resume normal activities, if only temporarily. It was still cold, but it had not rained for two days. Despite its being later than her usual morning ride, Retta was determined to give her precious Moonstar a good run and welcomed her uncle's company for at least the beginning and end of the ride. Having made a remarkable recovery, Uncle Alfred had returned to his normal routine, though he still worked from home. He received visits from a number of his cronies, including not only Dr. Lindstrom, but also the Duke of York who had brought with him a packet of papers that required Lord Alfred's attention. Retta thought the duke exaggerated, but she was grateful to him for giving her uncle something useful to do during his enforced seclusion.

Although she had continued to work with Mr. Bolton on a daily basis, she also welcomed his company. He was riding Blaze, so she looked forward to a short race. The three of them chatted as amiably as traffic allowed, marveling at their luck in the weather and commenting on newspaper accounts of both official negotiations and social events of the Congress of Vienna. The social news was full of balls and soirees hosted by this or that renowned hostess and dropping such names of aristocrats and nobles as to make the stay-at-homes in London envious. Retta was sure her stepmother was in her element. The official reports were full of a change in leadership: Lord Castlereagh was being recalled to London, and Wellington would replace him in Vienna. Because of winter weather and because the wheels of government, like of those of the gods, "grind exceeding slow," it would be some weeks before the change was accomplished.

"I do not understand this change at all," Retta said to her uncle as she skirted a woman selling roasted chestnuts on the street; because of the traffic, Mr. Bolton had dropped behind. "I thought Lord Castlereagh was deemed a huge success with his 'balance of power' proposals."

"He was—he is," her uncle said. "The truth is we must get Wellington out of Paris. Too many plots to assassinate him. The French don't like having him in Paris as our ambassador—he is a constant reminder of their defeat."

"Could he not lead the troops in America then?" she asked.

"He could," he replied as he, too, maneuvered around the chestnut seller, "but he refused that position early on. Said that war was a mistake to start with. He is probably right, too."

"Does this mean Papa and the countess are on their way home?" Her father, who communicated regularly enough with his heir and with his brother, rarely wrote Retta personally, and her stepmother never did; with Rebecca and Melinda in the country, such information came to Retta strictly second- or even third- hand.

"Oh, no," Uncle Alfred said. "Your father is to remain with the delegation." He emitted a rueful chuckle. "Besides, your stepmama is having the time of her life."

"That is not surprising in the least." When she thought about it—which was not often—she was still miffed that the countess had scotched Retta's own plan to go to Vienna. She glanced behind to see that Mr. Bolton had paused to buy some hot chestnuts. He now urged his mount forwarded and handed some of the treat to his companions.

"Never pass up warm chestnuts," he said amiably.

"Thank you," they both answered as the three of them entered the park.

Retta saw immediately that many others were taking advantage of the break in the weather to avail themselves of fresh air and exercise. And, of course, there was the usual "see and be seen" lot. Ladies in fashionable winter cloaks and bonnets trimmed in fur carried fur muffs and strolled beside gentlemen in many-caped great coats and tall beaver hats. Others rode in open carriages that stopped now and then—and held up traffic—as the occupants exchanged greetings. She also observed several nursery maids, their charges looking like colorful little bears, bundled as they were in layers of thick garments.

"Perhaps this traffic will thin out as we get farther along Rotten Row," Mr. Bolton said.

"Right." Uncle Alfred urged his horse onward.

They were on the verge of entering the central thoroughfare, when there was a great commotion just in front of them. Retta heard a loud scream, a shout of warning, and the thundering hooves of an out-of-control team attached to a flashy yellow and green curricle. Then, to her horror, she saw one of those overstuffed little bears toddle right into the path of the curricle. The driver was desperately trying to control his team as his fashionable female companion screamed. Retta wanted to call out a warning, but she felt the scene was transpiring in suspended time and that she herself was frozen in place, helpless. My God! That child! That poor babe!

Paralyzed with horror, she was scarcely aware of the blur of motion streaking past her until she saw Jake Bolton lean precariously from his saddle, snatch up the child, and carry it to safety off to the side.

The curricle rushed on, then slowed; the driver turned the team and brought the vehicle back. He called out, "Is the child all right?"

Bolton grasped the child firmly in front of him with one hand and managed to rein in his prancing horse with the other. "I think so. But good lord, man, what were you thinking to be driving at such a pace in the park?"

The tension of the moment was released when the child giggled in delight and said, "Horsey. Horsey ride!"

Bolton tightened his grip. "Yes, young fellow, you have indeed had a 'horsey ride.'" Retta heard sheer relief in his voice.

Two females were screaming hysterically.

One was the young woman in the curricle, berating her companion. "Oh, my goodness! Oh, my heavens! I might have been killed! How could you allow this to happen to me?"

The other was a distraught nursemaid. "Oh, Master Tommie! Master Tommie! Is he all right, sir?"

"I believe he is," Jake said, handing over the child to a sturdy woman of some forty years or so.

"It happened so fast!" the woman said to Retta who was only now regaining control of her emotions. "He snatched his hand out of mine and was gone before I could grab 'im. Master Tommie! You gave me such a fright."

She hugged the child to her, but the little mite just giggled again and said, "Down!"

"No!" the nurse said. "Absolutely not. Not 'til we get home." She shifted the child onto a hip and turned to look up at Jake. "I don't know how to thank you sir. I'm sure the boy's parents, Lord and Lady Davenport, will be ever so grateful. Now, Master Tommie, we must find your sister and go home."

Meanwhile the screams of the woman in the curricle had reduced themselves to hysterical sobbing and the driver, a young man of perhaps twenty, dressed as one of the dandy set, was trying ineffectually to comfort her. Finally, he said, "Miss Farnsworth, please. Please just be quiet. You assured me you knew how to handle a team, and just look what happened!"

"Oh! Oh! You are such a brute to make this all my fault."

"No," he replied. "It was truly my fault for taking you at your word."

"Take me home at once! I fear I may faint."

"Don't you dare do so!" The driver turned to Jake and said, "My sincerest gratitude to you, sir. That was a magnificent feat of riding. You saved that child and saved me untold regret."

"Take me home!" The girl's shrill demands elicited more annoyance than sympathy from bystanders.

By now the group had attracted quite a degree of attention from strollers and occupants of other vehicles. The story had to be told and retold several times. The girl in the curricle began to preen, obviously seeing herself as the heroine of the moment. Her demands to return home were forgotten, but to his credit, her companion kept asserting that the real hero of the day was the rider who had rescued the little boy. Retta thought Jake Bolton seemed uncomfortable with the attention, and she managed to get him and her uncle on their way once again. They finished their outing at a more sedate pace than she had anticipated—and with less conversation as Retta kept replaying the incident in her mind—and recalling a dockworker's telling her that yes, he had once ridden farm animals in Yorkshire. She also observed Uncle Alfred kept casting inquisitive glances at Jake.

* * * *

Jake knew immediately that he had made a mistake. He could almost sense the questions swirling in the minds of his companions. He had acted on instinct, but how could he have behaved otherwise? One could not just ignore a child in deadly peril—or anyone else, for that matter. The ride back to the stable was slower and uneventful. At this slightly later hour, street traffic had increased appreciably, but when they arrived at the mews, they found that by that mysterious system of communication among servants, the news of Jake's rescue of the child had beat them home. The stable hands wanted a first-hand account and to a limited extent Lady Henrietta and Lord Alfred were willing to accommodate them. Both were lavish in their praise of Jake as the hero of the day. But Jake could not shake the feeling that there was more to come.

And there was.

As the three of them walked from the stable to the house, Lord Alfred said, "Mr. Bolton, might I have a word with you in the library in, say, half an hour?"

Lady Henrietta gave Jake an enigmatic look, but shrugged her shoulders to suggest that she did not know what her uncle was about.

When Jake had changed from his riding clothes and showed himself in the library, Lord Alfred was alone, behind his desk. Either Henry Morrow had not shown up for work yet or his lordship had sent his secretary off on some made-up errand.

"Close the door please, and have a seat there." Lord Alfred pointed to a straight-backed chair in front of the desk. So. This was to be an interrogation, was it?

Jake sat, his arms folded across his chest and waited for the other man to begin. Lord Alfred got right to the point.

"Who are you, sir, and just why are you here?"

"I am not sure what you mean, my lord."

"What are you doing here? In Blakemoor House."

Jake decided to be as straight-forward as he could be, mindful of his last conversation with Peter Fenton. "But, sir, I thought Lord Heaton and Lady Henrietta had explained—"

Lord Alfred cut him off with a dismissive wave of his hand. "Oh, yes, they told me of the bet and that Bow Street Runner nonsense. But, frankly, I knew that was humbug before their attack of honesty struck them—Hendrickson, head of Bow Street, had never heard of you."

"Well, sir—"

"No. No more dissembling. Gerald and Retta think they picked up a dockworker off a pier on the river, but you, sir, are no ordinary dockworker. You may actually have come from Yorkshire at some point, but you are no ordinary farmer's son, either."

Jake stalled. "I am not sure how you arrived at that conclusion, my lord."

"I'll admit you had me fooled for a bit. That accent, for instance. But no dockworker of my acquaintance reads Homer. I watched you put that book away that day. Did you enjoy Chapman's translation, by the way? It's a bit dated, but—"

"Well, actually—"

Again his lordship cut him off. "And then we come to that display this morning. Your rescue of that child. That was a cavalryman's maneuver—not the clumsy action of one familiar only with farm animals. I would wager my entire fortune that you are or have been an army officer."

Jake sat silent for a minute, trying to sort out how to respond to this challenge. He decided truth—so far as he was safe with it—would be the best route.

Lord Alfred held Jake's gaze in the glare of an army officer dressing down a subaltern. "Look, Bolton. Do not seek to play games with me. Bolton. Is that even your name?"

"No, sir, it is not, but I am not at liberty to—"

"And why did you invade this home?"

"My—uh—work required that I be in this neighborhood, this part of London."

Lord Alfred gave a derisive snort. "And my brother's children just happened to give you the opportunity?"

"Well, yes, sir. They did not know that, of course. It truly is somewhat incredulous, but it was one of those coincidences that do happen sometimes."

Lord Alfred merely stared at him for a moment, then he sighed. "Your 'work'—and what would that be?" He paused, holding Jake's gaze. When Jake did not answer immediately, Lord Alfred's eyes lit up. "Hah. Government, I'll bet. Who? Home Office? Foreign Office? Parliament? I know it is not the army. York would have told me that much. But perhaps Prinny has decided to meddle in intelligence work now."

"I am truly sorry, sir, but I am not at liberty to—"

Again Lord Alfred held Jake's gaze for a long moment; he seemed to be trying to come to a conclusion. Finally, he muttered, "Government." He shook his head. "Sometimes the right hand does not know what the left is doing."

"Yes, sir."

Lord Alfred was silent for several weighty moments, then he shook his head as though he were arguing with himself. "Well, look, Mr. Bolton, if you can give me your word that you mean no harm of any sort to my niece or her brother, I shall let the matter continue as it is for the time being. But rest assured that I intend to keep fully aware of whatever goes on in this house."

Jake stood and offered the older man his hand. "I can do that, sir. I give you my solemn promise that I intend no harm to them at all."

Lord Alfred, too, stood and held Jake's gaze as he gripped the offered hand in a firm clasp.

Jake started to leave, then turned back. "Oh. And, sir? I did enjoy Chapman's work."

"Cheeky bastard," but it was said with a chuckle.

* * * *

For Jake, the next few days brought some minor changes to the routine of his life at Blakemoor House. Lord and Lady Davenport made a formal call and asked to be presented to the man who had rescued their son. Heretofore, Jake had not been included when callers were entertained in the drawing room. He was glad that his "lessons" had progressed to the point that he could drop the countrified accent entirely now and that Lady Henrietta had professed confidence in his social behavior. However, he thought she reflected his own apprehension—albeit for different reasons—as he joined the group in the drawing room that included Lord Alfred and Viscount Heaton as well as Lady Georgiana and Madame Laurent.

Immediately as Jake entered the room and was introduced, Lord Davenport rose and extended his hand. "Words are simply inadequate to express the gratitude Lady Davenport and I feel for your saving our son."

Somewhat embarrassed at the fuss over what had been an instinctual act, Jake took the man's hand and said, "I am glad to have been of service, my lord."

Lady Davenport rose from where she had been sitting next to Lady Georgiana and came to stand next to her husband. She, too, offered her hand. "You simply cannot know how very, very much we are in your debt, Mr. Bolton."

Jake bowed over her hand, then looked directly into her eyes and just barely prevented himself from revealing startled recognition. She was some fifteen years older than when Jake had last seen her, but as a young girl Lady Davenport had been one of half a dozen school friends his sister had brought home one school holiday. Hastily digging in the recesses of memory, he recalled having very little interaction with the gaggle of female guests of his sister. Still, there was no doubt. Lady Davenport was the former Miss Lucy Dennison!

Her brow wrinkled in consternation. "Do I know you, sir?"

"Oh, I shouldn't think so, my lady, unless ye be from a village in south Yorkshire." Jake deliberately slipped partly into his countrified dialect as he released her hand.

"No. I am from Kent," she replied. "Canterbury, actually. But I once had a friend in north Yorkshire. You look so familiar to me." She continue to stare at him.

Feeling panicky, Jake nevertheless controlled himself enough to shrug and turn slightly away, back toward her husband. "I suppose it is true that God has only so many patterns and outlines for his creations."

Everyone chuckled softly at this near joke and the conversation veered to safe topics of the weather and the coming Christmas season. The

Davenports again expressed their profound thankfulness to Jake as they took their leave.

Lord Davenport bowed to Jake and said, "Mr. Bolton, should you ever have need of anything—anything at all—you must allow me to be of service to you."

"Thank you, my lord." Jake breathed an inward sigh of relief as the couple left the room.

However, the incident had impressed upon him again that people tended to see what one told them they were seeing, and that the *ton*—those two hundred or so families of England's social elite—was truly a very small circle. He was simply not going to be able to carry on this charade forever. This fact was brought home to him again soon after the Davenports' visit.

Lady Henrietta and her aunt were busily planning their party set for the week before Christmas. Since there would be fewer than thirty guests, they would not open the huge ballroom, but they would decorate with festive greenery other public areas of the house—the dining room, drawing room, music room, and the library, as well as the entrance hall. This, of course, necessitated shopping trips to the flower market for the greenery and to various shops for ribbons and banners to put finishing touches to everything. Lady Henrietta insisted that Jake accompany her and her aunt to keep up his guardian guise—and to serve as an errand boy of sorts: that is, to carry their purchases. On these outings, the ladies chatted enthusiastically about their plans and about the invited guests.

Two names, especially, stood out for Jake: that of Colonel Lord Peter Fenton and that of Angus Middleton, Lord Ralston. Also, the ladies had invited Lord and Lady Davenport after their visit. He knew Peter would never give him away, and Jake thought he could finesse the situation with Lady Davenport, but Ralston was another matter.

"Oh, my. The plot thickens, eh?" Peter joked quietly when Jake met with him in the back stacks at Hatchard's Book Shop to tell him of his encounter with Lord Alfred after the incident in the park and his meeting the Davenport couple. "Did I not tell you years and years ago that your interest in Greek literature was not quite the thing? Has Lady Henrietta challenged you too?"

"Not yet. But at times I think she suspects things are not exactly as she thought them to be. Her interest in winning that bet is of foremost importance to her, though. She is now bent on teaching me how to address properly the likes of you in social situations."

Peter laughed. "I shall be my haughty best that evening."

Jake returned one book to a shelf and retrieved another, making a show of leafing through it as he said softly, "Ralston could be a problem, though. I can hardly ask her to uninvite him and Lady Ralston. Nor can I suddenly develop a case of the plague."

"Perhaps Ralston is not as much of a threat as you think. He was, after all, two years behind us in school, and you know how school boys stick to their own age groups. He went to Cambridge later when we were already at Oxford. Also, his eyesight is not what it should be. He wears a glass on a gold chain and squints through it like a veritable dandy, but for Ralston it is not merely an affectation."

"Well, in that case—"

"Besides," Peter added, "I will do my best to deflect any untoward curiosity, though you and I must be as strangers at this soiree."

"Of course. Now, have you had any luck with Morrow?"

"None. The man does his secretarial duties and goes home to his rented rooms. His landlady provides his meals, but he occasionally dines with friends or attends an entertainment of some sort. He is not a recluse. Not much of a gambler, either. He does not have a mistress, but goes to a certain brothel now and then. His needs seem rather modest. Whatever he is doing, it does not appear that money is his motivation."

"His companions?"

"Unexceptional." With a sigh, Peter turned to shelve the book he had been pretending to peruse. "We are following up on a couple of them, but, frankly, I still think the key lies in Blakemoor House. Or maybe Trentham's. Morrow is a friend of Trentham's butler, Talbot—yet another French émigré."

Chapter 12

Retta lay in her bed, once again robbed of sleep as she wrestled with her inappropriate attraction to Mr. Bolton; she could not deny the qualities of the man that were at the core of that attraction. Nor could she ignore the contradictions: a farmer's son, a sailor on a cargo vessel, a London dockworker. But he played the piano with a degree of expertise that was simply inconsistent with the level of training to which he admitted. Had he lied? Dissembled? If so, why?

He claimed a local vicar had allowed him to join lessons the churchman had conducted for paid pupils. Retta knew this was not an uncommon practice, nor did she discount a person's ability to educate himself beyond any level of formal education he might have had. And then there was the vicar's incredibly talented wife who had taught him music.

Retta was sure that casual reference to Shakespeare's famous line about music came from something other than seeing a single performance of a play performed by traveling players in a country village. Come to think of it, Mr. Bolton had let other such references slip in their conversations. She recalled their once discussing the self-indulgent behavior of the Prince Regent. She had said something about how the Prince and his royal siblings had been reared. Mr. Bolton had replied, "Well there is some truth in that line that 'the child is father of the man.'" She had been impressed by his cleverness at the time, but now she wondered how much more of Wordsworth's work he had committed to memory?

And, finally, there was that display of incredible horsemanship. Such skill had not come from working with draft animals on a tenant farm! She recalled other details he had shared of his life in their prolonged lessons. Details about the make-up of his family, for instance. How much of it was even remotely true? And how could she possibly challenge him at this stage when so much depended on his winning that infernal wager for her?

Concerned that he might be uncomfortable in such exalted company, she had been nervous when he came into the drawing room to receive the accolades of Lord and Lady Davenport—parents of the child he had saved. She need not have worried. He carried on as though he had been born to such company.

He rarely lapsed into the country dialect anymore. She was proud of his progress in that area. He had learned proper speaking very easily. Too easily? She dismissed this idea when she recalled the ease with which she herself had learned German. When she was thirteen, Retta had taken it into her head to learn the native language of England's Hanoverian king and queen. Her father had indulged her in this and hired a tutor for her. The countess had dismissed the whole thing as a waste of time; when, pray tell, was Henrietta likely to hold a dinner table conversation with the royal family? It had taken Retta a mere three months to become reasonably fluent. She could have put that skill to use in Vienna! She gave herself a mental shake and returned to the issue of Jake Bolton's language skills. After all, she noted, he was merely refining on his own language, was he not?

Still . . .

She pounded the pillow in frustration and willed herself to some semblance of sleep.

As the holiday season picked up momentum, she cut back on her protégé's lessons. There would be time for a serious review after the New Year had been ushered in. And there would be time after that for any serious consideration of her own future and the liberation her grandmother's legacy would give her. Besides helping her aunt prepare for their own party to occur only three days before Christmas, Retta accepted any number of invitations from others. She knew very well she was doing this in part to avoid thinking about the possible loss of her beloved Moonstar. Also, in moments of unguarded honesty with herself, she welcomed the fever of activity that kept her from dwelling on Jake Bolton's eventual departure from her life.

Just why had he become so important to her sense of well-being anyway? Then she would remember that kiss, the comfort of being in his arms, and dozens of not-quite-accidental touches and shared glances of mutual understanding. She was behaving—if only in her own imaginings—like some bird-witted schoolgirl. This would simply not do.

So she welcomed distractions, especially those offered by David Manning, Viscount Willitson. In recent weeks, having allowed him to renew his suit, she was at least half aware that she was using one man to avoid facing the obstacles of loving another. She accepted Willitson's invitations to go driving whenever the weather permitted; she urged him to prolong his visits when he called. He often appeared in her box at the theater or sat beside her at a concert. She liked David; he was comfortable. *Viscountess Willitson.* There was a certain ring to that, was there not? So what if his conversation sometimes lacked depth, or if she did not experience intensely physical responses to his touch, or if an idea or play on words went right over his head? He was kind, attentive, and sought to please.

It was in this frame of mind that she attended a ball given by the Duke and Duchess of Sutherlin. She suspected that David might this night press his suit more forcefully, though she had no idea how she would respond. Nevertheless, she thought a woman about to receive a marriage proposal should dress to suit the occasion. Having discarded two other choices Annie laid out before her, Retta finally chose a light orange silk gown with a bronze lace overskirt. The colors, Annie insisted, perfectly complemented the bronze streaks in Retta's light brown hair. A necklace of small topaz stones with a larger teardrop-shaped stone that nestled at the top of her cleavage, along with matching earbobs and a soft paisley shawl of the same colors, completed the outfit.

Gerald had agreed to escort his sister and their aunt to this ball, and as the three of them met in the entrance hall to don outer garments before taking on the winter weather, Retta noticed that the door to the library was ajar allowing a soft stream of lamplight to escape. Assuming Uncle Alfred was working late or just reading, she popped in to tell him good night and was surprised to find he was not alone. Jake Bolton sat in a winged chair opposite the one her uncle occupied. A small table between the chairs held a chess game. Retta, having not seen him since the early morning, had thought Mr. Bolton to be away doing whatever it was he did on his days off. The two men seemed to be quietly enjoying snifters of cognac as they lost themselves in their game. Both rose at her entrance.

"Oh! I thought you were alone, Uncle," she said, feeling a little foolish. "I just wanted to wish you a good night."

Uncle Alfred extended his hand to clasp hers. "Here. Let me see you." He turned her around. "Hmm. Well done, my dear. You will be the belle of the ball."

"Oh, you have been telling me that since my very first ball a hundred years ago," she said. "And it has not happened yet!"

"Well, it should," he said, giving her a kiss on the cheek.

But it was a gleam of appreciation in Jake Bolton's eyes and a silent nod of approval that made her body sing. She held his gaze for a moment, then quickly dropped her eyes, bade the two of them good evening, and rejoined her brother and her aunt in the foyer. Jake Bolton had not said a word, but it was his approval that she hugged to herself all the way to the ball.

As she climbed the stairs to the Sutherlin ballroom, she had a stern conversation with herself and firmly put a certain dockworker out of her mind. Having greeted her host and hostess and seen her brother stroll off with a group of his particular friends, she took a seat beside her aunt in what she thought of as the wallflower section of the room. She knew this was not quite fair as she was regularly sought out for a sufficient number of dances at any affair such as this. Sure enough, David materialized in front of her to claim the dance he had bespoke during a morning call two days earlier.

"You are looking especially lovely this evening, my dear. You quite put all the other ladies to shame," he murmured as they took their places in the dance that was forming.

"Thank you," she said, wondering why this effusive compliment seemed so weak against the approval she had seen in a pair of blue eyes earlier. They chatted amiably as the twists and turns of the dance permitted. When it ended, David sought to secure her hand for an additional two dances.

She laughed at him. "David, you know that would never do. Three dances? With the same man? Tongues would be wagging over every breakfast table. That would be tantamount to a declaration and you know it."

He gazed at her, warm friendliness replaced with something more serious, more intense in his usually laughing brown eyes. "Would that be so very bad, Retta? I think you know how I feel about you."

She looked away, but her tone was gentle. "You will have to be content with the waltz later. All right?"

He sighed. "If that is your wish." He leaned close as he returned her to her aunt. "I shall look forward to that waltz."

"Willitson seems especially attentive of late," Aunt Georgiana remarked as Retta sat down and the gentleman departed.

"He is a dear friend," Retta said.

"A friend? Nothing more?" Aunt Georgiana plucked at an invisible bit of lint on her dress. Her voice took on the quality of an indifferent afterthought, but Retta was not fooled for an instant. "A viscount. Heir to an earldom. You could do worse, my dear. Much worse."

Retta refused to get involved this discussion. She was relieved when Sir Michael Hamilton came to claim her for the supper dance. Immensely rich, Hamilton had earned his knighthood—as he was quick to point out—because he had rescued George, the Prince Regent, from his creditors on more than one occasion. Hamilton's remarkable sense of humor extended to himself. Retta loved the fact that he did not take himself overly seriously, that she could go driving with him or dance with him and know that he would joke with her, pointing out the more entertaining foibles of their companions. And so it was this evening as he entertained her and others at their table throughout their supper. It occurred to her that she could do worse than Sir Michael Hamilton too, should he seek to enter the non-existent competition for her hand.

As Retta came out of the supper room on Sir Michael's arm, David was waiting for her.

"Unhand that beautiful woman, Hamilton," David said with a mock growl. "She is mine, now."

Hamilton "protected" her by gripping her hand that lay on his forearm, and took a step toward his "adversary."

"The lady may choose otherwise, Willitson. In that case, I shall defend to the death her right to do so. What say you, oh lady fair?"

Retta laughed. "Do stop, both of you! Surely you were taught better manners in the school room." She looked up at Hamilton. "Thank you for charging into the fray for me, though. When next I need a champion, I shall call upon you, Sir Michael."

"Alas. I must be content with that promise." He grinned and bowed as she moved into David's arms with the first strains of a waltz tune from the orchestra.

"Did you miss me?" David asked.

"Oh, of course. We were separated *such* a long while. Why it must have been all of thirty minutes!"

Without missing a step, he pulled her closer and said in a tone only slightly more serious, "But I would have you near me always, my dear."

"Lord Willitson. Really. You must behave."

"If you insist, my lady. If you insist."

They gave themselves up to the music and the elegance of the dance for a few moments. Not only was David an accomplished dancer, but he had often been her partner and they danced well together, almost unconsciously. Which was not entirely good, for it allowed her to recall another waltz partner, one in her father's music room with only a single piano to supply the music. As the dance continued, Retta was scarcely aware that her partner had maneuvered them near and then through the open doors leading to the balcony.

"Too warm in there," he said, still moving in tune with the music.

"Yes, I think you are right." She noted that they were not exactly alone on the spacious balcony. Three or four other couples stood close and chatted quietly. The outer walls here were covered with ivy and there were several large potted plants strategically placed to allow guests a sense of privacy.

"This is better, eh?" he said as he danced her into a darker corner. Light from the ballroom and lanterns hung in the garden below provided a cheerful atmosphere and the strains of the music helped to carry one away from the everyday world.

"For the moment," she answered. "But it *is* December, and it is likely to become quite chilly, you know."

"I shall keep you warm." Pulling her close, he wrapped both his arms tightly around her and lowered his mouth to hers.

She had anticipated that at some point in the evening this might happen. Perhaps she had even willed it. She returned his kiss with a degree of enthusiasm that seemed to surprise him, for he broke the contact to look into her eyes. "My love," he murmured, pulling her even closer and kissing her even harder. She felt her breasts pressed against his chest. But instead of losing herself in the moment, she found herself taking an objective view of it—almost as though she stood outside her body as an impersonal observer. She pushed against him to separate the connection slightly, but she remained in the circle of his arms.

He drew a deep breath. "Retta, I know you are not one to tease and lead a man on. Please do say you will marry me. My feelings have not changed since I asked you before. We can make the announcement at your Christmas party."

She had seen this coming. Perhaps she had even willed this too. So why was her immediate reaction panic? "No! I mean—that is, I cannot—I need time . . . Please, David. . . "

He removed his arms from around her and took a step back as he held her gaze with his own. "How much? How much time do you think you need? My God, Retta, we have known each other for years."

"I know." Then she grasped at the first thought that floated into her mind. "My father is not here to give permission."

"I will write him tomorrow, if that is all that is causing your hesitation. I can send a letter by special courier. But, Retta, you know very well that he was agreeable to a match before he left England. And you *are* of age, my dear." There was a slight edge to his voice with the last sentence.

"I know. I am so sorry, David. I . . . I—" She grasped at another straw. "I cannot make such a decision until February."

"February?"

"It is only a few weeks."

"Why? Why February?"

"My birthday." She could not tell him of the wager. Not only was it imperative that as few people as possible know, but she was not at all sure how David would react if—when—he found out about it. Viscount Willitson sometimes showed himself to be rather strait-laced and conscious of his position in the world. "I will come into full possession of my fortune then," she added lamely.

"Retta, hear me clearly: I. Am. Not. Interested. In. Your. Fortune. Good God, woman. My father is the third or fourth richest man in all of Britain. It may have escaped your notice, but it just so happens that I am his heir."

"I know. It is just—well, it is important to me. Please do try to understand." She was genuinely sorry that she could not be more forthright with him. He deserved better of her than this. *My God! How many more people are likely to be hurt by that infernal bet and the secrecy surrounding it?*

"Easter."

"Easter?" She was perplexed.

"I give you until Easter to make up your mind. In the meantime, we just carry on. I shall not press you again."

She looked up at him. "Thank you, David. You are—you are more than generous."

"Men in love are fools," he said flatly. He pulled her close again and kissed her on the forehead. "Come. Let's go inside. It is getting cold out here."

* * * *

When Lady Henrietta left the library, Jake and Lord Alfred had gone back to their chess game. In the days following the rescue of the Davenport child and his confrontation with Lord Alfred, Jake had achieved a degree of rapport he had not had previously with the somewhat austere Lord Alfred. Jake suspected Lord Alfred's overtures of friendship stemmed from the man's desire to keep an eye on a person he viewed as an imposter. But the new relationship suited Jake very well, for he often shared the library with Lord Alfred and the secretary—and with any chance visitors.

Unless Lady Henrietta made particular demands for his presence, Jake now spent a good deal of time in the library, often ensconced in a big overstuffed chair off in a corner of that massive room, where he would not distract the men who worked there, or interfere with their business. In fact, neither Lord Alfred nor his secretary paid Jake much attention. He thought they mostly forgot he was there, buried in a book—at the moment Gibbon's treatise on the decline and fall of the Roman Empire. Jake hoped to make it through all six volumes.

But it had not escaped Lord Alfred's notice. "I say, Bolton. First Homer and now Gibbon. Careful, lad, you are likely to turn into whatever the male equivalent of a bluestocking is."

"I notice this copy has some interesting notes in the margin that look distinctly like your handwriting, sir."

"Oops. Guilty as charged. Have you got to his discussions of Christianity yet?"

"Not yet."

"Interesting stuff, that." Lord Alfred had been standing next to a table on which there was a chess game set up, toying with chess pieces as he talked. He gave Jake a direct look and asked abruptly, "Do you play chess?"

"I used to," Jake admitted.

"My brother is my usual opponent, but of course he is not here now. Care to join me?"

Thus had begun what were regular chess matches between the two. Jake was sure the games, like his freedom of the library, were part of Lord Alfred's plan to keep an eye on him, but the truth was they both enjoyed the games and they were fairly evenly matched.

Often enough, Jake was alone in the library, with no one taking undue interest in his being there. This suited Jake very well, for he was able—surreptitiously—to keep track of some of the documents that passed from one of those desks to the other. However, of late there had been very little to excite any interest. Then one morning from his corner, Jake observed as a courier from Whitehall delivered a packet to Lord Alfred.

"Sir, the duke would like your opinion of certain of these proposals by tomorrow morning if you can manage it," the courier said.

Lord Alfred examined them briefly, then nodded. "I shall deal with them right away."

Jake was annoyed when Lady Henrietta demanded that he accompany her and Annie on yet another shopping trip, and he was thus unable to hear any of the discourse that passed between Lord Alfred and his secretary regarding whatever it was the courier had delivered. When he returned late in the afternoon, both his lordship and his secretary had left the house and a hurried inspection of both desks revealed nothing of interest. Jake cursed his luck as he closed the secretary's desk and started toward his favorite chair across the room. But something caught his eye. The corner of a piece of paper stuck out from under the edge of the desk blotter. He pulled it out to see that it was a small card, about five inches square, and filled with notations such as he had deciphered before. He made a hasty copy and returned the card precisely to where it had been.

That evening as he and Lord Alfred were well into their second game, Lady Henrietta had bounced in to bid her uncle good night. And ruined any chance Jake had of winning that game. He rarely took notice of a woman's apparel, but her gown this evening was perfect for her. Her hair was arranged so as to leave a long strand along one side of her neck. A topaz necklace drew attention to that most delectable bosom, and he had caught a whiff of her usual scent. He ground his teeth silently cursing every man who was likely to dance with her this night.

When Jake lost that game, Lord Alfred said, "Somehow I don't think your mind was focused. Sure you are up to another game?"

"Of course. You just got incredibly lucky that time."

Lord Alfred gave him a knowing look. "Uh-huh. Have it your way. I will replenish our drinks as you set the board up again."

But again they were deep into a game when they were interrupted. This time, it was Sir Cecil Lindstrom dressed in formal evening attire.

"I am on my way to a small gathering at Carlton House," he announced, casually dropping the name of the Prince Regent's residence. "But I thought I would pop in to see how my favorite patient is doing."

Lord Alfred snorted. "Your favorite patient, indeed. What happened to the Duchess of Devonshire?"

"Off to the country, it seems. So—how are you? Breathing all right, are you?" He grabbed Lord Alfred's wrist to feel for the pulse. "Hmm. Seems fine."

"May I get you a drink, Lindstrom?" Lord Alfred asked. "We are having cognac, but I can offer you port."

"Ah, yes. Cognac is fine."

"Such exalted company you keep tonight," Lord Alfred said as he went to the sideboard for the drink. "I suppose I should feel flattered."

Lindstrom had not sat down and as Lord Alfred got up to pour the man's drink, the doctor wandered about the room. Had Jake not been watching keenly he would have missed his pause at the desk normally used by Henry Morrow. Pretending to study the chessboard, Jake saw the doctor slip that card from under the blotter and hastily consign it to an inner pocket of his coat.

Lord Alfred returned with the drink and motioned his friend a chair nearby. Lindstrom sat and chatted amiably, often dropping a name of this or that notable of society. He was not exactly rude, but his conversation

barely included Jake. Which was all right with Jake. He wanted a moment
to absorb the implications of what he had seen. He wished he could follow
the man, but that was probably foolish. It could very well be that the man
was off to precisely where he said he was going.

Lindstrom swallowed the last of his drink. "Well, I must be off. Prinny
hates for his guests to be late. Glad to see you doing so well, my friend."

Lord Alfred saw him to the door and returned to the game.

"Now, where were we? Hmm. Better watch that queen of yours."

Jake lost this game too.

Chapter 13

The Christmas party at Blakemoor House was small. During the season—only a few weeks away—it would scarcely be noted by the gossip mongers, who had to be satisfied now with whatever crumbs they could pick up. As one tabloid writer put it,

> *With so many of London's renowned hostesses out of town during this holiday season, it comes as welcome news that one of our great houses is keeping up with tradition. The question on everyone's mind is: Might we expect there to be an "important announcement" at this soiree? Lady HP and a certain viscount are keeping mum.*

Retta ignored such speculation as best she could, but she surmised this was the primary reason not one person had sent regrets to her invitations. The guest list had grown beyond what they had originally intended to that point that Retta and her aunt had briefly considered opening the ball room. "No, our guest list is not *that* large yet," they had agreed and neither of them wanted the overwhelming numbers that seemed to please so many *ton* hostesses.

For Retta, one of the happiest aspects of this event was that her brother Richard would be there to enjoy it with her and her other favorite relatives. Unbeknownst to her, he had arrived one night when she was out late attending a play. She had squealed with delight as he walked into the breakfast room the next morning.

She jumped up from her place at the table to hug him. "You might have warned us!"

"What? And spoil the surprise?" He hugged her tightly. "I heard you were having a party. Couldn't let you do that without me."

Gerald continued in his place to slather butter on a piece of toast. "The truth is the army discovered what a useless tool he is and sent him home. Is that not right, Uncle Alfred?"

"Not exactly," Uncle Alfred said, lowering his coffee cup to its saucer. "We have repositioned several regiments. Richard's is one of them."

"I like my story better," Gerald said.

"You would," Richard responded lightly.

"I do not care at all," Retta said, giving Richard another squeeze before returning to her seat. "I am just glad to have you here. And doubly glad you will be here for the party."

"So where do you go next?" Gerald asked, shoving a forkful of scrambled egg into his mouth.

"I am not sure," Richard answered as a footman placed a full plate of sausage and eggs in front of him. "The rumor is Belgium. Uncle?"

Uncle shook his head. "You know very well I cannot answer that."

"You mean *will not*," Richard said in an amiable tone. Then he asked in a false display of addressing the room at large, "Does it occur to anyone else how wholly useless it is at times to have relatives in high places?" Uncle Alfred merely snorted, and Richard turned to his sister. "So—oh wise and lovely eldest of the Blakemoor brood—is that tattlemonger right? Are you planning to make an interesting announcement at this party?"

Retta felt herself blushing. Involuntarily she looked at Jake Bolton two seats down on the opposite side of the table. He looked up and held her gaze. She thought she read amusement and curiosity—but something else too. Something more intense. Something that set her pulse to fluttering.

She quickly lowered her gaze and said brightly to her brother, "No. Not yet. Believe me, you will know before the tabloids do!"

In the last two days, Retta and Aunt Georgiana had worked diligently themselves or supervised servants in making and hanging decorations for their Christmas party. Garlands of greenery with bright ribbons woven into them draped fireplace mantles. Retta loved the tangy scent of evergreens that permeated the public rooms and hallways and the bright shiny green leaves and red berries of the seasonal holly. They had decided that the primary entertainment—caroling and dancing—would take place in the music room. Musicians hired to provide soft music during supper in the dining room would later move to the music room.

The music room received special attention as they decorated. Swags of greenery draped the fireplace and were hung along one wall as well, but the center of attention was a giant kissing ball suspended from the ceiling. Made of evergreen sprigs interspersed with holly and an abundance of mistletoe, it, too, had colorful ribbons woven through it. A good deal of giggles and teasing had accompanied its construction.

Retta also took special care in "decorating" herself for this occasion. Earlier she had commissioned a new gown of a blue so pale as to be almost white. An overskirt of silver lace gave the garment an ethereal look. Annie had twirled bits of the lace into Retta's upswept hairdo. She wore her mother's simple diamond necklace and earbobs.

"Oh, my dear," Aunt Georgiana said when Retta presented herself in their shared sitting room, "you look like the snow princess of Russian legend."

"Indeed yes," Madame Laurent murmured.

"You are in very fine looks yourselves, ladies," Retta said gesturing at her aunt's rich burgundy silk and the companion's soft green gown. "Shall we go down?"

In the drawing room they found that her uncle and her brothers, along with Mr. Bolton, were already sipping at before-dinner drinks. All four men were dressed in formal evening wear. While Mr. Bolton's attire did not seem to be in the first stare of fashion, he certainly did not stand out as some sort of aberration. In fact, Retta thought him strikingly handsome. She recalled Melinda's having said something to the effect that he would "clean up well." *Well,* she thought with an inward sigh, *Melinda certainly called that one right.*

The ladies were supplied with drinks—sherry or ratafia—and there was the usual anticipatory chitchat until guests began to arrive. With fewer than forty guests, they had decided against a formal receiving line. Despite the fact that so many people were out of town, Retta and her aunt felt they had put together a group that would have pleased any hostess at any time of the year—and that they had achieved not only a nice balance of males and females, but also had seen to adequate representation of both their generations. Retta's one regret was that her friends, Hero and Harriet, would not be here to enjoy it with her. But she had promised to write them afterwards with anything of note.

* * * *

Drink in hand, Jake wandered around the room, refusing to be drawn too deeply into any conversation. The family and he had agreed earlier that he would be introduced simply as "Mr. Bolton" with the implication that he had once been associated with Aunt Georgiana's late husband, though many guests would probably conclude that he was the Bow Street Runner they had heard about. There were a couple of raised eyebrows, and Sir Cecil Lindstrom more or less ignored him, but no one gave him the cut direct, and most people greeted him cordially.

Jake had been unable to contact Fenton since learning that Lindstrom was involved with Henry Morrow and the leak of information, so he welcomed being introduced to Colonel Lord Peter Fenton who, Jake was told, worked with the Foreign Office. Jake acted suitably impressed and offered his hand in greeting, thereby passing to Peter a copy of the information he had retrieved from the card Lindstom had later filched from Morrow's desk. As both he and Fenton wandered from one group to another, Jake was able, in small snatches of discreet conversation, to alert Fenton to the doctor's interest in the matter.

* * * *

Later Jake saw Fenton join a group that included Lindstrom and Madame Laurent. Jake had worried about this before-supper mingling of guests. If Lady Davenport or Lord Ralston were to recognize him, it would probably be then.

Lady Davenport did seek him out to thank him again for saving her child. "I just cannot get over the feeling that I should know you, sir."

Jake looked at her blandly and said, "As I said before, it would seem that I just have one of those very common countenances."

"Perhaps . . ." she said doubtfully.

Jake excused himself and retreated to a different part of the room.

His meeting with Lord Ralston had gone much as Fenton had predicted. Ralston lifted his quizzing glass to peer at Jake briefly, murmured a proper "How do you do?" and moved on. A short while later, Jake saw Fenton chatting with Ralston and even later Fenton managed to tell Jake, "Had to remind him who I was. I think you are safe."

Everyone seemed to understand that Lady Henrietta and her aunt had instigated this gathering, but Jake noted that the "honors" of hosting went to Lord Alfred and Lady Georgiana who, at supper, respectively occupied the head and foot of the table. The two ladies had assigned places to their guests with some eye to social protocol, while also taking into consideration that this was an informal affair and paired people according to perceived interests. Thus Richard was partnered with a young lady with whom he seemed enchanted at moment and Jake went into supper with Lady Henrietta. Jake felt a moment of triumph that he had won out over Viscount Willitson, whose name was so often linked with Lady Henrietta's, but she quashed that idea by explaining quietly, "This way I can deflect any awkwardness that might come up."

"Afraid I will use the wrong fork, are you?" he asked in an undertone.

"Of course not," she declared. "But in case you have questions about how to go on . . ." Her voice trailed off.

He noted that across the table, Dr. Lindstrom was seated with Madame Laurent, and the two often had their heads together in private conversation that Jake knew his mother would have considered "not quite the thing." Jake was glad that both Lady Davenport and Lord Ralston were seated some distance from him and on the same side of the table. Earlier Jake had been introduced to the Marquis of Trentham and his wife. They were among the age group that included Lord Alfred and Lady Georgiana. In the course of small talk before and during the meal, Jake was reminded that Trentham was one of Lindstrom's patients; the doctor often treated the Marquis for gout.

Following the meal, the ladies excused themselves to the drawing room and servants set out decanters of port and brandy for the gentlemen.

"I must caution you, gentlemen," Lord Alfred said, "I am under strict orders to minimize this part of the evening."

"The tyranny of women," someone said with a laugh.

Then, as such conversations were wont to do, their discussion turned to politics and news from the continent. Jake was alert to what others were saying, but he was particularly attuned to any comment or reaction of Sir Cecil Lindstrom, though he knew how unlikely it would be that Lindstrom would let slip anything of interest in this setting. The topic of major interest was, of course, the impending change in leadership of England's delegation to the Congress. The group was evenly divided in favoring Secretary Castlereagh or his replacement.

"I'm sure Wellington is a fine soldier," said Lord Jamison, a particular friend of Lord Alfred. Jake knew that Jamison, who wore a rather old-fashioned wig, was a retired veteran of the wars in the colonies some thirty years and more ago. "I never served with him, but it seems to me diplomacy should be left to diplomats. Castlereagh is a diplomat. Knows his way around those Russians and Prussians."

"Not to mention the Austrians and the French," someone muttered.

"My wife and I were in Paris this September," Lord Davenport said. "Wellington seemed to get on well enough in diplomatic circles there. He should do as well in Vienna."

"We hope," Gerald said, handing a decanter to the man next to him.

"I just returned from two weeks in Paris," Sir Michael Hamilton said as though to establish his credentials. "The duke may get on well there in high places, but all those ex-soldiers on the streets hate him mightily."

"To the point that one of them took a shot at him a few weeks ago," Richard offered.

"Well, now," Sir Cecil Lindstrom said, "with Wellington, you never know. Could just as well have been a jealous husband exacting revenge."

Polite laughter greeted this as the decanters were passed around again.

"The duke does have a way with the ladies," Peter Fenton said, "but real danger is more likely to come from those disgruntled soldiers." Jake glanced at him, surprised that Fenton would exert himself even to this extent. Fenton shrugged and turned to Richard. "So, Ensign Parker, what are they saying in the Horse Guards?"

"Word is that French soldiers are not faring well as civilians. No jobs. Life is tough. They are looking to Napoleon to save them by some miracle," Richard said. Jake was both surprised and irrationally pleased at the young man's insight.

"They are cagey about it, though," Hamilton said. "One fellow asks another, 'Do you believe in Jesus Christ?' The other responds, 'Yes, and in his resurrection.' Then they drink heartily to *his* health. Everyone knows who *he* is."

Jake glanced around the table to see how others might be responding to this. He focused his attention on Lindstom, but the man's countenance remained impassive while others expressed concern or outrage.

Lord Alfred stood and said, "Gentlemen, fascinating as this discussion is, we had best rejoin the ladies or I may be consigned to exile along with Bonaparte."

As soon as the men rejoined the ladies in the drawing room, Lady Henrietta clapped her hands and announced, "We shall all repair to the music room where there will be tea or other drinks of choice as well as biscuits and sweetmeats."

"I like the sound of 'drinks of choice,'" Lord Jamison said jovially.

"She also mentioned biscuits and sweetmeats." His wife's stern tone was belied by a smile.

"Oh, did you hear her, Alfred? If I'm not careful, I shall be joining you in exile."

"That you will, Phillip."

The men all chuckled at this exchange; the women mostly just shook their heads knowingly.

Jake brought up the rear as the guests followed their hostesses to the music room below. The ladies in their colorful gowns, the men in pristine black and white, and the buzz of chatter put him in mind of an assortment of exotic birds. He was not surprised to find Peter at his side.

"Had you heard of that toast of Napoleon's soldiers?" Jake asked quietly. "It was not a common salute when I left Paris in the spring."

"I have heard of it," Peter admitted. "If it as common now as Hamilton implied, it would bear watching. But right now, I am more interested in 'watching' that fetching Miss Henshaw."

"You were fortunate in your dinner partner."

"As were you, my friend. As were you."

Although a number of chairs and benches were strewn about the walls, the center of the room had been cleared for dancing, and when Jake and Peter entered the room, Lady Henrietta was already organizing the dancers into pairs and groups. Jake managed to suppress his grimace of disgust at seeing her partnered by Willitson. So? *Would* there be an announcement?

Lady Georgiana was at the piano and in effect "supervising" the three professional musicians who were playing a bass and two violins. The music was a rousing tune that had the dancers swinging from one partner to another. Periodically, Lady Georgiana would signal the music to an abrupt stop, catching a couple under the mistletoe decoration hanging from the ceiling. Other dancers and onlookers would then chant,

Come one, come one, come all, come all,
Look who's under the kissing ball.

Whereupon the gentleman would pluck one of the white berries, present it to his partner, and kiss her.

The nature of the kiss, of course, varied with the couple. Lord Alfred gave his friend Lady Hermiston a chaste peck on the cheek, and the two of them—both battling degrees of arthritis—escaped to the sidelines. Gerald gave his lady, whom he had known since they were children, a kiss of such length and mock passion that they had the whole room laughing and clapping.

Jake had seen Lady Henrietta "caught" under the kissing ball not once, but twice, first with Hamilton, then with Willitson. He tried, despite his gritted teeth, to force himself to be indifferent as Hamilton drew her close and kissed her soundly. Jake thought Willitson's kiss, though, was more intense and more meaningful. He was sure their audience saw it that way as well, for they expelled a collective sigh. Then the music struck up again and other couples were caught—or managed to be caught.

In the twists and turns of the dance, Jake had had several partners, even Lady Henrietta twice. But suddenly when the music stopped and the chanting started, it took him a moment to realize that it was he and Lady Henrietta under the kissing ball. It took him another moment or two to find a white berry to present to her; after all, the ball had seen to a good many kisses at that point.

"Oh, just kiss her," someone said—Jake thought it was Richard.

Nervous and thinking only of kissing her, he found a berry, placed it in her outstretched palm, and closed her fingers over it, holding her gaze as he did so. He found it hard to read her expression, but in any event it was not rejection. He drew her close, pressed his lips to hers—and nearly lost control at her response and his response to her response. Friendly catcalls, clapping hands and stamping feet brought them to their senses and he handed her off to her next partner in the dance—but not before seeing the wonder in her gaze that precisely mirrored what he was feeling.

Looking back at it later, Jake thought he had been in something of a daze through the rest of that long "kissing ball" dance. Afterwards, there had been caroling with many of the company gathered around the piano and others on the sidelines, all singing enthusiastically the time-honored tunes, himself included. It was in the midst of "Deck the Halls" that disaster struck.

Suddenly Lady Davenport, who had a pleasing soprano singing voice, stopped in mid note on the other side of the piano from Jake, and, staring right at him, her voice in a high pitch of excitement, said, "I have it! At last it has come to me! The Duke of Holbrook! You are the very image of one of his sons! But I forget which one."

Lady Georgiana had stopped playing and all eyes turned toward Jake. He looked around pretending to search for the person she was addressing, then feigned surprise to realize she was talking to him. "Oh, unlucky man, he then," he said with an embarrassed laugh.

Lord Ralston, who stood some distance away from Jake, raised his quizzing glass to peer at Jake for a long moment. "Can't see it myself," he said. "And I went to school with two of Holbrook's boys."

Jake was glad when Peter Fenton jumped in with, "Nor can I and I have known that family forever it seems."

Lady Davenport was clearly embarrassed as she said, "Oh, I am so sorry. It just burst out of me—and the resemblance seemed so very, very strong to me. But of course it has been years and years . . ." Her voice faded.

"Never mind, my dear," Lady Jamison said. "I make such mistakes all the time."

"Very understandable," some gentleman mumbled. "Now, where were we?"

Whereupon Lady Georgiana and the musicians started the tune again and everyone joined in, the incident apparently forgotten. But Jake happened to glance at Lord Alfred and the found the man staring at him rather intently.

Shortly after that servants wheeled in a flaming wassail bowl and a wassail song brought the caroling to an end. And then the party had broken into small pockets of conversation and finally people began to leave amidst many a "thank you" and "we had such a good time."

When he climbed into bed, Jake thought he had survived that scare with Lady Davenport. And he thought the tabloids would correctly report, "A good time was had by all." But at least there had been no "interesting announcement" for them to crow about. Most of all, his mind dwelt pleasantly on that kiss, and even at the memory, his body tightened, and he dreamed of something beyond a kiss.

* * * *

Retta kicked off her slippers, stretched her legs out straight before her, and leaned back in her favorite barrel chair in the sitting room. Her mind went to that kissing ball dance and focused on the one kiss that had meant the most to her: Jake's. She relived the feel of his lips on hers, the way her whole body seemed to awaken to his touch.

She accepted the nightcap her aunt offered her and Madame Laurent. She sniffed at it and raised an eyebrow. "Cognac?"

"I thought we deserved something more than lemonade or ratafia," her aunt replied.

"And so we do," Retta said. "I think our Christmas party went very well."

"Very well, indeed, my lady," said Madame Laurent.

Retta sat up straighter and waved her glass at her aunt's companion. "Oh. And you, Madame. What is this thing between you and the good Doctor Lindstrom?" Retta was by no means inebriated, but she knew she had drunk enough this evening to loosen her tongue.

Madame blushed and said primly, "I am sure I do not know what you mean."

"Doing it too brown, Celeste," Aunt Georgiana said languidly. "Besides, we think it is wonderful—do we not, Retta?—that you have . . . an interest . . . at this point in your life."

"Well." She sounded reluctant. "Sir Cecil did send me flowers this week."

"Which I noticed you wore tonight," Aunt Georgiana said.

"I think it is nice—very nice," Retta said stifling a yawn.

"We have much in common," Madame Laurent said. "He, too, lost property in France during the revolution. We both have hopes in the new Bourbon regime."

"I hope it works out for you," Retta said politely. She turned to her aunt. "And you, my lady. I think I may have a bone to pick with you."

Her aunt set her empty glass on a nearby table. "I have no idea what you are talking about."

"As you just said to Madame Laurent, 'doing it too brown, my dear.' You know very well that it was no accident that I was caught three times—three times!—under the kissing ball. At a party I was hosting!"

"'Tis hard sometimes to see who is where in the midst of a lively dance."

Retta merely snorted softly, stifled a yawn, and excused herself. Despite feeling sleepy only moments before, once in bed, she lay there staring at the canopy, which was faintly visible in light from the banked fire. As a social gathering, the party *had* been a success. As a means of sorting out her feelings about Jake Bolton, it had been a disaster. That kiss. Oh, that kiss. That kiss had complicated her life immensely. There was no way she could be so unfair as to accept David's proposal when she was in love with another man.

She turned her face into the pillow. *Oh, my God! It is true. I am in love—in love!—with Jake Bolton.*

The next day, still struggling with her feeling for Jake Bolton, she sought to gain a better handle on the situation by trying to bring her friends, Hero and Harriet, up to date:

> *Dear Hero and Harriet,*
>
> *I am assuming that, as my dearest friends in all the world, you will forgive my writing you together and sending one of you a copy. Remember those lengthy missives we used to share during school holidays? We poured our hearts out to each other and worked through such monumental problems! I wish the issues in my life today were so simple.*
>
> *First of all, your reservations about that bet were well-founded, though not entirely for the reasons you stated at the time. I previously wrote you both about going to the docks and Rebecca's choice of a "suitable specimen." As I have come to know Mr. Bolton, I am more and more certain that he is capable of winning that bet for me, though I am sure he thinks the whole thing is a bit silly.*

I admire so much about this man! And yet—I have so many unanswered questions about him! In many ways he is honest and straightforward in his dealings with me, but I always have the feeling that he is holding back, that there is much, much more to him than he is allowing the world—well, me at least— to see. Did I mention before that he is quite handsome and has absolutely gorgeous blue eyes? I am sure you can tell that I find him most intriguing. I am equally sure that you understand how thoroughly unsuitable that idea is! If only I had met him at a ball or at some ton soiree. And yet . . .

Our lessons proceed apace, and he is learning faster than I hoped. Perhaps too fast? But I dare not challenge him, for I simply must win that bet! I find the idea of giving up Moonstar far more devastating than I ever imagined when I so glibly agreed to that wager. Why must I always learn the lessons of life too late????

Finally, on the topic of that infamous bet: I am sure the two of you foresaw better than I the intrigue and secrecy that would be necessary to keep up this charade. I find I am not comfortable with that aspect at all.

She went on to recount social affairs she had attended lately and finished by telling her friends of the Christmas party, though she found she was not quite ready to share—even with Hero and Harriet—the truth of her overwhelming reaction to that kiss—or the previous one.

Chapter 14

Retta would have liked to withdraw into herself to try to come to terms with her feelings for Jake, but there were still traditional Christmas activities to get through. In the absence of the real mistress of Blakemoor House—her stepmother—Retta felt she should try to keep those traditions for the rest of the household. To this end, she and her aunt requested that Jeffries, Mrs. Browning, and Monsieur Aubert, the Blakemoor chef, meet them in the morning room to discuss plans for a festive Christmas dinner. The five of them sat around the wicker and glass table, the chef with a notebook at hand.

"We simply must have a plum pudding," Retta said. "I know that is not something that appeals to you, Monsieur Aubert, but it is traditional in English homes."

Monsieur Aubert nodded. "I made one last year, if you remember, my lady. I shall prepare two or three other desserts as well. And for the main course, my lady?"

"Ham would be nice," Aunt Georgiana said.

"Last year I was instructed to roast a goose," Monsieur Aubert suggested.

"Oh, yes, by all means," Retta said. "A Christmas goose. And ham. And filet of sole. And those wonderful Brussel sprouts you do, and peas, and—oh, whatever else you wish, Monsieur. I trust your judgment fully. But the real reason I ask you to meet with us this morning is that I should like you to produce a like menu to be served in the servants' hall on Boxing Day—with only a limited buffet for the family then."

"My lady?" Monsieur Aubert seemed confused.

"Boxing Day should be for those who make our lives easier. We will limit duties of all staff as much as possible that day. Mrs. Browning? Mr. Jeffries? You will see to that, will you not?"

"Yes, my lady." They spoke in unison.

Then Jeffries as the highest ranking servant in the household, cleared his throat and said, "Uh, my lady, I am wondering if Lady Blakemoor left these instructions? Or perhaps sent them from Austria?"

"As a matter of fact, she did not. But she is not here to object, is she? Both Lord Alfred and Lord Heaton endorse this plan for the holidays."

"Yes, my lady." Again the two spoke in unison, and Retta caught them exchanging a look of mutual understanding. When the three had left, Retta looked over her own notes again.

"I do miss the yule log ceremony we always have in the country," she said.

Her aunt nodded. "'Tis hard to go out into the forest in the middle of London to choose a yule log. Perhaps we could send your brothers among the trees of Hyde Park."

"Do be serious, Aunt!"

Aunt Georgiana's tone did turn serious. "I miss the children. Christmas should be about children. What with siblings and cousins galore, the Blakemoor country house always had a gaggle of children about for the holiday house party. Seeing their faces light up when Father Christmas made his appearance was such a treat! I remember one year—you must have been about three—he gave you an orange the size of a small melon. Your little fingers could barely grasp it." She sighed. "But then you all had the lack of grace to grow up."

"Such a lamentable action on our part."

"And none of you seems in any hurry to produce the next lot for me to dote upon."

Retta laughed. "Rebecca is the only one of us in any position to remedy that situation—and she has been married less than six months. You must allow her time."

"Yes, she is. And is that not a shame? *You* are the eldest. It is high time *you* were settled, my girl." Aunt Georgiana shot her an inquiring look.

Retta, who almost never felt uncomfortable with her beloved Auntie Georgie, did so now. She shrugged and looked away. "When a suitable partner presents himself . . ."

"Perhaps he already has."

"What do you mean?" She could not control the anxiety that even she heard in her voice.

"Retta, my dear, I have watched you for several weeks now with Willitson and Sir Michael and that other fellow—what is his name? Oh, Mathisson. Baron Mathisson. A baron, a viscount, and a knight. And you find none of them 'suitable'?"

Retta busied herself with jotting a note, then merely twirled the pencil in her fingers. "When you put it that way, it makes me seem terribly shallow."

"No, my dear. *Shallow* is not a word anyone could toss at you. Your work with the Fairfax sisters, as well as your attendance at the literary league's meetings, belie that term immediately."

Both were silent for a moment, then Retta ventured, "Auntie Georgie, are you happy? I mean do you regret not having had children of your own?"

"William and I wanted a family, of course, but life just did work in that direction for us."

"But you were young when we lost Uncle Mickelson. Did you never think of remarrying?"

"Not really."

Retta leaned forward. "But why? That is, if I am not being too intrusive."

"I do not mind your asking, my dear." Her aunt seemed lost in the past for a few seconds. "I hardly know how to respond. What William and I had—well, it was special. Anything else would have seemed second best and I just could not accept second best."

"But are you sorry now that you did not?"

"I do not regret my choices," her aunt replied slowly, her hands clasped before her on the table. "You asked if I am happy. Yes, I think I am. One does not miss what she never had. I have always had you and your brothers and sisters. And since I am *your* godmother as well as aunt to all of you, I feel a bit more possessive about you—and more concerned. I want *you* to be happy in whatever choices you make in life. But know this, my dear: I approve—in advance!"

Retta reached across the table to grasp her aunt's hands. "Thank you," she whispered. Then in a stronger voice, she added, "I may need that assurance more than either of us knows."

Her aunt gave her a questioning look, but Retta did not elaborate.

* * * *

Jake hoped he could just get through these holiday weeks without endangering his mission or losing his sanity. He was irritable and despondent—two moods that were simply out of character for him. He knew the source of his irritability was this ridiculous situation with Lady Henrietta. That kiss under the kissing ball had been some sort of turning point—and he was sure she knew it as well as he did. But he also was absolutely sure that so long as she thought him a common dockworker, she was not likely to entertain the possibility of their being anything more than they already were. But what was that? Friends? Teacher and pupil? Or two people sincerely attracted to each other and unable to break through the constraints that held them back?

As long as he was in the midst of this spy mission, he could not just throw caution to the winds and declare to her and the world at large who he was. He had not counted on this situation becoming even more difficult because of the winter holidays. Always before when he had been engaged in a mission during this time of the year, it had been on foreign soil. He was sure his family would have all gathered at the family seat in the country for the holidays—that was just what Bodwyns did. And, damn it, he wanted to be there too! Nevertheless, he went by Holbrook House twice just to make sure, but saw no sign that any of the family was in residence. He dared not march up to the door—or even to the stable—and ask. And what would he have done had they been there? Show himself and possibly compromise the mission?

With Lady Henrietta occupied in planning this or that festivity or attending some social gathering elsewhere, he found himself with a good deal of empty time on his hands. He was grateful whenever the weather permitted the morning rides, but those rides did not fulfill his need for meaningful work, and the weather did not permit them often. So, he spent a good deal of time in the library reading off in his corner, or playing chess with Lord Alfred.

He had slunk deep into the comfort of his corner chair one afternoon when Sir Cecil Lindstrom dropped in. Lord Alfred had been working at his desk earlier, but had excused himself to "look in on what was going on above stairs" where his sister and his niece were holding court with afternoon callers.

"Do you have anything new for me, Morrow?" the doctor asked of the secretary. "I am just on my way out."

"For you, sir? Why no, sir, but Lord Alfred has just stepped out for a moment, if you'd like to wait for him." Jake could not see the secretary from his own position, but he imagined this bit of dialogue was taking place with a good deal of head gesturing and rolling of the eyes in Jake's general direction.

After a long pause, Jake heard the doctor say, "Oh, I see. Yes, I believe I shall wait for him. Thought maybe he'd left a note for me." Jake sat up straighter as Lindstrom strode across the room to say, "Hello, Bolton. Didn't see you there. Shouldn't you be out protecting Lady Henrietta from dastardly fellows?"

"Not today," Jake replied. "They are right here today." He paused and saw a shadow of alarm cross Lindstrom's eyes before Jake added, "The ladies are still entertaining in the drawing room above, are they not?"

The doctor gave a nervous laugh. "Ah, I see."

He was saved any further dissimulation as Lord Alfred entered the room and said, "Ah, Cecil. Jeffries said you were in here. Did you require something else of me?"

"No, no. I just wanted a quiet word with you—outside the presence of the ladies—to ensure that you are really feeling all right. We don't want a repeat of that episode earlier in the month, now do we?"

"No, *we* do not." Lord Alfred's voice dripped sarcasm. "Did I or did I not just see you at the club last night? And fifteen minutes ago in the drawing room? I do not need you hovering over me like a hen with one chick."

"No, of course not. We medical men tend to be overly solicitous at times. I'll just be going now."

"Right." Lord Alfred plopped himself down behind his desk waved the doctor onward.

Jake saw the doctor exchange a look with the secretary who just shrugged. Then the doctor was gone and Jake hid his grin behind the book he had been reading.

* * * *

Christmas Day came and went. Boxing Day came and went. Both days had passed pretty much as Retta had planned them.

Christmas dinner had been made more festive by the addition of several guests: fellow soldiers from Richard's regiment, the Dean of St. Paul's Cathedral along with his wife and two marriageable daughters, Lord Jamison and his wife, Sir Cecil Lindstrom, Madame Laurent's brother, Henry Morrow, and her son, Charles Laurent, who came in from the country to spend Christmas with his mother and uncle. Neither of the last two guests interested Retta much, but it *was* Christmas and the Laurent-Moreau folk had a long-standing relationship with the Earl of Blakemoor.

The dinner went very well and Retta was glad to see Madame Laurent exert herself enough to ensure that her brother and her son, as well as Sir Cecil, were properly entertained. She was not glad to see one of the churchman's daughters openly flirting with Jake Bolton or to see that traitorous man responding to the girl's wiles. What had possessed her to seat them next to each other anyway? After the meal, the men chose to forgo the ritual of drinking port or cognac absent the ladies, and the whole party trekked down to the music room, which had been restored to its usual appearance with chairs and settees arranged in comfortable groupings. Aunt Georgiana again performed as the principal purveyor of music, though other ladies—and some gentlemen—took their turns as well.

Afterwards, Retta would have been hard-pressed to explain what bit of perverseness had inspired her, but when it was her turn to perform, she insisted that Mr. Bolton join her. Aunt Georgiana and other members of her family were clearly surprised. She could tell that he was reluctant to do so, but she had made it something of a challenge and she was sure he would not back down from it. Nor did he. As he sat next to her on the piano bench, she immediately felt herself responding to his being near—the warmth of his body so close to hers and that tantalizing cleanness that she associated with him.

"Do you know this piece?" she asked as she put a sheet of music in front of them. "It is one of my favorites."

"Vivaldi. Yes. One of my favorites as well." He laced his fingers together and stretched his arms before him, then laid his hands on the keys.

He nodded for her to start, and then both became engrossed in the music, though her attention was not so grounded that she did not notice how his hands—those big hands, those long fingers—fairly coaxed the music out of the machine. Occasionally their fingers brushed against each other to elicit an instant twinge of awareness in her. When they were finished, she chanced gazing into his eyes and found herself so mesmerized that she was scarcely aware of the applause they were receiving. And it was enthusiastic applause, not the polite appreciation one usually had on occasions such as this. As they both rose and relinquished the bench back to Aunt Georgiana, he gave a formal bow.

"Well done, my lady."

She gave him a slight curtsey. "And you too, kind sir."

"That was simply splendid!" Aunt Georgiana said, then raised her voice to address the room at large. "I doubt any of us will want to follow that performance, so let us all join in singing our hearts out with traditional carols."

As the entire party did so, Retta had servants bring in a wassail bowl and serve drinks and small cakes to everyone.

The next day, Boxing Day, went exactly as Retta had planned, ending with a group of mummers who performed in the servants' hall where tables and benches has been pushed aside to provide a "stage" around which the entire household gathered to watch the traditional slapstick plays. Again, the evening ended with wassail and cakes. Seeing the genuine enjoyment and gratitude of the staff, Retta knew these festivities were worth every bit of the effort to prepare for them. Had she had any doubts on that score, Annie would have dispelled them later, for the maid simply could not stop chattering about what a wonderful day she had had playing in the snow in the park with the footman Baker and three or four other members of the staff, but Retta noted that it was Baker's name that was threaded into the conversation repeatedly.

The following day life in Blakemoor House returned to its normal routine—more or less. Retta was determined to take holiday goodies to Fairfax House. Food left over from the two feasts—and deliberately planned as well—went into covered hampers. Oranges and clusters of sweetmeats tied into small packets with colorful ribbons went into another basket. She had ransacked her own closet and those of her friends—especially those friends who had children—to collect clothing to take to the sisters and their current charges. Jake Bolton would, of course, accompany her and Annie, but in view of the harshness of the winter and the vulnerability of any carriage on some of London's streets, Retta thought it prudent to have one of the footmen accompany them too. Annie's raptures over Baker made him the perfect choice, though he would have to ride on the top and Bolton would ride beside the driver because the coach was so loaded.

* * * *

Jake was not at all comfortable with the idea of a journey to Spitalfields when the weather and limits on seasonal jobs would make folk more desperate. And here was Lady Henrietta, her coach so loaded that bags and parcels literally stuck out from the top railing, blithely assuming she would be safe going through of the roughest sections of the city! He made sure that he and Baker and the coachman were well armed.

Baker took the loaded pistol and held it gingerly. "I ain't never shot no gun afore."

"Let's hope you won't do so today, either," Jake said, trying to project far more confidence than he was feeling.

"But if you have to, don't try to aim the gun—just point and shoot. The mere sight of a gun—and the noise—will likely scare off anyone trying to do us harm."

"If you say so," the young man said doubtfully.

"Lady Henrietta will have two pistols inside the carriage and she knows how to use them. We should do all right."

"If you say so," Baker repeated.

They aroused little interest until they reached the edges of the Spitalfields area. Jake was aware of some rough-looking types eyeing the loaded carriage. "Be alert now," he told Baker. He knew the coachman needed no such instruction.

Suddenly two men darted toward the front of the team and tried to grab at the harness to slow the horses. The driver was having none of this and cracked his whip in their direction, the sound of the whip urging the animals forward. Jake saw two other men rush toward the carriage, apparently ready to grab a door handle as soon as their accomplices managed to slow the team enough.

Following his own advice to Baker, Jake simply pointed his pistol at one of those grabbing at the harness and shot. The man howled and dropped away. The driver was busy trying to manage the team, so Jake snatched up the pistol on the seat beside him and pointed it at the other fellow trying to halt the team. That one looked up to see the gun pointed straight at him and quickly lost interest in stopping this team.

Jake heard a shot from within the carriage and saw one of those on the side of the vehicle grab at his shoulder and stagger back.

"Other side," he shouted at Baker, who quickly shot his pistol at the man grabbing at the handle on that side. He missed, but the mere fact that they had so many firearms aimed at them discouraged the would-be robbers.

Jake reloaded, traded his pistol for Baker's, then reloaded that one and the coachman's. "Stay alert now," he told Baker. "There may be more of these bastards."

"Are you all right up there?" Lady Henrietta called through a slit under the coachman's seat.

"Yes. Are you?" Jake yelled back.

"Shaken, but whole," she said.

He grinned at her sheer bravado.

They arrived at Fairfax House without further incident and while the coach was unloaded, Lady Henrietta was invited for tea in the drawing room while Jake, along with Annie and Baker, was given tea in the kitchen. Mrs. Boskins sent a boy out with a mug for the coachman. Amid exclamations of wonder and concern, they informed the Fairfax people of what had happened and learned of similar incidents in the area in the last few weeks. As they prepared to depart, the sisters, along with a few of their charges, stood on the front steps.

"This has been such a hard winter for so many folks," said tall, gray-haired Miss Fairfax. "We do what we can, but we still must be cautious. We hired two more men to help Mr. Boskins. People know we are armed."

"And they also know they can come to us for help, so people in the neighborhood truly do help protect us," her sister said.

"I do not mean to be ungracious at all, Lady Henrietta," Miss Fairfax said, "and we are ever so grateful that you have come, but as soon as your baskets are emptied, you really should be on your way. Darkness comes so early these days."

"And darkness seems to bring forth the worst in folks," her sister added as a man came out with the empty baskets.

Lady Henrietta hugged the sisters and Jake handed her into the carriage.

"You and Baker will ride inside with Annie and me," she told him.

"As you wish, my lady."

He noted that the coachman or Baker had lighted all the lanterns in and on the coach. As he handed Annie in as well, he saw her take the seat opposite her mistress. When Lady Henrietta said nothing, Jake motioned Baker into the carriage beside Annie, leaving him the seat beside her ladyship. Which was just fine with him, though he harbored a wish that the others might just disappear. The trip back to Blakemoor house was uneventful if one discounted the fact that Jake Bolton was so very aware of the warm female body on the seat next to him and that flowery-woodsy scent he would always and forever associate with her. He wanted to pull her close and kiss her senseless, but of course he did not do so. That couple on the other seat were very effective as chaperons, though Jake suspected Baker was holding Annie's hand under the drapery of her skirt. Lady Henrietta tried initially to keep up a running patter of conversation, but then gave it up and they completed the journey in relative silence.

Chapter 15

The New Year made its appearance rather quietly. Retta had feared the tradition of the "First Footing" would be ignored this year, but apparently either Uncle Alfred or Aunt Georgiana had seen to its fulfillment. Thus, on New Year's Day when members of the household were all seated at the breakfast table, Mr. Jeffries announced the entrance of the first guest to step across the threshold of Blakemoor House in the New Year. As custom demanded, he was a tall, dark man dressed in black and bearing the symbolic gifts of coal, salt, and cake, which he presented to Uncle Alfred as apparent head of the household while wishing them all warmth, wealth, and food in the coming year. Retta was delighted and led the applause that greeted his performance. He refused their invitation to join them, but Retta saw her uncle press a coin upon him. She assumed he was scheduled to be the "First Footer" at some other household. She was glad that, symbolically at least, they might all look forward to good fortune in this new year of 1815.

January weather took a turn for the worse in the first week. Snow piled up on all but the most traveled streets, though in wealthier neighborhoods, servants were sent out with shovels to clear the walkways and make the streets navigable. Robbed of her morning rides, Retta nevertheless made a daily visit to the stables, armed with apples or carrots for her favorites, especially for her precious Moonstar. Each day she confided to the mare her confidence or apprehension about the culmination of that infernal bet.

"Happy New Year, Moonstar," she murmured, holding an apple in the palm of her hand. "Only five or six weeks to go. Oh, dear God, I do not want to lose you too."

As the mare gently took the apple, Retta realized what that *too* meant: losing Jake. No matter how the bet turned out, he would disappear from her life.

"So, I'd best treasure what time I have left," she said into the softness of the mare's neck.

To this end, she cut back on her social outings and was "at home" to fewer callers as she tried to be absolutely sure that Jake Bolton would be ready for his big introduction to society.

Or that was what she told herself.

She knew very well he was probably as ready as he ever could be. Nevertheless, she worried that they might have overlooked something, that some little detail might trip him up—and doom her chances to win the bet. But, far more importantly now, she wanted to protect him from the public humiliation that might ensue were he found to be a fraud. Despite the diversions of the holidays, she was still intensely conflicted when it came to one Jake Bolton. However unsuitable, however inappropriate, she savored her time with him, treasuring a grin, a shared view of some story in the morning paper, the warmth of being near each other, the occasional brush of a hand or an arm. She simply could not deny the physical attraction, even as she recognized and distrusted the anomalies associated with him.

One day as her aunt and Madame Laurent were entertaining callers in the drawing room, Retta commandeered the morning room for a tutorial session with Jake. Mr. Bolton. She really must stop thinking of him as *Jake*. Both were dressed casually. She had donned a soft blue print muslin with a dark blue woolen shawl to fend off the winter chill in even the finest of houses. He wore his buckskins with a gray wool jerkin over an open-collared blue shirt that emphasized the blue of his eyes. Her attention kept straying to a hint of dark hair she glimpsed at that open collar. *What would it be like to touch it? To kiss that hollow at the base of his throat?* She gave herself a mental shake and turned to the business at hand.

She made up improbable scenarios for him. What if he were introduced to a dowager duchess and her daughter-in-law at the same time? To a younger son of a duke—no, not the heir? To a high-ranking member of the clergy? To this or that member of the royal family?

"Do you really think I will need to know all this—these fine distinctions in ranks—for a single evening at a ball?" he asked, sitting back in his chair and waving a hand at the copy of Debrett's guide that lay on the table.

"Perhaps not. Heaven knows people with titles often make mistakes themselves—but they would get away with it, while you might be shown as an imposter."

"And you would lose your bet."

"And I would lose my bet," she said glumly. She could hardly add that the thought of losing him was far more troubling, now, could she?

"Does winning mean so much to you?"

"Winning for itself alone? No. But the very thought of losing Moonstar—" Her voice caught as she looked at him, not even trying to hide the worry and pain that seized her.

He sat up straighter and leaned across the expanse of the table between them to grasp her hand. "I shall do my best to ensure that you do not lose, my lady."

"Thank you." Without conscious thought, she turned her hand so as to grip his. She looked at their clasped hands and allowed the warmth and security of his touch to enfold her.

He cleared his throat and, still holding her hand, said, "Lady Henrietta, I fear we are drifting into dangerous waters."

She did not pretend to misunderstand, but she did seek to lighten the mood. "Is that a metaphor from your days at sea?"

He smiled. "Not exactly, but it fits, does it not?"

"It fits." She reluctantly withdrew her hand. "But this is a ship that should never have set sail."

"Floundering, perhaps, but not yet sunk, I think."

She laughed softly. "I like a man who is able to express optimism in the face of great odds."

"Well, then, I'm your man," he said lightly and sat back in his chair. Silence ensued for a moment or two as she idly riffled the pages of the book that lay between them, and then he added, "What next, oh Socrates of the fair sex?"

She had been thinking that she wished he really were her man, but his question brought a dose of reality. "Socrates? Where did that come from?"

He shrugged and would not meet her gaze. "I—I don't know. Just popped in from somewhere."

"Just as your other learned allusions have done, I suppose."

"I am not sure what you mean." He sounded guarded.

She sensed an immediate shift in the tone of their conversation—a chilly shift—but she doggedly pursued. "'If music be the food of love . . .' Or, 'the child is father of the man.'"

Again he shrugged, but this time he held her gaze. "One picks up phrases here and there. In three decades of living, things is likely to rub off, dinna ye ken?"

"Standard English will do very well," she snapped. "There is no need to revert to that countrified dialect."

"Yes, ma'am."

"I think there must be more to it than that."

"I am not wholly sure of what you mean by 'it,'" he said, and she wondered if he were stalling, trying to put her off.

"Those allusions. Your expertise with language. Your riding skills. Not to mention that you handled yourself *very* well at our Christmas party even when Lady Davenport made such a ridiculous scene. And the dinner on Christmas day. I am thinking there is far more to Jake Bolton than meets the eye."

"There is probably more to anyone than meets the eye," he countered. "I thought I was behaving as you wished me to. I simply cannot offer you any more than that."

"Cannot? Or will not?"

"Have it as you wish."

He was dissembling. She was sure he was, and it infuriated her. She wanted to demand flatly that he explain himself, but she dared not do so. Five more weeks. Six at the most.

She gathered up the book and some papers she had brought with her and said, "I think we shall continue this session at another time."

"Yes, ma'am."

He stood as she did and even his acquiescence annoyed her. She left the room abruptly and almost immediately began chastising herself. Lady Henrietta Parker, normally forthright and direct, had turned into the sort of equivocator that she hated. The more she thought about it, the angrier she became. Who did he think he was—to be playing such games with other people? Why didn't she just have it out with him?

But she knew why.

That damned bet.

She dared not upset the status quo at this stage, but, by heavens, before he just strolled out of her life, Mr. Jake Bolton would damned well explain himself!

* * * *

Jake knew and regretted that she was angry. Truth to tell, she had a right to be angry. His mind dwelt on the picture she presented: the blue of her garments, enhancing the gray of her eyes and her square neckline, allowing a better than usual glimpse of tantalizing bosom. He had taken her hand impulsively, but her welcoming the touch had aroused him as more erotic touches from others never had. He would try to smooth things over with her later in the day. However, he did not see her the rest of that day and at supper, Lady Georgiana announced that her niece was having a tray in her room as she had a theatre engagement that evening. With Willitson. Willitson again. Jake kept asking himself how a woman could kiss a man as she had kissed him—twice—and continue to encourage another man. His body tightened at the mere memory of those kisses, and he was convinced they had meant as much to her as to him. Well, he did not have time to dwell upon it now.

Early in the evening, he met Fenton at yet another out-of-the-way pub. This one was a shade more pleasant than the last one, with fresh rushes on the floor and the tables wiped clean. A short, stubby candle cast light on their table, though there were gas lanterns at either end of the bar. Seven or eight other patrons chatted among themselves, occasionally calling out a drink order or a joke to the barman.

"You look as though you'd like to plant a facer on the first bloke that crossed your path," Fenton said when they were seated and nursing tankards of ale.

"Can't plant a facer on a lady," Jake said, sliding his stein on the table from one hand to the other.

"Oh-ho. The Lady Henrietta proving difficult, is she? I thought the two of you looked to be in some accord under that kissing ball."

"She grows increasingly suspicious of me. So does her uncle. I need you to get me out of there. I need to contact my family. The last letters you gave me indicated that my father might be seriously ill." He took a drink from the stein and set it down forcefully. "I need to be me."

Fenton nodded sympathetically. "Can you hang on for a bit longer? We are seeing some progress. With his permission, we planted some deliberately misleading information in the packet Trentham carries around from time to time. We are waiting now to see where it ends up."

"You suspect Trentham?"

"Not Trentham. Someone close to him. His butler, Talbot. He is French and he once had a close tie to the family of the Comte de Laurent and, by extension of course, with Moreau. Talbot and Morrow are sometimes seen together in one of those gambling hells in Seven Dials."

Jake shook his head. "Seven Dials? That's rough territory. Worse than Spitalfields."

Fenton nodded his agreement and took a long swallow from his tankard. "And the play is deep there."

"So these two are selling information to foreign agents to pay off gambling debts?"

"Possibly. The Moreau-Laurent ties to the Bourbons in former times may offer another incentive if Talleyrand is offering a return of properties confiscated during the revolution."

"And then there is the good doctor, Sir Cecil," Jake said.

"He seemed very attentive to Madame Laurent at that Christmas party—but where the hell does he fit into this tangled web?"

Both drained their drinks and neither said anything for a moment. Then Fenton said, "Would you like another?" When Jake merely shook his head negatively, Fenton added in an almost pleading tone, "Can you stick it out for a few more weeks?"

"Yes. I promised Lady Henrietta I would try to help her win that ludicrous bet."

Fenton grinned. "At the party I thought you presented yourself quite well as a gentleman. Her lessons are doing some good."

"About this business of planting someone a facer . . ."

Jake took a hackney cab to within about a mile of Blakemoor House, then walked the rest of way in a soft but persistent rain, mulling over the information Peter Fenton had given him. The Marquis of Trentham, when he was not laid up with an attack of gout, was an active member of Parliament with a strong interest in the doings of the Foreign Office. Furthermore, he was a close friend of Lord Castlereagh. It was not inconceivable that the two men carried on an active correspondence in which they openly shared their views on just what England's interests would be in the new design of continental Europe now that Bonaparte's empire was a thing of the past.

So, Jake thought, *at least two parts of the English government might be sources of information for spies who work for a foreign entity—or, perhaps the information is being peddled to different recipients. Obviously, Morrow and Lindstrom are coding and passing on information from the office of the army's Commander-in-Chief. But to whom? To the same person or persons receiving information for which Trentham seems the ultimate, if unknowing, source? Trentham's Foreign Office information would logically be of most interest to negotiators in Vienna squabbling over who gets what in the way of territory. Is Talbot working with Morrow and Lindstrom? Are those ancient familial ties important to the investigation? Or are they merely coincidental? One thing is certain: one or more of these treasonous fellows had a hand in killing Richter. And—by God!—Richter's death will not go unpunished!*

As he entered Blakemoor House, the footman at the door this evening said, "Ah, there you are. Lord Alfred asked for you. He is in the library."

Jake hurried up to his room, quickly divested himself of his outer cloak, ran a towel over his wet hair, and dashed back down to the library. "You wanted to see me, sir?"

Lord Alfred was in his favorite winged chair near the fireplace. "Just wondered if you'd be interested in a game or two. Didn't realize you'd gone out."

"I met a friend for a drink, but his wife keeps him on a short leash, so we ended early. You sure you are ready for more abuse from lady luck?" Jake moved the small table and the chess board and set in front of the old man and pulled a chair opposite for himself.

Lord Alfred snorted as he began to set up the board. "Luck has nothing to do with it, my boy. Chess is a game of skill and strategy. But it does require fortification—so grab yourself a glass from the sideboard there—I have the bottle right here."

"You are well prepared, I see."

* * * *

Earlier in the day, Retta had welcomed the idea of going to the theater with Willitson. Anything to keep her from dwelling on her frustration with Jake Bolton. But she missed more of the performance than she actually saw because her mind kept swinging from that truncated session with Jake Bolton to what she was fast coming to view as her abuse of David Manning, Viscount Willitson. She might not be able to handle the problem of Jake for another month or more, but she could at least be honest with David right now. In the slow-moving traffic in the theatre district as several plays finished at the same time, she and David sat side-by-side in his carriage. The dim light of a lantern allowed them to see each other clearly.

"David, I feel I must be more honest with you than I perhaps have been lately," she began tentatively.

"I'm not sure I like the sound of this," he said.

"Nevertheless, I beg you to hear me out." When he said nothing in response, she swallowed and went on. "You gave me until Easter to make up my mind. I—I do not need until Easter. It—it just would not work for us, David. I want to release you from any sense of obligation you may feel toward me."

He moved on the seat so he could look at her directly; he did not say anything for some moments, but he wore a rather grim expression. "You are giving me my conge—as a man might break off a relationship with his mistress?"

She placed a hand on his arm. "Please don't say that. It—it feels so fleeting, so cheap when you put it that way."

"Well, it has been, has it not?"

"No. I have valued—I do value—your friendship."

"Friendship," he said bitterly.

She plunged on. "But I cannot marry you. If I did, we would likely drift into one of those marriages when the principals eventually just become indifferent to each other."

"There is someone else, isn't there? Is it Mathisson? No, more likely to be Hamilton. Eh? Is it Hamilton? Are you going to accept his suit?"

"No. I value his friendship as I do yours."

"For God's sake, Retta! I *love* you!"

She removed her hand from his arm and sat with her hands tightly clasped in her lap. "I know you do. And that is why I cannot allow this to continue—cannot let you go on under a misapprehension."

"If it's not Hamilton, it must be Mathisson, or—oh, my God—it cannot be that Bow Street Runner? I saw how you kissed him under the kissing ball. It's him, isn't it?"

"Does it have to be anyone?" She hated hearing herself equivocating. "Can you not simply accept that you and I would not be happy as partners in a marriage?"

They sat in silence, listening to the sound of traffic: carriage wheels and horses' hooves on cobblestoned streets, splashes of water kicked up, and occasional greetings or curses of drivers. Finally, their vehicle stopped at Blakemoor House; Willitson handed her from the carriage and, shielding her from a light drizzle with an umbrella, walked her to the door.

"I do not share your view at all," he said rather stiffly, "but since you do not share mine, you may be sure that I will not press my suit again."

"May we continue to be friends, though?"

"You want friendship?" He held her gaze, his expression one of suppressed pain. "Of a sort, I suppose. But not right away, Retta. I can promise you civility, though."

She stood on a step above him and kissed him on the cheek. "I'm sorry, David, I truly am." He turned back toward the carriage without saying anything further. She lifted the knocker and a footman opened the door.

"Good evening, Spencer," she said, handing him her cloak and bonnet. She heard men's voices at the library door across the foyer. Her uncle and Jake seemed to be calling it a night and were about to climb the stairs to their chambers.

"Retta, my dear," Uncle Alfred greeted her. "Was the play as good as it is reported to be?"

"Mr. Keane's performance truly is exemplary," she said, glancing at Jake who was standing politely aside.

"Bolton and I just finished a chess game. He turned the table on me tonight—but I must say it took him a while. He is as skilled a player as you are, my dear."

She gave a small embarrassed laugh. "I think there is high praise for one of us in that, Mr. Bolton, or perhaps a bit of a set-down."

"I shall take it as praise, my lady."

Lord Alfred stifled a yawn and said, "I am off to bed. 'Tis cold here in the foyer."

Bolton moved to follow him, but Retta said, "Mr. Bolton, might I have a word with you?"

He nodded. "Of course, my lady."

He followed her into the library, which was several degrees warmer than the entrance hall. Servants had not yet come to douse the fire or the lamps. The comfort level notwithstanding, he gave her a questioning glance when she deliberately shut the door.

"Come and sit down," she said, pointing to the other half of a small couch on which she positioned herself. When he had done so, she turned to face him directly and held his gaze. "I am not sure that I do owe you an apology, but I did not want to let the strain under which we ended our session earlier to continue."

"I think I understand." His blue eyes holding hers were warm and accepting.

"Do you? If so, you are far ahead of me on that score. I have been thinking about it—and you—a great deal. I am ever so grateful that you have agreed to this charade I foisted on you, but you are entitled to your own person and your own life. I vow I shall henceforth control my curiosity—no matter how much it eats away at me."

"I think," he said softly and slowly, "that as human beings we are each a mass of contradictions."

"See?" she cried. "That is precisely what I mean. That is not the observation of a common laborer! But I forget myself already."

He laughed outright and moved closer to put an arm around her shoulders. "I did not think you could keep that vow for very long, my lady." And slowly so as to give her every chance to reject him, he put a hand on her chin to lift her face even more towards his and settled his mouth on hers.

She gave herself up to responding with the sort of intensity she had, without quite realizing it, dreamed of since that kiss under the Christmas kissing ball. As he sought to deepen the kiss, she pressed herself closer and opened to his entreating tongue—he tasted of cognac. She welcomed the caresses of his exploring hands. His mouth moved from hers to nibble at her neck and then nuzzle the tops of her breasts at her stylish, but almost scandalously low neckline. One hand cupped her breast and she drew in a sharp breath as she felt her nipples harden and knew that he felt them do so as well. She groaned and twisted in his arms, but did not pull away. Instead she turned her face into his neck and drank in the smell of him. He lifted her chin and moved his mouth to hers again, softly nipping at her lower lip, silently urging her to open to him.

Which she did.

Then she moaned softly and pulled away, but only slightly. "I . . . I . . . this is . . . it is not . . . we must not . . . I cannot allow—"

"Cannot allow what?" he teased as he kissed her again and she—God help her!—responded again.

She pushed away from him and sat with her hands clasped in her lap. Her voice became steady as she managed a stronger hold on herself. "I cannot allow this to go any further."

"Why not? You want it as much as I do. I know you do." He had released her, but his hand still idly caressed the nape of her neck.

She spoke more firmly. "I lied. It is not that I *cannot*, but that I *will* not. We—we are wholly unsuited to each other, Mr. Bolton."

"Jake. In view of the way you just kissed me, at least call me by my name. Jake." He sat up straighter and moved farther away from her.

She instantly regretted the loss of his touch, but she would not weaken her resolve now. "All right. Jake. I will not indulge you—or myself—in some sort of tawdry affair."

"And I suppose marriage to the likes of me is out of the question, though that kiss alone would put the lie to our being 'wholly unsuited to each other.' We—you and I—are more 'suited' than you care to admit even to yourself, my lady."

"Retta. If I am to address you as *Jake*, you must use the name I prefer in private conversation." She sounded rather stiff even to her own ears.

"Whatever you say, my la—uh—Retta."

"Thank you for understanding."

"I am not admitting to 'understanding' anything of whatever it is that is between us."

Her tone softened as she added with a sigh, "Perhaps one day we can both be more honest with each other."

"Perhaps." He leaned towards her and kissed her cheek. "Meanwhile, if you change your mind about an affair, do let me know."

"I will," she said lightly. "Meanwhile, though, we just carry on as before."

"As you please, my lady. Retta."

Chapter 16

Retta had spent some time that evening reassuring Annie that whatever might come of the incident, the young maid was to feel secure in her position. The truth was, though, that this event could very well become the latest bit of salacious gossip if it became widely known that a certain lady of the *ton* had as her personal maid a former prostitute. She would stand by Annie, but Retta knew the countess would, as Jake might have put it a few weeks ago, "throw a reet proper tantrum" at such a woman remaining in her household. *Another reason to welcome the freedom my birthday is going to give me,* Retta thought grimly.

Once she had calmed Annie down and sent the girl off to her own bed, Retta settled into trying to come to grips with the event—and the man who, for her, was at the heart of it. Having eased her conscience with regard to Willitson, Retta was able to clear her mind of him at will. Try as she might, she could not do the same with Jake. He simply dominated her waking thoughts and her fretful dreams. Three times now she had seen him leap into action to rescue others. Yet he had treated each incident as less than the extraordinary feat that it was. Was she just some starry-eyed schoolgirl looking for a hero? Perhaps she had missed that stage of her growing up years and was reverting to it now.

As she had repeatedly noted before, there was far more to this man than he allowed others to see—or at least more than he had allowed *her* to see. She sensed a depth in him that was simply absent in other men of her acquaintance. She had spent hours and hours in his company in the last four months, watching his expressions as they discussed this or that topic, watching as amusement or empathy stirred him. She felt that much of what he had told of her of his childhood and family was true, but what had he left out? She had actually *seen* him working on the docks, but had no real knowledge of how skilled he truly was at that job. He told a good *story* of being years on a merchant ship; now she questioned that—but, again, she had no concrete reason to disbelieve him. He seemed knowledgeable about farm work, but had clearly learned riding skills that exceeded those of an ordinary farmer. His speech was impeccable now. Too much so? Two women from very different elements of society had thought they recognized him and both times he had brushed off such a possibility. The second woman's comment about "college boys" would explain some of what was troubling about Jake Bolton, but there was more—much more.

And there were those kisses. She recalled every nuance of those encounters: the way his lips moved on hers, the rough feel of his shaven chin pressed against her skin, the scent she had come to recognize as his, the controlled power she sensed in his body, the gentleness of his touch. Most of all, she kept reliving the way her body responded to him—and that aching desire for more—much more. She was nearly twenty-seven years old, but never had she experienced the sheer physical attraction she had for Jake Bolton!

If it were only physical and only desire, she thought she might be able to cope with losing him in a few weeks. But it was not. He might not have been forthcoming about his life experiences, but she was sure that the values and interests he had expressed were real—and that they fit in perfectly with her own—just as his body had fit hers so perfectly during that waltz and beneath the kissing ball. Feeling wicked even as she thought about it, she wondered if their two bodies would, indeed, fit perfectly in other circumstances.

In three weeks she would be twenty-seven years old. *And still a virgin,* she muttered to herself. But—she would be in total control of a very considerable fortune. She would no longer be dependent on her father's allowance—generous though it was. No longer subject to the strictures of a stepmother who disproved more often than not of a daughter who just happened to have come with the marriage certificate. Retta could establish her own place, be her own person. And if she were to invite Jake Bolton to share her life, who was there to say *nay*? Of course there would be talk; they might even be ostracized from the most exalted circles. Members of her own family would be divided, though she was sure she could count on the loyalty of Uncle Alfred, Aunt Georgiana, and her brothers. Harriet and Hero might advise against what she was contemplating—what she had not thought through enough even to verbalize fully to herself yet—but they, too, would stand by her.

She slept only intermittently that night, engaged as she was in the on-going argument with herself.

Such improper behavior for one who has always at least technically observed the rules.

Sometimes the rules just need to be broken. As an ancient writer put it, Carpe diem—*seize the day.*

But at what cost? Which friends and relatives are you willing to forego?

The countess, surely. Papa? Perhaps, but he and I have not been close since he sent me away to school. True friends will stick by me.

You will have no place in society.

I will still have my work with Fairfax House and the Literary League—and music. I will still have music—we will have music.

What if Jake flatly rejects your overtures?

In that case, my life, on the surface, will not change much. I shall be heartbroken, but people do survive broken hearts.

Having slept so fitfully, it was very late in the morning before she woke, far too late for her morning ride even if the weather cooperated. Still not absolutely certain about what course of action she would take with Jake, she dawdled over her morning ablutions and even in choosing what to wear.

Finally, she sent Annie to summon Mr. Bolton to the drawing room. Annie returned very shortly.

"Mr. Bolton is not here, milady. He left early as you hadn't sent for him. This is his half-day off, you know."

* * * *

Jake, too, had spent a rather sleepless night. The object of his turmoil was mostly Lady Henrietta. Though he was well aware of her charity work with the Fairfax sisters, her taking a former prostitute under her wing came as a surprise. Or did it? Retta was a rare woman. She conformed to behavior that society expected of women of her station, but she flouted conventions when doing so suited her sense of right and wrong. Witness her trips to Spitalfields. Still—a former inmate of a brothel as a ladies' maid? He doubted that would go down well. A society that tolerated eccentricities in the rich and powerful would probably not accept such aberrant behavior in a young woman of marriageable age, no matter who her father was.

But Jake Bodwyn loved her all the more for it.

Loved her?

Yes, loved her. He might as well admit it, at least to himself. He loved her spirit of generosity, her determination to help the less able. He also loved the way she toyed with a strand of hair as she thought seriously about something, the way amusement started in her gray eyes and erupted in an honest laugh, her sense of loyalty to people she loved such as her aunt and her uncle, and the easy rapport she had with her brothers. And there was more, of course: the honest enthusiasm of her kiss, that woody-floral scent she wore, and a body that had a man fairly salivating—this man, anyway.

He tried to reason with himself. This was ridiculous so long as he was in Blakemoor House under false pretenses. But as soon as this damned mission was finished . . .

Thinking of the mission brought him to an idea he would discuss with Peter Fenton.

At Jake's request, they met for lunch at one of their pub haunts that served an excellent shepherd's pie, a tasty apple tart for dessert, and good selection of beer and ale. For the midday meal, the place was rather crowded, but they were able to secure a corner table in the back. When their food and drink was spread before them, they turned first to the serious business of appreciating good food, discussing other matters as the drift of conversation took them.

"Thought you would like to know that your brother has returned to town," Fenton said. "The Marquis of Burwell and his lovely wife have taken up residence in Holbrook House."

"I know," Jake said. "At least I surmised such when I observed increased activity around the house. Did anyone else accompany them?"

"Not yet, but others are expected. Have you been lurking around Holbrook House?"

"Couldn't help trying to satisfy my curiosity. But I am not going back on my promise to keep my distance for another few weeks."

"Good. I know it is hard, but it is for a good cause, you know."

Jake snorted. "Don't lay that sanctimonious rubbish on me. I'm good for the time I said I would be."

Fenton shoved his dishes aside, and reached for his beer. "Now, just what was is it that you have in mind?"

Jake finished his last bite of the tart and pushed his own dishes aside. He leaned toward Fenton. "You won't like it, but I think we should bring Lord Alfred into the picture."

Fenton thought about this for few moments before replying. "I take it you no longer have any reservations about his lordship's involvement?"

"I suppose there is an outside possibility—who knows why some people do the things they do? But his being party to this?" Jake shook his head. "It comes down to motivation, and it simply makes no sense for him to be involved. He'd have nothing to gain and I'd stake my life on his being totally loyal."

"If you are proposing what I think you are, you may be doing just that," Peter said flatly. "You do remember what happened to Richter, do you not?"

"Yes, I do. But I believe that Lord Alfred is unaware of what his secretary is doing."

"Right under the old man's nose?"

"Even under his very nose. Lord Alfred is a trusting soul and he comes from the old school of loyalty to country and to family. And distant though the relationship is, he considers Morrow family. I think he also trusts that Morrow has a natural sense of gratitude to himself and to the earl. After all, Blakemoor and his brother rescued three of them from utter penury once they escaped to England during the revolution."

The barmaid came to replenish their drinks and retrieve their dirty dishes. Fenton watched idly as she did so. When she left, he asked "So what, exactly, are you proposing?"

"I think we should go on the offensive with these scoundrels. Ask Lord Alfred to give Morrow a phony list of regiments and locations, complete with logistical support for them to make it look authentic. He gives the list to Morrow who encodes the information and passes it on to Lindstrom who, in turn, passes it on to his contacts."

"Without involving Lord Alfred's superior? If the Duke of York finds out, he will not be very happy about his being overlooked. And, as you well know, an unhappy duke is a force to be reckoned with."

Jake took a long drink from his beer, then set the stein down. "Yes. I, of all people, am aware of that."

"Ah, God, Jake, I did not mean—"

Jake waved his hand to dismiss his friend's apology, "I know. Back to York. I doubt not that York himself is all right, but that business a few years ago of his mistress selling commissions and lining the pockets of her friends is troubling."

"York spent years out of favor for even seeming to be involved in the scandal that erupted."

"But he still has the same mistress, has he not? And even if there is a new one, well . . ." Jake allowed his voice to trail off.

"I see your point. And you are right that we should take the offensive however we can. Feeding them false information is a start."

"Were you able to find out who lives at that address I gave you?"

"Yes. The house is occupied by a deputy to the ambassador of Rome."

Jake's eyebrows darted upward. "Rome? Now the Italians are involved too? What a rat's nest."

"It gets worse. You may remember that Napoleon tried to establish ties with major provinces on the Italian peninsula—made one of his brothers king of Naples."

"And . . . ?"

"And his sister, Pauline—his favorite relative, by the way—is married to a Roman nobleman. Mind you, she is separated from him, but she maintains her home in Rome. And she and their mother have not only visited Bonaparte on Elba, but are rumored to have smuggled money and jewels to him."

Jake leaned back in his chair, stunned. "My God, it never stops, does it? So now Napoleon Bonaparte is back in the picture?"

Fenton nodded. "He may be. So feeding them false information about our army positions on the continent is a good idea. Though, truth to tell, Boney is pretty well trapped on that island feeding his grandiose dreams with false hopes."

"I've always thought his 'prison' was a little too plush. Should treat him like those poor bastards—French enlisted men—we assigned to the hulks." Jake referred to the English practice of using old, unnavigable navy ships as makeshift, overcrowded prisons.

"I agree, but you and I, my friend, are not in charge." Fenton finished the last of his beer. "Nevertheless, I see no problem with your enlisting Lord Alfred's aid, if you are absolutely sure of him."

Returning to Blakemoor House, Jake took his customary position in the library, well out of the way of Lord Alfred and his secretary, who were discussing the disposition of troops in Ireland, the secretary making notations on a map as Lord Alfred directed. Then his lordship outlined points he wanted in a letter regarding a local militia to be stationed in Derbyshire.

"There. It is late, Morrow. That letter can wait until tomorrow. You are free to leave now."

"Thank you, sir."

Pretending to be absorbed in his book, Jake waited until the secretary had gathered up his papers and neatly stored them away in the desk. When Morrow left, Jake stood and tucked his book under his arm. "Sir? Might I have a word with you?"

"Of course, Bolton, but what say we do that over a drink before it is time to change for supper?" Lord Alfred went to the cabinet housing the bar and poured out two generous servings of whiskey. He handed one to

Jake, motioned him to one of the winged chairs flanking the fireplace, and took the other himself. "What's on your mind, lad?"

"The truth."

"Hmm. A weighty subject, but usually a good place to start." Lord Alfred sipped at his drink.

Jake was finding this harder than he had anticipated. "Do you recall how you challenged me after that incident with the Davenports' child?" Lord Alfred nodded and Jake went on. "You were right, of course. Like you, I am an army man. I served in the peninsular as a corresponding officer. My name is really Jacob Bodwyn."

"Bodwyn?" Lord Alfred sat up straighter. "That is Holbrook's family name."

"Yes, sir. Holbrook is my father."

The older man's expression hardened. "So—what are you doing in this house as Jake Bolton?"

"As I told you, I needed to be in this area of London, and events just fell into place to put me here. I am temporarily, at least, assigned to the Foreign Office. We have been trying to locate the sources of leaked information—a leak that is, to put it mildly, causing frustration among our people in Paris and Vienna."

Lord Alfred's temper flared immediately. "I am well aware of that—the Commander-in- Chief is not entirely uninformed, you know. And you come here suspecting me and my family? How dare you?"

Jake continued in the dogged "reporting" tone he had started with. "Actually, sir, it boiled down to either this household or that of Lord Trentham. Turns out it was both, but with very different people and different purposes involved."

"Now, see here—" his lordship protested.

"Just hear me out, please, sir."

"This had better be damned good," Lord Alfred said, setting his glass down with a thunk on a nearby table.

"Actually, we think information from the Foreign Office is finding its way through Lord Trentham, though he was unaware of that until just recently. That information, as you can guess, is of great interest to persons trying to interfere with Lord Castlereagh's proposals in Vienna. They must have been very happy indeed to know what England wanted before our negotiators even presented their proposals."

"You said 'until recently.' What does that mean?"

"Trentham's butler has been filching information from his lordship's portfolio and feeding it to the French and to the Austrians."

"Talleyrand and Metternich," his lordship muttered. "Early on, we worried that those two would have something of the like going on. But how does Trentham figure into it?" Some of the anger had gone out of Lord Alfred's voice, but he was still suspicious.

"We did not know immediately. We put a man in his household as a footman–Richter. He turned up murdered."

"Good God."

"When we had cleared Trentham himself of any of this business, we enlisted his aid in making sure that his butler had access now to only false information. We think that particular route has been stymied, at least for now."

"Good. So your mission is completed then."

"Not quite, sir."

"What?" Lord Alfred rose and stood glaring down at Jake. "Are you suggesting that I or either of my nephews are under suspicion?"

"Not anymore."

"But we were? You've got some kind of nerve coming into this household under false pretenses and now telling me that my family and I have been suspected of treason! I want you out of this house within the hour."

Again Jake struggled to keep his tone even. "Please, Lord Alfred, hear me out. We need your help." He pulled out two sheets of paper that had been tucked into his book and handed one to Lord Alfred. "I think you will recognize this list."

His lordship glanced at the paper, then sat down and read it more thoroughly. "Where did you get this? You have no authority—"

"Now look at this one." Jake leaned forward in his chair to hand over the second list.

Lord Alfred frowned. "This is gibberish!"

"Actually, it is the same list, only in code. I obtained both of them from that desk." Jake pointed at the one usually used by Morrow. He explained the code to the older man so he could see more clearly the parallels between the two.

Finally, Lord Alfred sat back in his chair and, in almost a whisper, said, "Morrow? He did this? Morrow? I cannot believe it."

"Yes, sir. He did." Jake was silent as he allowed Lord Alfred to digest this information.

I just cannot believe it," the old man repeated, shaking his head. "Why we—my brother and I—have exerted great effort and not a little funding to help him and his sister and her son."

"We do not yet have the whole story, but we are sure he is not working alone." Jake explained fully how he had discovered the code, starting with the fragment that Richter had provided and then seeing a note pass between Morrow and Lindstrom.

"Lindstrom too?" This came as a cry of pain. Lord Alfred reached for his glass and took a healthy swallow. "This is just incredible! Why, I've known Lindstrom for nearly twenty years—he's been my doctor since I came home from the colonies very near death."

"I am sorry, Lord Alfred. I do understand what a shock this must be."

Neither of them spoke again for several moments. Jake sipped at his drink and Lord Alfred sat staring at nothing. Then the old man said, "I cannot believe it, but there it is—right before my eyes." He gestured at the papers. "And to think it was going on right here, in this very room. I trusted them—both of them."

"Yes, sir," Jake said sympathetically. He could see that the old man was still reeling from a sense of betrayal, so he spoke more forcefully as he added, "But we need your help now."

"Of course. I shall discharge Morrow immediately and cut ties with Lindstrom. I gather we haven't evidence solid enough to have them arrested."

"No, sir, we do not. However, we think we can put our knowledge to some use and manage to put a spoke in their wheel."

"I will help in any way I can." The older man sounded weary and deflated.

"We should like you to do as Lord Trentham has agreed to do—that is, pretend nothing is amiss and feed these scoundrels false information. If we are right, our plans in Vienna will no longer be compromised."

"But this information," Lord Alfred motioned at the papers he had returned to Jake, "is not going to Vienna. It has nothing to do with victors dividing the spoils of war."

"You are right, sir. We think this information is going to Napoleon."

"Napoleon? Oh, my God."

Jake explained about the connection with the deputy ambassador from Rome and from there the possible connection to Napoleon's sister.

"So the 'little corporal' still has ambitions to conquer the world, eh?"

"You might say that. In any event, we think he may as well be playing with his toy soldiers on our terms rather than his."

"Good God, yes. Should he ever escape Elba, the whole of Europe will be ablaze again."

"So—will you help us, my lord?"

"I will help you, though I do not approve of the tactics you have used in gaining access to my home and my family. My brother will be most displeased about all this. Do Heaton and Lady Henrietta have any idea what you are really about?"

"No, sir. And I would ask that you keep that confidential—at least until after the Lenninger ball. I have promised Lady Henrietta that I will see her through to the end, no matter how that silly bet turns out."

Lord Alfred heaved another weary sigh. "So be it." He drained his glass and added as he rose to his feet again, "We'd best see to dressing for supper."

Jake also heaved a sigh—of relief.

Chapter 17

As the month wore on, members of the *ton* began to trickle back to town, many complaining bitterly of road conditions and delays caused by inclement weather. Technically, Parliament had been in session continuously since autumn, but now their numbers increased as more members returned to town and began to open their townhouses and make and receive calls. Retta wondered how her own life might change when her sisters and their retinue returned to town.

She needn't have worried.

In a letter addressed to Gerald, Viscount Heaton, who as the heir was the nominal head of the Blakemoor House in the absence of his father, Rebecca, Lady Lenninger, informed her brother that, until the earl returned from the continent, their sister Melinda and Cousin Amabelle would take up residence with her and her husband in the newly renovated Lenninger House, located in another—equally exclusive—section of town. The letter was followed a few days later by a visit as three of these persons descended on Blakemoor House for a morning call. They were received in the drawing room by the current residents, including Mr. Bolton. Lady Georgiana, at her nephew's request, acted as hostess.

Retta noted that Rebecca and Melinda had somehow found time to visit a modiste before calling on their family. Rebecca's day dress was an exquisite little number of polished cotton with yellow and brown stripes; Melinda's was a rose-colored muslin. Both gowns displayed the high waist and low neckline that seemed de rigueur for contemporary fashions. Retta noted that Lenninger, too, was decked out in the latest fashion with a coat of blue superfine and an emerald green waistcoat embroidered with a peacock feather motif. Next to all this finery, Retta felt a positive frump in a medium blue printed cotton that was actually a holdover from the previous fashion year.

Rebecca, having first greeted everyone rather effusively, explained Cousin Amabelle's absence: "The trip was exhausting and we have just worn her out since arriving back in town. The poor dear is resting today." She went on to declare, "It is such a joy to be back in town! I do love the country, but it offers little in the way of stimulating company and truly interesting activities."

"I thought you were to attend not one, but two lengthy house parties," Retta said.

"Oh, well, yes. We did so, but some of the more interesting members of society either stayed in town or went to their own country estates."

"Or to Paris," Melinda said in a dreamy voice. "I do wish Mama had approved of my going to Paris with my friend Barbara and her parents."

"You know very well Mama disapproves of Lady Tourland," Rebecca said.

"Because of something that happened ages and ages ago," Melinda said, pouting.

"Your mother has her reasons." Aunt Georgiana lifted the teapot as she reigned over the tea table. "Would anyone care for more tea?"

"I think not," Rebecca said. "We have made three other calls this afternoon and were offered the same lemon tarts at two of them!"

"I'll have more, please." Richard passed his cup over to their aunt. "And another of those tarts too, please."

"Good job the army makes you fellows march in circles as much as it does," Gerald commented. "The way you scarf up those tarts, you should weigh thirteen or fourteen stone at least."

"I can tolerate them. I lead a more active life than you do."

"Balderdash!"

"Enough," Uncle Alfred said. "Tarts or no tarts, you two look as much alike now as you did in your cradles."

"And they enjoy needling each other as much as they did as schoolboys," Retta said with an indulgent smile at her brothers. "'Tis truly a wonder they made it through childhood without killing each other—or having someone else perform that feat on both of them."

"Ah, but you'd miss us, would you not?" Richard teased. "Who else would you have to boss around?"

"She still has Mr. Bolton to boss around," Rebecca said.

"Not exactly." Retta leaned forward to set her cup on the table in front of Aunt Georgiana. She shared a secret twitch of a smile with Jake, then glared a warning at her sister and nodded towards Madame Laurent.

Rebecca got the message, for she waved a hand dismissively and said, "All I meant was you always have enjoyed being the one in charge, so to speak."

"Would that were true," Retta said, thinking, *Lately, I am not even in charge myself—especially where Mr. Bolton is concerned.*

Aunt Georgiana set the teapot back on the tray, and said, "You children have been together for only a few minutes, and here you are—squabbling just as you used to do in the nursery."

The siblings sat mildly chastened for a moment, then Rebecca offered a change in subject. "Lenninger and I have decided to give a ball."

"We have?" her husband asked, but in response to a speaking look from his wife, he added, "Oh. So we have."

"We want to show off the renovations to Lenninger House. It will have to be early—about three weeks from now—as there is no telling if I will be up to hosting such an entertainment later in the season."

She paused dramatically to allow the full import of this pronouncement to sink in.

Aunt Georgiana was the first to respond. "I assume this means you are increasing?"

Rebecca blushed prettily. "Yes."

A blend of congratulatory comments and good wishes directed at both the prospective parents followed this announcement.

"When is the new arrival to make his or her appearance?" Aunt Georgiana asked.

"Late June or early July."

"This is wonderful news indeed," Retta said, feeling magnanimous.

"Yes. A spinster at my wedding, you will now be a spinster aunt," Rebecca said with a toothy smile that Retta assumed was intended to mitigate the cruelty of the snide remark.

Retta's magnanimity vanished. "Does your mother know?"

"I wrote her as soon as I was sure."

Retta replied without thinking. "Somehow, I have difficulty seeing the countess as a doting grandmother."

Rebecca's expression took on a cold look. "I am quite sure Mama will welcome her first grandchild." Then she brightened. "Now, about my ball. I am planning it for February 17. That is three days prior to your birthday, is it not, Retta?"

Retta merely nodded, knowing full well this was a two-pronged jibe from her sister: a reminder of her age and of the bet.

"I shall be inviting just everyone," Rebecca continued airily, "including the patronesses of Almack's and anyone else of note who happens to be in town so early. It is sure to be a positive crush, and mine could very well turn out to be the most significant entertainment of the season, despite its being so early. Melinda is helping me with the invitations."

"We are planning three waltzes," Melinda said, "and since I received permission from the patronesses last year to waltz, I shall dance every one of them with a different, exceedingly handsome partner."

"One would certainly not wish to have a homely dance partner, no matter how well that person executed the steps," Richard said.

"If you make fun of me, I shall not allow you to sign my dance card at all," Melinda said with a pout.

"Oh, no. The most dire of threats," he said.

"In any event," Rebecca said, rising to signal to her party that she was ready to leave, "I will be sending invitations within the week, but do save the date for me. I want all my family to attend—those who can be there, that is. I shall miss Mama and Papa terribly."

As the Lenninger party left, Jefferies announced the arrival of new guests, including Baron Mathisson, Sir Michael Hamilton, and Sir Cecil Lindstrom. The conversation centered on new topics of more general interest, but, lively as it was, Retta noticed as Jake quietly excused himself to Aunt Georgiana and left the drawing room.

* * * *

Jake had felt twinges of nostalgia as he watched the Blakemoor twins and their sisters engaged in the kind of sibling repartee that he had once enjoyed with his brothers and sisters. But it was not nostalgia that gripped him when Mathisson and Hamilton were introduced and Retta set about being charming and flirtatious. No, it was not nostalgia. It was insipient jealousy. He recognized it for what it was and cursed himself for allowing it to materialize to the point of being recognizable even by just himself. However, he did notice with some glee the absence of Viscount Willitson.

Since the principals of the house were all gathered in the drawing room, he escaped to the music room. He lifted the lid over the piano keys, idly hit a few notes, then sat and began to play in earnest. Mozart for a bit, then he switched to Vivaldi. Would he ever play or hear those works again without thinking of her?

He had known the conditions of that bet from the very beginning, but not exactly how it would culminate. A public forum of some sort. Now, it seemed that the public forum would be the Lenninger ball to occur in three weeks. Once that bet was won—or lost—there would be no more reason for Jake Bolton to be a member of the Earl of Blakemoor's household. He had three weeks to resolve the issues of this spy business. He shook his head. It truly was rather weird. Usually, he and his team were trying to identify spies. Now, they knew who the spies were—in fact, there was an overabundance of them—and of motives for their behavior too. Jake stopped playing as his mind explored ideas that might help end this infernal mission. Lindstom was above stairs right now. He may have dropped in on Morrow before climbing the stairs to the drawing room. What, exactly, was his interest in Morrow's sister? Well, they were both single and of similar age and members of a like level of society. But was there more?

Not at all sure of where it might lead him, he thought now might be the time to develop this thread of the investigation. Impulsively, he decided to follow Lindstrom when the man left the gathering upstairs. He dashed up to his chamber and hastily changed into his buckskin breeches and a wool shirt over which he donned a dark overcoat. Then he went out to the mews and helped a groom saddle Blaze.

As darkness began to drape itself over the town, he stood with Blaze beneath a large fir tree some distance from the entrance to Blakemoor House and waited for Lindstrom to leave. Both he and the horse were impervious to the cold rain that was falling, but he hadn't long to wait. Lindstrom stepped out, unfurled an umbrella, and walked in the direction of a more trafficked street where, Jake knew, he would be able to find a hackney cab. Jake waited until the doctor was some distance ahead before cautiously leading Blaze in pursuit. When Lindstom hired a cab, Jake mounted and followed the vehicle, keeping his distance to avoid detection.

Though it was not easy, what with traffic and the rapidly diminishing light, Jake managed to keep the doctor's cab in sight as it traveled into a section of the city that hosted less elegant houses than those of the highest echelons of the *ton*. Modest as they were, these were houses of people of means and the neighborhood was one that could afford street lights that were even now being lit. Jake hung back as the doctor's cab stopped at a particular house. Lindstrom got out, paid off the driver, and dashed through the rain to a covered porch. He was given entrance the instant he knocked. Could he be visiting a mistress? Jake knew from discussions with Peter that this was not Lindstrom's address. He duly noted the street and number and waited for a few minutes, but clearly Lindstrom would not be exiting the building any time soon. After all, he had dismissed his cab. So Jake gave it up and returned to the Blakemoor mews. Leaving Blaze to the care of a groom, he entered the house from the rear. He just had time to change and join the family for supper.

The next day he met Lady Henrietta in the morning room and they went through the motions of yet another lesson. Both knew he was as ready as he was likely to be for his big come out. He was sure that she was as reluctant as he to give up these sessions that allowed them simply to be together. They sat side-by-side at the glass-topped table, books and papers scattered in front of them. She had convinced him to read that new novel, *Pride and Prejudice*, and they discussed it after exhausting news items and gossip that appeared in both the more respected press and the tabloids.

"Do you not agree that Elizabeth Bennett is just as arrogant as she accuses Mr. Darcy of being?" he asked as much to tease her as to elicit a considered response. They were only now getting into the third volume of the book.

"No. How could she possibly accept the suit of a man who not only holds her family in such contempt, but must force himself to accept the fact that he loves her?"

"What if the situation were reversed? What if his status and his connections were of such dubious worth that she would be demeaning herself to accept him?"

He held her gaze until she looked away, her gaze directed, unseeing, at the wet foliage just outside the French doors of this room. She shifted slightly in her seat before saying, "I think Elizabeth would be in a very difficult position, given that her family has such limited prospects."

"But what about him? And her? Would she throw caution to the winds and love him anyway?"

She brought her gaze back to his and said slowly, "She—she might do so. If she truly loved him enough."

He knew that neither of them was discussing the book any longer.

"And does she?" he asked softly.

"Perhaps. Probably." She looked down at the open book and her tone was filled with a resigned sadness. "But it is not merely a matter of loving another person, is it? The world always has a way of intruding."

He leaned closer to her and placed an arm around her shoulders, aware of that woody-floral scent she always wore. "Devil take the world," he said in that same soft tone and kissed her very, very thoroughly.

She put her hand to his cheek and responded in kind, emitting a small moan of desire, but she quickly pulled away when they heard footsteps outside the door that had, as usual, been left ajar.

"That intruding world," he whispered and leaned back in his own chair as the footman Baker knocked perfunctorily, entered at her bidding, and handed her a message on a salver.

She opened it and said nervously, "The invitation to Rebecca's ball. She made certain to include you."

* * * *

Besides being called upon to report for his usual lessons, Jake was also still being asked to accompany Lady Henrietta on certain outings. Thus he and Annie attended her on a visit to a modiste for a fitting of the gown she would wear to Rebecca's ball. From there she went to a shop specializing in buttons, ribbons, lace, and other decorations for ladies' dresses and bonnets. Jake found this sort of outing utterly boring, but he remained alert as he waited outside the shop. The weather being relatively dry this day, he leaned against the outer wall of the shop a few feet from the entrance. He saw a hackney cab pull up and position itself immediately in front of the Blakemoor carriage. Jake exchanged a glance with the Blakemoor coachman who merely raised an eyebrow and shrugged. The cab did not move and Jake was about to stroll over to ask if there was a problem when Annie emerged from the shop with her arms full of parcels. Lady Henrietta was in the open doorway apparently saying farewell to the shopkeeper.

Suddenly, the door to the cab opened and a man jumped down to hand a buxom, middle-aged woman to the pavement. The woman wore an expensive brown traveling cloak and far more make-up than any respectable matron would be wearing in public. Before Jake realized what she was about, the woman had grabbed Annie's arm, forcing the maid to drop her packages.

"Now, I've got you, you little slut! There will be no running away from me again!" She pushed Annie toward the man who stood near the open door of the cab. Lady Henrietta saw what was happening and instantly jumped into the fray, screaming and shoving at the woman as she tried to get hold of Annie herself, grabbing at the maid's cloak. Now the man was trying to force a fighting, yelling Annie into the cab. Lady Henrietta rushed at him and tried to keep Annie away from the open door. The buxom woman was slapping and punching Lady Henrietta. At this point, with no regard for what was supposed to be the fair sex, Jake shoved the older woman hard enough to set her on her backside on the curb.

"Just get 'er in the cab and go!" the woman yelled at her companion.

He, however, was having a hard time fending off Lady Henrietta, who still had hold of Annie's cloak. She pulled hard and she and Annie fell into a noisy heap of flailing arms and legs near the step of the cab. The man kicked at Lady Henrietta and tried to make another grab for Annie. Jake threw a strong punch at the man that, in the melee, hit the man's shoulder and spun him around. At this point, the hackney driver, probably seeing the quality of the folks involved in the altercation and aware of the attention it was garnering, decided he wanted nothing to do with it, whipped his team into action, pulled his vehicle into the street, and dashed away.

The scene had transpired in only a very few minutes—maybe seconds—but it was accompanied by yells, screams, and loud grunts. Customers from the shop and the one next door, as well as other shoppers on the street began to gather and gawk.

"Someone go for a watchman," Jake ordered. "There must be one in this area with all its shops."

"Be a while," a male bystander said. "Office is three streets over, don't you know?"

"Just go!" Jake yelled, keeping a firm hold of the man and shoving the woman back down as she tried to get to her feet. "You just stay right there," he ordered.

"You got nothin' on me," the woman screamed, partly at him and partly for the benefit of the gathering crowd. "That girl is a runaway an' she belongs to me."

Annie and her mistress had struggled to their feet; Lady Henrietta's bonnet was askew and Annie's lay on the ground. Annie picked up her muddied bonnet, put it back on her head, and stood strangely quiet, a blank look in her eyes. Shock, Jake surmised.

Lady Henrietta placed an arm about the maid and replied, "She 'belongs' to no one! She is her own person!"

The woman managed to get to her feet and made a grab at Annie. "She's mine. Bought and paid for."

Annie squealed and Lady Henrietta gave the woman a very unladylike punch to her face. The woman screamed and clutched at her nose. Her man jerked away from Jake and tried to intercede for her, but Jake punched him again, catching him on the chin this time; the man slowly sank to the pavement and did not move.

The woman yelled, "You've killed him!"

"I doubt that," Jake said. "And you'd best stop your caterwauling until the watchman gets here."

"Better do as he tells you," someone among the bystanders said. "That fellow packs a wicked punch, he does."

The crowd seemed interested in the show, but Jake felt they mostly favored him and Lady Henrietta, who had now helped Annie into the Blakemoor carriage and stood nearby as the woman in brown persisted in trying to win over the bystanders. "He's got no call," she argued. "I paid good coin for the girl's services and that one"—she pointed at Lady Henrietta—"just stole her right away from me."

"Hey! I know her!" a surprised male bystander yelled out, pointing at the woman who was holding a handkerchief to her nose. "That is," the man said, suddenly seeming embarrassed, "I know who she is. She's the madam at The Bird's Nest, a brothel out in Spitalfields area."

"A brothel! Well, I never—" said a well-dressed woman next to him in a shocked tone as she backed away from the scene, but not so far away that she would miss anything.

Now the crowd was firmly against the woman in brown. Her protests turning feeble, she seemed to accept defeat as they awaited the watchman's arrival. She kept looking at Jake, her brow furrowed in curiosity and anger. Jake ignored her stare, but a twinge of apprehension kept nipping at him.

Finally, she said, "Hah! Now I remember where I seen you before! Years ago—more'n fifteen at least—you was with a bunch of college boys come to my place an' 'bout destroyed it."

Jake looked directly at her and shook his head. "You are out of your mind, woman." He had recognized the name of that brothel, The Bird's Nest, and reaching into the recesses of memory, he brought up an alcohol-soaked vision of a bunch of overzealous and overly drunk university students who let themselves loose on the town one spring. As he recalled, that was one of the incidents that had been the last straw for his father. Ordinarily the woman's accusation would have been meaningless, and Jake could have shrugged it off. But he had to protect his identity at this point. Now, more than ever.

"I never forget a face," the woman said.

"Well, you have the wrong one this time," he snapped, turning away from her and catching the speculative gaze of Lady Henrietta.

A few minutes later the watchman, a tall, thin man who might have fulfilled the role of the "First Footer," arrived with enough enforcements to take the two miscreants into custody. He jotted down the names and addresses of the principals in the incident and those of a few willing witnesses on a pad, then turned to Lady Henrietta. "I doubt you will be called to testify when this comes to court, my lady, but the magistrate will surely want to hear from your maid, so it would best if you see that she remains available."

"We both shall be," she replied as Jake handed her into the carriage to sit beside Annie; then he climbed in himself to sit opposite them. A young man handed in the packages that had been dropped; Lady Henrietta thanked him and signaled the coachman to go before turning her attention to the still distraught Annie. Both women bore evidence of their encounter: patches of mud on their skirts, mud and scratches on their faces. Lady Henrietta has lost a glove in the encounter.

"Oh, my lady," Annie wailed, "I knowed it couldn't last. You never should've took me in like you did. Now ever'one will know I come from that—that place, an' it'll come back on you."

"Never you mind, Annie. You are going nowhere," Lady Henrietta said, putting an arm around Annie's shoulders.

"But when the countess comes back and the whole house knows, you'll have to sack me. I know you will."

Lady Henrietta gave the girl a firm shake. "Stop that now. I have put far too much effort into training you as a proper lady's maid to give you up at this point. Unfortunately, there are people who will hold your past—which you could not help—against you. Some may even hold it against me. But those are people of small minds, people lacking in charity towards others. As for the countess—we shall deal with that issue when we must, but now—"

"Oh, my lady." Annie dissolved into a fresh spate of sobs.

In part to help bring Annie around, Jake said in a calm voice, "Would you care to explain what that incident was all about?"

Lady Henrietta sighed. "Annie was twelve when that—that female— bought her from the mistress of a flash house. She'd already been put on the street as a pickpocket, but those two beldames took another look at her and decided a pretty young thing like that would bring in more coin in the brothel. The madam put her to work immediately."

"In the brothel." Jake was careful to keep his tone neutral for Annie's sake.

"In the brothel," Lady Henrietta repeated. "God knows how many times that despicable woman sold Annie's 'virginity' or quite how she managed that trick, but she did."

"She done it to lots a girls." Annie's sobs devolved into hiccups, then sighs.

"By the time a judge is through with her, she will be lucky if she is selling her wares in New South Wales," Jake said.

"Transportation?" Annie asked wonderingly.

"Transportation," he affirmed. "Kidnapping is a hanging offense and that is precisely what she had in mind. Actually, she will be lucky if she is merely transported to a penal colony."

Annie sat silent for a few moments, then said, "Still, I don't want to bring shame to you, my lady. Mayhap Miss Fairfax can place me as a scullery maid or some such."

"Absolutely not. I will not hear of it," her ladyship replied. "I do not want to hear of it from you again, either."

"Yes, ma'am," Annie said.

"Now," Lady Henrietta said decisively, looking directly at Jake. He thought she looked decidedly fetching despite a streak of mud on her cheek, her bonnet askew, and strands of hair flying about with each breath she took. "Just what was that business about college boys tearing up the premises of a brothel?"

He knew this was coming, but he merely shrugged. "The woman was clearly mistaken."

"As Lady Davenport was mistaken?"

"Can I help it if I have a very common visage?"

Her ladyship merely sniffed and turned back to comforting Annie.

Chapter 18

For a full day and into the night Retta had struggled with what she thought of as "the Jake dilemma." When the bet was won—or lost—he would leave Blakemoor House. The thought of no longer sharing time with him had become far more devastating than the prospect of losing Moonstar. She could not face the possibility that he would not be there to offer his take on what the newspapers were reporting or arguing with her about the actions of some government minister who was making a mistake—or had got something right. Lately, she had introduced into their lessons more discussions of literature. The *Pride and Prejudice* novel of course, but also works by some of her favorite poets and she was delighted to find he enjoyed the works of Blake and Wordsworth as much as she did. She challenged him on that—how had someone with the limited education he claimed to have be familiar with such works. He shrugged off her questions with "I've been reading—that is, I have read a great deal in many areas since I left the vicar's day school."

She did not push the conversation regarding his own learning—she dared not bring her doubts into the open yet, but she was sure there was more to it than he admitted. Soon enough she would have the truth about this man. In thinking about it later, she was surprised that she was able to control her curiosity enough *not* to push him. Instead, she had shifted the subject to the general topic of public education and was pleased to find his views more or less coincided with hers on that topic. "Though the Methodists have a narrow goal in mind," he said, "their insistence that people of all classes should learn to read is most laudable—as a start at least."

When he was no longer there, she would profoundly miss little personal things about him: the way he twisted his mouth when he was contemplating an idea, the twinkle in his eyes when he was teasing her, the way his fingers coaxed music from piano keys, that faint twitch of a smile when they both happened to think of the same thing in the midst of company, and his touch—accidental or not.

If I am to lose all that, she told herself, *I will, by all that is holy, seize what I may while it is still possible. "Carpe diem" as the ancients said.* Was she being too impulsive, just as she had been with that infernal bet that had brought Jake into her life to start with?

Probably.

But she would not be deterred.

She waited until she was quite sure that all the inhabitants of the house were settled into their own chambers and likely off in dream land. She threw back her covers and donned a silk dressing gown over her nightgown of thin lawn. She peeped from her own bedchamber into the adjacent sitting room to be sure both her aunt and her companion had retired to their own rooms, then she crossed that room and cautiously opened the door to the hall. She listened for any activity there, and finding nothing but silence, she let herself out the door, and hurried down the hall, and down the stairs to the floor on which she knew Jake's room to be. She stood before his door for a moment. *Am I really going to do this?* Before she could answer that even in her own mind, she knocked softly.

She heard him rustling about, then he opened the door. "My lady?" he asked in surprise. "Is something wrong? Why . . . why are you here?"

She had planned to be ever so sophisticated—a true woman of the world at this point, but that plan was lost as the words just came tumbling out. "You told me to let you when I was ready for an affair. I am ready."

"What?" His eyebrows shot up.

"Don't make me repeat it, Jake," she pleaded.

He took her hand, pulled her into the room, and closed the door. "Are you sure of this? I mean, really sure?" He still held her hand and gazed into her eyes. His touch and the raw hunger in his gaze were doing strange— wonderful—things to her body.

She saw that he had partially undressed, having removed his shirt and his boots and tossed a dark blue robe over his breeches. She recognized the robe as having once belonged to her brother Gerald. She saw that he had been reading in a big overstuffed chair. The lamp beside it and the one on a night stand next the bed were both lit. The bed had not been turned down. *At least I am not disturbing his sleep,* she thought nervously, then reminded herself that was precisely what she had in mind.

"Yes, I am sure," she said.

"Well, ah—"

"You don't want me." She turned away, acutely embarrassed, her cheeks virtually on fire.

"Oh, yes, I do. I do." He pulled her close and kissed her fiercely, then whispered, "I do indeed want you, Retta. It is just that you caught me by surprise."

"Pleasantly so, I hope," she murmured. She put her arms around his neck and nudged his face back to a kissing position, pouring into her kiss the pent up desire she had felt for days now.

"Very pleasantly so," he said, his voice growing husky.

He trailed his tongue across her lips, teasing them open then plunged her into a maelstrom of sensation. Not only were his lips and tongue wreaking havoc on her mouth and neck, but he had slipped his hands inside the dressing gown to caress her sides, her back, and her breasts. She felt her nipples harden and a burning need lower in her body. His hands cupped the rounds of her buttocks and pulled her even closer. Something firm pushed against her belly; she knew immediately what it was and what it meant. The knowing made her hungry for more.

He pulled away slightly. "You can change your mind if you want, Retta. But once I take you to bed, there will be no turning back."

"I don't want to turn back." Her own voice was rather husky too.

He let her go for a moment as he turned out the lamp near the chair and turned the one next the bed down to spread only a soft glow about the room. He grabbed a towel from the washstand and placed it beside the lamp on the nightstand, then he threw back the covers of the bed, and reached for her again.

"Last chance to change your mind," he said softly as he undid the loose braid of her hair, let it drape about her shoulders, and buried his face in its tresses.

"I am not changing my mind," she said firmly, and pushing his robe off his shoulders, pressed her lips to his skin, the hair on his chest tickling her face. She licked at his bare chest, noting that he tasted slightly salty. His robe fell to the floor.

"My God, Retta. Oh, my God, I want you."

"That *is* why I am here," she said in a saucy tone that belied the butterflies of doubt she was feeling at the sheer boldness of what she was doing. She put her arms around his neck again and pressed her body against his.

He shoved her dressing gown off her shoulders and the silk fell to the floor with his robe. He stepped back and for a moment merely looked at her in that thin nightgown. She knew it revealed not only that her nipples had hardened, but also showed clearly the dark patch of hair at the juncture of her legs. She felt shy and wanton at the same time.

He drew in a sharp breath and, quickly divesting himself of his breeches, shoved her gently towards the bed.

"That nightgown must go, too," he said. She slowly removed it, aware of his steady gaze all the while, and let it drop to the floor with the rest of their clothing.

She lay on the bed and scooted over to allow him room as he lay beside her and took her in his arms. He kissed her and nuzzled against her neck as one hand toyed with her hair. She was immediately lost in the sheer sensation of skin against skin as he kissed her lips again. She kissed him back, reveling in the way her whole body responded to his every touch. He trailed kisses down her neck and to her breasts. As he kissed and nibbled at one hard nipple, he stroked the other, gently pinching it. She whimpered her pleasure in the sheer ecstasy of what he was doing, but she knew there was more, and she was torn between wanting it all now, or savoring each little nuance of his lovemaking.

Savoring could be had in memory.

He placed a hand on her inner thigh and she instinctively opened to allow him access. His fingers stroked and probed, awakening her very core of sensuality; he stroked gently, then with increasing intensity as he kissed her mouth, his tongue echoing the rhythm of his strokes below.

She jerked her mouth away from his to say, "Oh, my God, Jake, what you're doing to me!"

He gave her a knowing grin and whispered, "We are not there yet, Retta. Touch me, sweetheart." He positioned her hand around his erection and she wondered at the smoothness and warmth of it. He uttered a groan and inserted a finger and then two fingers into her and she could feel the wetness.

When she had reached a fever pitch of sheer desire, he positioned himself between her legs. "Put your legs around mine," he whispered. She did, thus allowing both of them better traction as he continued to stroke her, but not with his fingers. His hands were braced on either side of her head and his gaze locked with her own as he entered her with slow strokes at first, then more rapidly as she responded thrust for thrust. His moans of pleasure blended with hers. She felt a twinge of pain, then an incredible sense of euphoria as her body reached for—for what? She strained harder and suddenly, there it was! She cried out, but he quickly caught her cry in a long kiss. She began to relax as she felt him building to the same pitch. With a soft groan, he withdrew from her and reached for the towel into which he spilled his seed. He rolled to her side, buried his face against her neck, and just held her close as he regained control of himself. After a while he rose and, retrieving a wet cloth from the washstand, he gently cleaned her and himself before again lying next to her, kissing her neck and nibbling at her earlobe. He reached to spread the blanket over them and they lay quiet for a while, he trailing a hand idly over her body, and she savoring their closeness.

His care in not spilling his seed inside her and his tender ministrations in cleaning her moved her profoundly. These actions bespoke a man whose thoughtfulness was somehow ingrained in his character. No wonder she loved him so.

"*That* was pretty wonderful," she said. "Wherever did you learn that? No. Don't tell me. I don't want to know."

His chest rumbled with a laugh. "*You* are wonderful, my lady of surprises. How will I ever be able to let you go?"

It was a rhetorical question and an idle one at that, but she said, "Who says you must?"

He rose on one elbow and held her gaze. "Are you suggesting what I think you are?"

"Probably. In less than a month, Jake, I will be a very rich woman in my own right, and, frankly, I want to keep you in my life. There. I've said it." She buried her face in his neck and said against his warm skin, "Does that make me a bad person?"

"No, my darling, of course not." He continued to idly caress her body. "I cannot like the idea of a future without you, but circumstances are against us, you know. At least for now. I doubt your family would approve your marrying a dockworker—or a Bow Street Runner, for that matter."

"I am of age," she said. "Their approval is not really necessary. And in about two weeks, I will be very rich. You need not stay a dockworker—if, indeed, that is what you were—are."

He laughed and drew her closer. "Are you proposing that I become a kept man? A rich woman's plaything?"

"Oh, please, don't put it that way."

"Why don't we just leave things as they are for the time being?" he asked. "I am not going anywhere soon. Now. How much time do we have before this house starts stirring?"

"Enough," she said, surrendering again to his exploring hands and kisses, but she also noted that he had ignored her challenging his status as a dock worker.

* * * *

They made love twice more, dozing between encounters and joking about how the teacher had suddenly become the student—and an eager one at that. Jake always slept with his window open and when he began to hear the familiar morning sounds coming from the stable yard, he nudged Retta, then kissed her awake.

"Hmm. What?" She snuggled closer.

He chuckled. "If you do not wish to be caught in my room, love, you'd better wake up and return to your own."

"Oh, my goodness." Fully awake now, she scrambled off the bed to reach for her clothes. She hastily tied her hair back and tightened the sash on her dressing gown. He grabbed his robe too, and pulled it on as he went to the door to open it and peer into the hall.

"All right," he said, keeping his voice low. As she passed by him, he kissed her and said, "Later."

He went to the window to check the weather. He heard rather than saw that it was raining. Sunrise was late this time of the year, and all he could see were vague shapes of surrounding buildings. Well, that rain answered one question: there would be no riding this morning.

No longer sleepy, he quickly pulled on his buckskin breeches, a wool shirt, and his boots. He had opened the door when a thought hit him. He closed it and returned to the bed to throw aside the bedcovers. *Aha! Just as I thought.* There was a telltale spot of blood on the sheet. He wet a cloth in the basin and scrubbed at the spot until it was hardly visible. He hoped it would dry by the time the maid came to clean his room, but as a precaution he made up the bed himself. The maid might wonder at the already made bed and an excessive number of cloths near the basin, but that could not be helped.

At this hour and with all the bedchambers on the second and third floors, he would be disturbing no one by playing the piano. The Earl of Blakemoor had installed gas lighting within the last two years, so the halls were dimly lit as he made his way down to the music room on the ground floor. The room was cold, so he lit the fire and heaped the coal high, glad that in this well-run household the fireplaces were cleaned every day and a ready supply of coal was always available. He thought briefly of the cold, dark room he had shared with those other dockworkers only a few months ago.

But mostly he thought of Retta as he began to play the piano softly, just letting his fingers find the keys as they would. Well aware of what she was risking, he was humbled by her willingness to give up her life—a life in which she had always been an important and respected figure in society—merely to be with him. He did not doubt that she meant every word, and it made him love her even more. He was growing used to the idea that he was in love with her. A few months ago—during that first meeting in The White Horse, for instance—he would have scoffed at such a possibility. But here he was, loving her and hating the fact that he could not throw everything aside and court her as he wanted and as she deserved. He wondered how she would take the truth of his identity . . .

Jake had met with Peter Fenton, but neither had much to report as they simply waited. When he thought about it, it occurred to him that intelligence work involved a good deal of that: waiting. Two weeks ago, the Marquis of Trentham had reported to Fenton that he was ready to take home his carefully contrived false documents showing what England wanted at the Vienna Congress in the way of distribution of territories that Napoleon had conquered. Fenton had then made sure to have Trentham's butler under surveillance whenever he left the house. The butler was seen visiting the docks where he met with an officer on a French ship visiting the London harbor. Since that ship was one that carried passengers as well as cargo, it was not difficult to put an English spy on board to follow the trail once the information made its way to France. Once Colonel Lord Peter Fenton was certain the information had been passed to French recipients, he would give the order to arrest Trentham's butler.

The information that Lord Alfred manufactured—ostensibly from the Army Commander-in-Chief—supposedly showed locations of various units of the army and their strengths now that England, no longer at war on the continent, was reducing its numbers. Jake had actually had some small input to this misleading information, and he was glad to see that Lord Alfred included just enough verifiable information to be fully believable about the English army of occupation in France and Belgium. Again Lindstrom was seen visiting the home of the deputy ambassador of Rome. Because this information would go into a diplomatic dispatch, it would be harder to trace on the continent. It was a now a matter of waiting to hear when Napoleon might have received it. The British commander overseeing Napoleon's exile on Elba sent regular messages regarding the prisoner's daily life and his visitors. When the British Foreign Office was informed that the Countess Borghese had visited her brother again, Jake and Peter would put into motion the arrests of Morrow, his sister, and Dr. Lindstrom. *When,* Jake thought, *and if nothing goes wrong. After all, it was just a stroke of luck to find that we are dealing with two lots of these bastards with different, albeit overlapping motivations.*

Motivation was a key element. What on earth was Napoleon to do with the information he was seeking, incarcerated as he was on a small island?

The only explanation was that he was planning an escape. He had tried that in the early days of his exile and had been suitably foiled in the attempts. The question was now: When would the next attempt come? And why were the powers that be in the entourage of England's Prince Regent so reluctant to beef up security on that island? Instead they had allowed the former dictator to increase his number of "servants." Jake did not know the exact number, but it was over a thousand. What individual—even a former dictator used to every luxury known to man—needed that many "servants" to keep him entertained?

Jake had discussed this at great length with Lord Alfred and with Peter Fenton; the three of them agreed on possible motives of the man who had once sought to rule all of Europe, if not the whole world. And all three complained that those in power—especially the Prince Regent and the Prime Minister—seemed so unconcerned about the possibility of having "the Corsican Monster" unleashed on the world again. Jake and his cohorts only hoped that the Foreign Secretary and the man chosen to replace him would take a more practical view of the situation: Castlereagh and Wellington would surely have a better grip on the issue than the armchair diplomats here at home had.

Jake decided he would deal with these issues when they received word that the false information had been delivered to its intended destinations—namely Talleyrand and Napoleon. Surely it was a matter of only a few days. Meanwhile, his life was consumed not only by finding reasonable, believable activities to fill his days, but also by his nights with Retta. Three times after that first encounter, she had come to his room and stayed until nearly dawn. Both complained that these nights were far too short, and he worried aloud about her being caught leaving his room, a worry she tried to kiss away. While they did, indeed, spend a good portion of those hours simply exploring each other's bodies and sharing the incredible bliss of the most intimate union known to mankind, they also spent a good deal of time just talking, sharing small details of their lives as lovers since the dawn of time have done. On his part, Jake was careful to screen whatever he shared. He trusted her implicitly, but he did not want her involved in this messy spy business—at least not until it was necessary. And by then, he hoped it would be over. So, he withheld the vital information of his identity, but he shared truthfully as much as he could, telling her of escapades with his friends and with his brothers and sisters. Nor did he share only the happiest stories of his childhood. He told her of his estrangement from his father and how he hoped one day to mend matters with him.

She, in turn, told him of the loss of her mother and how her stepmother had never quite been able to accommodate for that loss. She told him how Uncle Alfred and Aunt Georgiana had helped fill the void, and how her school friends, Hero and Harriet, had become essentials in her life. She confirmed what he had already deduced about her relationship with her brothers and sisters—her closeness and shared interests with the boys and how she had always felt a sense of distance between her and her sisters.

He treasured these nights with her.

* * * *

For Retta, these nights were a taste of what she imagined paradise to be. The discovery of his male body, and discovering the raw sensation her own was capable of, thrilled her beyond anything she had ever experienced. She simply never wanted it to end. In the back of her mind, there was a persistent worry about keeping the relationship—that is, the change in her relationship with Jake—secret from members of a household of literally dozens of people, some of whom had known her all her life. But again and again, she found herself gently knocking at his door once it seemed all was quiet.

On returning to her bedchamber after her fourth night with Jake, she entered the sitting room quietly and was surprised that a lamp was on. She was sure she had extinguished it. Then she saw Aunt Georgiana sitting in a chair near the table that held that lamp. She had been reading, but Retta immediately surmised that the book she held on her lap was really just to while away the time as she waited.

"Oh! You startled me," Retta said. "Did you have trouble sleeping too? I—"

"Do not even think of dissembling with me, Retta." Aunt Georgiana spoke softly, mindful, Retta thought, of Madam Laurent who slept in an adjoining room. But the tone and expression on her aunt's face were stern, disapproving. She held up a blue ribbon she had been using as a bookmark. "This is yours, is it not?"

"Why, yes. I wondered where it had gone." Retta also kept her voice low.

"Mrs. Browning brought it to me yesterday. The maid who cleans Mr. Bolton's chamber found it beside the bed and gave it to the housekeeper."

"Well, I—

Her aunt ignored her. "Have you any idea at all of the consequences of what you are doing?"

"I—I think so," Retta admitted, sinking into a seat opposite the older woman.

"I think *not*," her aunt said emphatically. "Servants talk, my dear. So far, you are just incredibly lucky that that maid was Martha who has been with this family since I was a girl and that she went to Mrs. Browning who has served this house almost as long and feels remarkably protective of us. Neither of them will be able to cover for you forever—nor should they be expected to do so."

"No, of course not." Totally chagrined at being caught out so, Retta sat twisting her hands in her lap. She wanted to defend herself, but the stark reality was that there simply was no defense.

Her aunt went on unrelentingly. "This sort of scandal would be devastating to the whole family. We have whispers enough about Mr. Bolton's actual residence in this house. Now, if this gets out too, *your* reputation will be ruined. I doubt not your sisters and stepmother would disown you, and the men in the family will have to deal with sly jokes at their expense. Is that what you want?"

"No, of course not," Retta repeated. She felt tears welling and did not bother to wipe them away. "But please, Auntie Georgie, please understand. I love Jake and after Rebecca's ball—what, ten days away?—I may never see him again." Overwhelmed by soul deep despair at that thought, she stifled a sob.

Her aunt's tone softened. "I do understand, my child—truly I do. I would have found it very difficult to stay away from my William, but you simply cannot—can*not*—carry on this way in your father's house. What *were* the two of you thinking? I could see what was happening—that is, how you feel about each other—but really, my dear—"

"I—I don't suppose we were *thinking* at all."

"Well, it is time you did," her aunt said flatly. "Servants talk and you know how Celeste," she nodded at Madame Laurent's door, "loves gossip."

Retta rose. "I—it won't happen again. I'll tell Jake this morning. I'm sorry."

"I am sorry, too, for both of you," her aunt said rising herself and enfolding Retta in her arms. "Perhaps when this—this bet business—is all over, you will be able to work something out."

"With a dockworker?"

"Who knows?"

They kissed each other on the cheek and both went to their own chambers where Retta, at least, dissolved into a bout of tears.

Chapter 19

For Jake, time in the next few days seemed to declare itself his enemy. In terms of the mission, it crawled at an excruciatingly slow pace. He could see that it was hard on Lord Alfred, too, as they waited for word that those messages had been delivered. Even then, they could not immediately deal with their known scoundrels. Only when word came that the French and Austrian negotiators at the Congress in Vienna were acting on that false information could they pick up Trentham's butler, Talbot. And they could not confront Morrow and Lindstrom without alarming Talbot. Jake knew that Lord Alfred, heartsick as he was at the personal betrayal of his secretary and his old friend, just wanted the whole thing to be over. And so did Jake, but for different reasons.

Retta had confided her aunt's discovery of their affair and she had not come to his room any night since. They still managed to snatch a few hours together, but other than a stolen kiss or two, there was nothing else as they kept up the routine of before—conducting their "lessons" in full view of others or with doors left ajar. He wanted this damned spy business tidied up so he could devote his time to righting himself with Retta. Knowing her as he did by now, he was sure she knew he had been deceiving her—had she not said as much?—but she did not know the exact nature of his deceit. When she found out, she would be angry and hurt. He also knew her to be impetuous and stubborn. Would she even be able to accept him after knowing how he had hoodwinked her? These few remaining days before the big come-out at the Lenninger ball moved slowly. Jake was tagged to accompany Retta to another fitting for her ball gown, but of course they were accompanied by Annie, leaving them little opportunity for more than a passing touch or squeeze of hands as he helped each woman from the carriage. He and Retta often exchanged rueful glances with each other.

Under the guise of a social call, Peter Fenton, who had, after all, been invited to that Christmas party, called at Blakemoor House and in the course of the visit managed to have a private word with Jake and Lord Alfred when they accompanied him downstairs as he was leaving. In his earlier disclosures, Jake had revealed to Lord Alfred that Colonel Lord Peter Fenton was Jake's immediate superior in the Foreign Office. As the three of them stepped into the entrance hall, Lord Alfred silently motioned them into the music room rather than the library across the foyer where Morrow was still at work. He closed the door and confronted Peter.

"I take it you have news, Colonel Fenton?"

"Yes, sir, I do. The French have received the information we gave them, and they seem to have shared it with the Austrians. Wellington left Paris a few days ago to travel to Vienna and Castlereagh is preparing to come home. He may already be on his way. It is my understanding that there is not much serious business occurring in Vienna at the moment."

"Then we have stopped that leak, but what about the other one—the army postings?"

"We just today received word from the English guard on Elba that Napoleon was visited by his sister last week. That is why I am here, my lord. We can rid ourselves of the whole lot of them at your discretion."

Lord Alfred heaved a sigh. "The sooner the better."

"The day after tomorrow—in the evening, say?" Fenton suggested.

Lord Alfred considered this a moment. "Yes, my sister and I had intended to go the theatre that night along with my niece, but I can invent some pressing work from the office that will necessitate my cancelling—and require the presence of Morrow. I shall ask Heaton to escort the ladies to the theatre."

"We shall arrest Talbot in the afternoon and keep him under wraps until we have them all," Fenton said. "There is a holding cell in the basement of the Foreign Office. We can do nothing at the moment about the deputy ambassador from Rome who received the information from Lindstrom and passed it on, but we can have him declared *persona non grata* later. Meanwhile, let him wonder."

"What about Madame Laurent?" Jake asked.

Peter slapped the base of his palm against his forehead. "I forgot about her. And her son."

"I doubt her son knows much about what his mother has been involved in," Lord Alfred said. "At most, Charles Laurent is a bit of a hanger-on. That is, when he is in town, and then he is always plaguing her for extra funds, but probably not aware of where they come from."

"Still, he is a loose end that must be dealt with—but he is not of high priority at the moment," Peter said.

"Will Madame go to the theatre too?" Jake asked.

"I think not," Lord Alfred replied. "We discussed this theatre outing at lunch yesterday and she distinctly said she was not interested in seeing a French play performed in English. I believe she will stay in. We can call her down when Lindstrom arrives."

"And he will be here because—?" Peter asked. Jake knew from working closely with Fenton on the Peninsula that Peter was meticulous about the details of a mission.

"I shall manufacture a medical malady and send a servant for him."

Peter nodded. "That should work."

* * * *

For Retta, these days were full of frustration and apprehension. The frustration came seeing Jake every day, yet never getting a chance to make love with him or even discuss anything meaningful about their relationship without fear of being interrupted or overheard. They did manage a couple of hasty kisses and there were a number of "accidental" touches. The apprehension came from the upcoming Lenninger ball. Would she win that bet? That is, would Jake win it for her? The possibility of giving up Moonstar still hung over her like a threatening storm.

Adding to her worry was the prospect of the details of that bet becoming public. If it did, it would create a huge scandal that would undoubtedly mean ridicule and social ostracism. Since the "setdown" she received from Aunt Georgiana, that particular fear had intensified. Her family did not deserve the condemnation that might come their way because of her actions. Well, Rebecca and Melinda might—they who had known just which of her strings to pull when that infernal bet was made. But the rest of the Parker family did not deserve such. And truth to tell, even her sisters did not bear as much blame as she herself did.

But without the bet, she would never have met Jake.

There were still obstacles to overcome in that part of her life, but she was certainly not going to give Jake up just because people like her stepmother would disapprove of him. Was this yet another example of her being "impulsive and intransigent" as Uncle Alfred had accused her of being? No, she could not accept that—not about her feelings for Jake.

She wished now that she had not agreed to go to the theatre with her aunt and uncle. With both of them out of the house, she and Jake might have managed some quality time together, for her brothers rarely spent evenings at home. *Too late to back out now,* she told herself; if she did, Aunt Georgiana would immediately know why and stop her.

In the event, Uncle Alfred had excused himself because of some urgent army work and Gerald had agreed to escort her and Aunt Georgiana. Retta was sorry Uncle Alfred had to bow out, but she welcomed the idea of Gerald's accompanying them. In the last few months, she had shared too little time with her brothers and she and Gerald nearly always enjoyed the same theatre works. In fact, some years ago, the two of them had read this play by Moliere together in French and she looked forward to its being produced in English.

* * * *

The theatre party had left an hour ago and now Jake and Peter Fenton sat in the music room with the door slightly ajar so they would hear Lindstrom arrive. As he entered the room, Fenton had informed Jake that he had posted three men just outside the main entrance to the house. Jake knew Lord Alfred had instructed the footman at the door to show Dr. Lindstrom to the library and then request that Madame Laurent join them there. Meanwhile, he and Peter whiled away the time with small talk.

"I've had an invitation to a ball given by Viscount Lenninger and his wife," Peter said. "Isn't she a sister to the Blakemoor brood?"

"Yes," Jake said. "You must remember that she had a central role in that bet that put me here in the first place."

"Ah, yes. Now that you remind me, I do recall your telling me that."

"The ball is to be the scene of my big come-out," Jake said.

Fenton laughed. "So at last you will enter the ranks of true gentlemen."

"Whatever that is."

"Then what?"

"I am thinking of selling out and retiring to my property and becoming not just a gentleman, but a gentleman farmer."

Fenton gave him a sharp look. "Good Lord, I think you are serious. You will be bored within a fortnight."

"I doubt that. I fully intend to be accompanied by my new wife."

"Wife? Who? Aha! You and the fair Lady Henrietta? Well, I'll be— Congratulations!"

"It is not settled yet, mind you, so please do not go bruiting it about."

"That ought to make tomorrow night's ball very interesting, indeed."

"Shhh. I heard the door knocker."

They sat in silence as they listened to the footman at the door greet Sir Cecil Lindstrom and then show him to the library. A short while later, they heard Madame Laurent come down the stairs. She knocked at the library door and they heard her say, "You wanted to see me, Lord Alfred? Oh, Sir Cecil. How nice to see you."

Fenton stood. "Show's on," he said softly.

Jake and Peter entered the library to find the three men, Lord Alfred, Lindstrom, and Morrow, standing at the entrance of Madame Laurent. Morrow, Lindstrom, and the lady all turned as Jake and Peter came through the door.

"What is going on here?"

"Is something the matter?"

Lindstrom and the woman spoke simultaneously.

"Please sit down, everyone," Lord Alfred said, reseating himself in a chair near the fireplace. "We all know each other, I think."

Jake saw Lindstrom and Madame Laurent exchange puzzled looks and then glance at Morrow almost apprehensively. All but Morrow sat in the chairs and a couch that formed a conversational group around the fireplace. Jake noted that Madame Laurent sat on the couch next to Lindstrom, but that Morrow had not moved from behind his desk. Jake and Peter occupied chairs set an angle to the couch, with Jake in the one nearest Morrow's desk. Jake sat casually with one leg resting on the knee of the other.

Lord Alfred leaned from his chair toward his long-time friend to hand Lindstom two sheets of paper. "I assume you recognize these, Cecil."

It took only a moment. Jake saw the doctor's face turn pale, and he made a choking sound, but quickly recovered and said in a rather blustery tone, "Why no. I've never seen these before."

"That is odd," Lord Alfred said in a deceptively mild tone, "for Mr. Bolton here saw you retrieve papers exactly like these from under the blotter on my secretary's desk. Now, I wonder how you might have known to look for such—and in just that place."

Madame Laurent buried her face in her hands and began to whimper.

Jake had been watching Morrow at the desk and saw a look of surprise cross the secretary's face and a surreptitious movement of his shoulders. Suddenly, the secretary had whipped a pistol from a desk drawer and rose to stand at the desk.

"Don't anybody move," Morrow said. "It's over, Celeste, Lindstrom. But the three of us are getting out of here right now."

Madame Laurent's whimpers turned to sobs. Lindstrom put an arm around her shoulders and she turned her face into his neck.

"Shut up, Celeste," her brother snarled. "Now is not the time for your histrionics."

"You might have some difficulty getting by my men posted at the front door." Peter Fenton sounded almost bored, but Jake knew that Peter, who had a gun tucked in the waistband of his trousers and covered by his coat, was poised like a panther, awaiting an opportunity to act. Jake had no firearm, but, typical of soldiers in the field, he did have a knife tucked into his boot.

"They'll not shoot at his high and mighty lordship, now, will they? He will shield us quite nicely, I think." Morrow waved his gun at Lord Alfred to move.

Lindstrom and the woman had risen and were moving cautiously. Jake noted that Lord Alfred was making a point of moving slowly. Madame uttered an unintelligible cry and her brother said, "Celeste, I told you to be quiet."

But he had made the mistake of glancing at her, and Jake used that split second to grab his knife and throw it at Morrow. It caught him in the shoulder and the gun went off. Madame Laurent screamed and would have collapsed but for that fact that Lindstrom still had an arm around her.

Peter had his weapon out now and pointed it directly at Morrow. "The tables have turned, I do believe."

Morrow was clutching his shoulder and blood seeped between his fingers. The bullet had grazed Madame Laurent's arm, which was bleeding rather profusely. She sank down to the couch again.

"Well, will you look at that," Peter said, still in his bored tone, "we have brother and sister with matching wounds." Then in a harsher tone, he said to Morrow, "At this point your gun is useless, but drop it anyway and get over there by her. And you, doctor, you who minister to the great and powerful, will see to their wounds, if Lord Alfred will be so good as to ring for a servant."

The doctor reached for the medical bag he had brought with him, but Jake intercepted him. "I'll just have a look inside, if you please." He opened the bag and removed a pistol. "Ah, I see you did not please. Ah, well . . ."

At that moment, the men Fenton had posted earlier rushed in, guns drawn.

"Lawks," one of them said. "We missed the fun."

"As soon as the doctor has finished with those two, tie the hands of all three of them," Fenton ordered, "and we will have a bit of a chat before you take them off our hands."

Both wounds were superficial, and when a Blakemoor servant had brought a basin of water and some cloths, the doctor made quick work of dealing with them, and then the three sat side-by-side on the couch, their hands bound with heavy cord; each wore a glum expression.

Jake noticed that Lord Alfred's expression was rather stoic, and he seemed tired, but he roused himself enough to offer his "guests" drinks all around. Jake rose to help him and cast an inquiring glance at Fenton before according the prisoners such hospitality.

Fenton shrugged and said, "All right. I am quite sure it will be their last drink for a while—a very long while."

Jake suspected Fenton also intended the drinks to soften the prisoners for interrogation. When these had been distributed, with the prisoners imbibing them somewhat awkwardly because of their tied hands, Fenton sat back, looking as relaxed as he might on an afternoon social call.

"You three may be interested to know that your friend Talbot was arrested this afternoon. He gave us much of the story, but perhaps you will be so kind as to fill us in on such details as he left out," Peter began.

The three sat across from him looking stubborn.

"Clever of you to divide your efforts, by the way," Peter went on just as though the prisoners were engaging with him in his conversation. "I mean you had us quite confused for a while there, with some information going to the continent and some being sent elsewhere. As I said, clever." He paused. "But you know, treason is a very serious offense. Actually, a hanging offense."

Madame Laurent let out a long sigh ending in a whimper.

"And then there is the murder," Peter added still in that conversational tone.

"Murder?" the woman said in shocked surprise and looked from one of her companions to the other.

"I know nothing of a murder," Morrow said.

"Ah, but the good doctor does, I think," Peter said and now directed his words specifically to Lindstrom. "Surely he remembers a young footman serving in the house of the Marquis of Trentham. His name was Richter. Fired for 'pilfering.' Talbot tells us he was caught looking through your medical bag, *Dr.* Lindstrom. He found something other than medical instruments, did he not?"

Lindstrom did not respond, simply staring blankly at the wall beyond Peter's head.

Lord Alfred made a choking sound. "Oh, my God! Cecil, that cannot be true, can it? It is hard enough for me to view you as an enemy agent, but murder? Murder! How could you—you a man sworn to heal, not destroy?"

Lindstrom shot a glaring look at his one-time friend. "Stuff you and your self-righteousness, Alfred. You have no idea what it is like to live just on the fringes of society all your life."

Lord Alfred's expression hardened. "I am willing to forgive a great deal because of how instrumental you were in my recovery from grievous wounds all those years ago. But I cannot—I will not—forgive your treasonous acts perpetrated right here in my home. And murdering an innocent man? That is simply beyond the pale." He shook his head in sorrow, leaned back in his chair, and closed his eyes. Jake thought he was fighting off tears.

The doctor merely shrugged and refused to meet Lord Alfred's gaze, so Peter went on with his interrogation. Jake had seen Peter question prisoners many times before, and he always marveled at his friend's ability to elicit more information than prisoners were aware of giving him. It was painstaking work, one question at a time, and each question leading to another, but eventually, Peter had ferreted out the whole story. Little of it was really new, and it fit with what they had already known.

Morrow—or Moreau—and his sister had been promised the restoration of their titles and property in France for their help in keeping the new French government informed regarding England's role in the divisions of Napoleon's empire.

"I did it for my son," she sobbed. "He deserves his father's title and wealth."

Further questioning revealed that Lindstrom, aware from Talbot of Morrow's willingness to help, had then approached Morrow for information about placement and strength of English troops on the continent. The emperor would be very grateful, he was told. Both Lindstrom and Morrow had seen this as a way to hedge their bets and ensure that at least one of these rolls of the dice would pay off. No, none of them knew to what *specific* uses their information would be put—just that they were paid well now and would reap even further, more meaningful rewards later.

Peter looked at Jake in silent question of "are we finished?" Jake nodded and Fenton ordered one of his men to accompany Madame Laurent to her chamber to gather a few necessities and to write a note to Lady Georgiana stating that she had decided to spend a few days in the country with her son. When she returned, carrying a small bag, and quietly weeping, her brother berated her again.

"Do shut up, Celeste. You knew the risks, same as all of us."

Unable to put his arms around her because of his bound hands, Lindstrom leaned close to her and glared at Morrow. "Have some consideration, Henry. After all, it was you got her into this mess." He managed to touch her hands with his and added, "There, there, my love. We will see this through together."

Colonel Fenton instructed his men to load the prisoners into the waiting carriage, but lingered behind for a few moments to speak with Lord Alfred.

"I know this came as a great shock to you, my lord, but I assure you that it will be handled with the utmost discretion."

Lord Alfred passed a hand over his eyes and gave Fenton a rather bleak look. "It always comes as a shock when you have trusted people for a certain role in your life, and they show themselves to have betrayed that trust." He sighed. "What is to happen to them now?"

"By the time the truth comes out, these three and their accomplice already in custody will, in all likelihood, have been quietly dealt with—probably hustled aboard a transport headed to New South Wales. We do not want to sound the alarm for their contacts, you understand."

Lord Alfred rose and extended his hand to Fenton. "'Tis a sad business, but—on behalf of my family and the Commander in Chief—thank you, sir."

Jake accompanied Peter to the door. "You handled that very well, Colonel Lord Peter Fenton," Jake said with a grin.

"I might add that, you, Major Lord Jacob Bodwyn, had no small role to play and the powers that be will be so informed."

"It will not matter. I am selling out, as I told you, but I appreciate the thought."

"Well, what will be will be. In any event, I'll see you at the Lenninger ball tomorrow."

Jake returned to the library to find Lord Alfred refilling his and Jake's glasses.

"I just assumed you would join me," the older man said and sat back in his chair.

"Yes, sir." Jake sat down, reached for the glass, and raised it to his lordship. "That cannot have been easy for you, my lord."

"No, it was not," Lord Alfred replied. "It will come as a shock to my brother when he finds out. To the rest of the family too. I am guessing that with the defeat of Napoleon and return of the Bourbons to the throne in Paris, Morrow—Moreau—and his sister were counting on their return to French society as well. Apparently over twenty years in this country failed to anglicize them." The old man sighed, looking older than Jake had ever observed of him before. "It is Lindstrom's behavior that I find just impossible to understand or condone."

"Sir? I understood that he, too, had property in France that was confiscated during the revolution."

"Yes, he did. But so did many Englishmen. Perhaps his being elevated to a knighthood for his doctoring the rich and powerful gave him delusions of grandeur. Who knows?" Lord Alfred set his glass down. "Who knows?" he repeated wearily.

"Will you be sharing this news with Lord Heaton and the rest of the family?" Jake asked, wanting to know what kind of face the family would be putting on at the night's events.

Lord Alfred pondered for a moment, then said, "I think not. I shall explain it all to them after Rebecca's ball. It will not be common gossip for a few days at least. Might as well let them enjoy the ball." He paused. "It has been one hell of a night, has it not?"

"That it has, my lord."

Chapter 20

On returning from the theatre, Retta peeped into the library hoping that Jake would be there, as he so often was, playing chess with her uncle. But the neither man was there and the room was dark. Assuming that they had retired earlier than usual, Retta accompanied her aunt up to their sitting room.

"I am ready to divest myself of this corset," said Aunt Georgiana, as she rummaged around in the sideboard. "What say you to our getting into our nightclothes and then having a bit of a nightcap? I'm sure the sherry decanter is here somewhere—ah, there it is."

"Sounds fine to me," Retta said absently, still disappointed at not having seen Jake this evening.

"You needn't exert yourself on my account," Aunt Georgiana said a bit caustically.

"No. No, I did not mean to sound reluctant."

Her aunt raised an eyebrow. "You will see him soon enough tomorrow, you know."

Retta felt herself blushing at being caught out so. "All right. If you just help me with the fastenings on this gown, I shall do the same for you, and we needn't disturb our maids. I'm sure they will appreciate our letting them sleep."

"By all means."

When they had performed those services for each other, they went to their own bedchambers and donned their nightwear. Retta was just reentering the sitting room when her aunt came charging into the room, her own dressing gown agape, and waving a bit of notepaper.

"Retta, you will not believe this."

"What?"

"Celeste has left us."

"What do you mean, 'left us,'?" Retta asked.

"I am not at all sure what it means. She writes that she has decided to go into the country to spend a few days with her son."

"She could hardly have arranged that and packed adequately in the time we were attending the theatre. Did you check her wardrobe?"

"No. But I will." Aunt Georgiana stepped into Madame Laurent's room and returned almost immediately. "Strange. Very strange. She took almost none of her clothes. Her hairbrush and a jar of cream I know she uses at night are gone. But she left an open book on her nightstand. Why would she not take a book she was reading?"

"That *is* strange," Retta said, then laughed as she filled the sherry glasses. "You don't suppose she has eloped with Sir Cecil?"

"Do be serious. Not only would that be out of character for Celeste, it would be totally unnecessary. Who would object—at their ages?"

"Well, I am quite sure I do not know what bee got in her bonnet. Here." She handed her aunt one of the glasses she had filled.

"'Tis a puzzle," Aunt Georgiana murmured, taking a seat in a barrel chair and propping her feet on a matching footstool. "I suppose we will know more in the morning. Maybe she will write a letter explaining beyond these few lines. This just is not like her at all."

They sipped silently for a few moments—Retta lost in thoughts of Jake as her aunt seemed to be thinking of the strange behavior of her friend. Then her aunt sighed and dropped that subject. "I thought the play tonight was very entertaining. I have always loved Moliere's work, but I had never seen this one."

* * * *

Jake greeted the next day with mixed feelings. With the spy mission completed, he no longer had reason to remain at Blakemoor house. The prospect of rejoining his own family was tempered by the thought that he would, for a time at least, see less of Retta. But while still there, he had one last chore to be got through before he could take up his own life again. His own life again. Just what might that be like?

After a restless night, he rose early and discovered that he was not the only one to find meeting this day head on was preferable to burrowing back under the covers in an attempt to postpone the inevitable. The weather having taken a pleasant turn, he surmised that Retta and Lord Alfred would already be at the stables for what might well be the last ride the three of them would have together.

And so they were.

At this hour, and because it was still wintery cold, they encountered little traffic. Nor did they engage in their usual back and forth chatter as they approached the park. He thought Lord Alfred might be preoccupied with the loss of his friend and secretary. Retta seemed in particularly low spirits and Jake was sure they stemmed from thoughts of perhaps losing her horse. She kept patting Moonstar's neck and murmuring praises to the animal. He felt sorry for her and tried to distract her.

"My lady," he called to her, "Blaze and I will give you and Moonstar a count of three and race you to that big overhanging willow down there." He pointed to the tree about a quarter of a mile distant.

She immediately perked up. "You're on!"

Jake held the eager Blaze back for the three count he had promised, then let the horse go. They finished almost simultaneously, both horses prancing at the end and both riders laughing.

"I needed that." Retta leaned forward to pat the neck of her mare. "*We* needed that, didn't we, my pretty?" The horse looked around at her rider just as though she agreed. Then Retta looked directly at Jake. "And that is not all I need, as I am sure you are aware." She pursed her lips.

"Stop, you wanton hoyden, you! You are wreaking havoc with a certain part of my anatomy with such talk." He wanted desperately to kiss her. For a moment, desire was almost palpable between them and Jake thought they were both a bit relieved as Lord Alfred joined them.

"So—who won?" his lordship asked.

"'Twas a tie," Retta said with a laugh.

Later, at breakfast, Jake noted that Lord Alfred avoided talking of what had taken place the night before. When his sister mentioned her missing companion, he had no comment beyond an absent "Is that so?"

"You were not aware of her leaving?" Lady Georgiana persisted.

"Um. No, I don't think so. I rarely notice any commotion in the entrance hall when Morrow and I are working."

She turned to Jake. "What about you, Mr. Bolton? Did you hear anything untoward last evening?"

Jake looked at Lord Alfred who gave him a slight shake of the head. "Um. No, my lady, I heard nothing. But I'm rather a heavy sleeper."

"Are you, indeed?" Lady Georgiana asked with a raised eyebrow, but she went on to note that, "This was most unlike Celeste."

Jake did not dare do more than glance at Retta, but he was sure she blushed.

That evening, he dressed carefully for the ball in the formal trousers and long-tailed coat that someone had supplied—he suspected Lord Heaton, perhaps at Retta's direction. There was even a polished onyx stickpin for his neckcloth. He joined Lord Alfred and Lord Heaton, dressed much as he was, as they waited in the library for the ladies to join them. Richard in the full dress uniform of a member of the King's Guard would join the rest of the family at the ball.

"Are you nervous, Bolton?" asked Gerald, Lord Heaton.

"Somewhat. I just it want to go well for your sister."

"So do I. Most sincerely do I wish just that."

Before anyone could add to that, the ladies joined them. Retta was wearing a splendid gown of blue silk with a deep-scooped neck and silver lace trim. Her aunt was outfitted in a maroon silk with touches of ecru lace. Jake raised an eyebrow to show his appreciation of Retta's appearance. Her hair was arranged in a rather severe French knot, but a few curls dangled at the side of her face to soften the overall image. A sapphire and diamond necklace with matching earbobs completed her outfit that also included a cape of matching silk with a silver lining.

"Nicely done, ladies," Lord Alfred said.

"Thank you, kind sir," Retta said, linking her arm with her uncle's. "But I see that we are to be accompanied by the handsomest men at the ball." Her gaze lingered on Jake.

Arriving at Lenninger House, they discovered their carriage to be one in a long line of vehicles waiting to disgorge society's elite, and that there was quite a crowd of people on the opposite sidewalk gawking at all the finery.

"Can we not just get out here and walk?" Retta asked when they were still seven or eight carriages back. "It has not rained all day," she added. "In that, Rebecca's timing has been excellent."

They all agreed and the men got out and as they handed the ladies from the carriage, Retta ended up on Jake's arm. He felt her hand trembling on his arm as they climbed the steps to the ballroom.

He leaned close to whisper, "No matter how this turns out, I love you and I will stand by you." Then he mentally kicked himself. That was not how he had intended to make that declaration.

She looked at him, startled, but whispered back, "And I, you." He was not entirely sure what that meant, but now was not the time to pursue it, for they were suddenly at the reception line that included Lord and Lady Lenninger, the dowager baroness, and Lady Lenninger's sister, the Honorable Melinda Parker.

Jake heard Lady Lenninger greet her aunt and uncle effusively and complain to her brother Gerald that he, along with Richard and Retta, had refused her invitation to join her in the reception line. "I was not surprised when Retta refused a wish of mine, but you?"

"Reception lines are always such bore, no matter which side one is on," Gerald said and moved on.

Rebecca glared at his back, but turned an overly bright smile on her sister. "Ah, Henrietta," she said in a voice that could be heard even by many who had already gone through the line, "how lovely you look, my dear. And, Mr. Bolton, how very nice to see you. I confess I was not at all sure you would accept our invitation."

"I would not have missed your ball for all the world," he said politely.

Rebecca lowered her voice. "Both the Countess of Sefton and Countess Cowper are among our guests."

"How nice for you," Retta said, and Jake saw her jaw tighten.

He was also aware of Melinda's boldly looking him over and then saying in a stage whisper to Retta, "I told you he would look splendid in formal wear!"

As soon as they were through the reception line, he asked Retta, "What was that all about?"

"Which?"

"Both of them."

"Lady Sefton and Lady Cowper are two of the patronesses of Almack's." Retta sounded a bit nervous to him, but then she grinned and said, "I think Melinda has her eye on you."

"Oh, really?" He rolled his eyes and she laughed. At least she sounded more relaxed now.

Along with Lord Alfred, Lady Georgiana, and Lord Heaton, he and Retta moved beyond the reception line and stood on the edge of the ballroom, as were a number of other small groups. Jake could see that Rebecca had achieved every *ton* hostess's dream in producing such a "crush" that he wondered how on earth she expected that many people to dance easily.

But in the event, after Lord and Lady Lenninger led the first dance, others did move about with a degree of freedom that surprised him. With Jake at her side, instead of taking part in that first dance, Retta moved from group to group, acknowledging acquaintances and always making sure to introduce Mr. Bolton. He could tell that she was searching for someone in particular, then he heard her indrawn breath and she tightened her hold on his arm. "Oh, Lady Sefton and Lady Cowper. How very nice to see you here. My sister is so glad you could come. May I present my

friend, Mr. Bolton? He has only just returned to town after several years
out of the country."

Jake wondered how she had come up with that last bit of information, but
it was ironically accurate, was it not? The two ladies were both attractive
and at least ten years older than Retta. They were both in very fashionable
gowns and each seemed aware of the place she held in society. He bowed
politely over the hands of both and he noticed that Retta stood slightly
aside as he engaged in small talk with them, discussing what a fine turn-
out Lady Lenninger had achieved and how sad that so many of society's
notables were on the continent yet.

Jake said, "Ah, but it is their loss to have missed such a fine gathering
as this with so many beautiful ladies." He smiled and winked at both of
them and they simpered like schoolgirls.

"When the season has really started in earnest, Mr. Bolton, we hope
to see you at Almack's," Lady Sefton said a bit coquettishly, "Do we not,
Emily?" she added to Lady Cowper.

"Of course," Lady Cowper agreed. "We delight in welcoming gentlemen
such as yourself."

As he and Retta moved on, Jake waited until they were out of earshot
and asked, "How did I do?"

She tapped his arm with her fan. "You know very well that you did
splendidly, you arrogant man!"

He chuckled as the orchestra was emitting the first notes of a waltz.
"You did promise me the first waltz, did you not?"

For several minutes, he just marveled at having her in his arms again.
"I have missed you so much," he said softly, drinking in that beguiling
flowery-woody scent of her hair. "When this night is over, there is much
that I must tell you."

"All those secrets you have withheld from me?" she teased.

"Well, yes, that too." He splayed his hand on her back and pulled her
closer. They simply reveled in the swirls of the dance, and he knew from
a small sigh that she regretted the end of it as much as he did.

* * * *

Retta was feeling exuberant as they left the dance floor. So far, the evening
was perfect. Jake had clearly charmed the patronesses of Almack's—those
most particular arbiters of London society. And he had said he loved her.
True, he had made that statement in a rather off-hand way, but he *had*

said it. She could not wait to tell him—and show him—just how much she returned that sentiment!

Suddenly a tall man standing on the edge of the dance floor, beside a pretty woman in a fashionable gown of sunny yellow, said in a loud, surprised voice, "Jake?" He grabbed Jake's other elbow and jerked him around so hard that Retta lost her very light grip on his arm. "Jake! Just what the h— What are you doing here? In London? At this ball? We thought—we were sure you were still in France! Why, we had a letter just last week—and here—here—"

"Oh, God," Jake said in a stricken tone. "Not here, Burwell."

Retta, concerned at what she perceived as pain in Jake's voice, quickly took charge. "The library is just down the hall from the ballroom entrance," she said, glad that she had allowed Rebecca to show the place off to her on a call one afternoon.

Burwell's outburst had attracted a good deal of attention, and the crowd parted as they made their way across the ballroom. Retta was aware that they had picked up an entourage as they went: the woman in a sunny yellow ball gown clung to the man's arm and Uncle Alfred fell into step beside Retta, who led the way to the library. It was well lit, intended, she supposed, as a place for guests to seek a temporary respite. She could hear the buzzing behind her. *Burwell. Burwell. I know I know that name. Ah! I have it! The Marquis of Burwell. Heir to the Duke of Holbrook. But why—? How does Jake—?*

Her thoughts were abruptly interrupted as the five of them went through the library door. She was vaguely aware of others crowding in behind them.

Burwell stopped abruptly in the middle of the room and whirled around to face Jake. He was obviously angry. "Well? I do hope you have a credible explanation for this. Or maybe you just forgot you had a family?"

"No, I did not forget. I—I was not free before." Jake sounded somewhat uncertain of himself—a condition that Retta thought she had never seen in him before. He put an arm around her waist and drew her close. She felt his arm trembling. "Lady Henrietta Parker, may I present to you Herald, the Marquis of Burwell and Deirdre, Marchioness of Burwell? My brother and his lovely wife."

"B-Burwell?" she stuttered. "Your b-brother?" She quickly recovered herself, incongruously thinking, *Miss Pringle trained her girls well.* She curtsied to the Marquis and his wife who acknowledged her politely; then she waited as impatiently as she supposed they did for Jake's explanation. She felt Uncle Alfred at her other side and then Aunt Georgiana pushed through the gathering crowd at the door to stand with Uncle Alfred.

There was a long, heavy silence.

"Well?" the marquis demanded, then his voice broke and he opened his arms. "For God's sake, Jake, we've not seen you in more than ten years!" He enfolded Jake in his arms and said against his brother's neck, "Years!" He stepped away enough to allow his wife to hug Jake as well.

"We truly have missed, you know," she said.

"Now, just what is going on here, Jake?" The marquis was back to sounding demanding, but both his and his wife's eyes showed glittery moisture. "Surely you cannot think you would be unwelcome in your own family? Not even you could hold a grudge that long and all your letters—"

"No. No, it was nothing like that at all." Jake's voice sounded a little "watery" too.

Retta saw him look about the room, his gaze resting on Lord Peter Fenton who had pushed into the room. Then he glanced at her uncle and both men nodded to him.

"Let us all sit down," Jake said, drawing Retta onto a couch with him as Burwell and his wife took the matching one opposite them. Retta saw that Lord Fenton was trying to close the library door against gawking onlookers.

"You will not deny me entrance to a room in my own house," Rebecca said in a shrill voice. Fenton stepped aside and Rebecca was followed by her husband, and Melinda, and then Richard and Gerald and several others, including Lady Sefton, before Fenton succeeded in closing the door. Retta closed her eyes for a moment. *My whole family. My whole family is to witness* . . . but she could not complete that thought because she did not know what was going on. But Jake still had an arm about her shoulders, so maybe it was not so very bad.

* * * *

Jake bent his head close to Retta's and whispered, "Trust me, my darling. This changes nothing between you and me. Nothing."

Then he sat up straighter and faced his brother. "I could not contact you, B'well," he said using the name the siblings had called the heir in the nursery rooms, "because I was—until yesterday—working on an assigned mission."

"What 'mission' kept you from your own family?"

Sensing some apprehension in Retta, Jake sighed. "It's a long, long story, my brother."

"I cannot wait to hear it," Burwell said.

"Nor can I," Retta muttered, moving away slightly.

Jake looked at Retta, but she refused to meet his gaze. He drew a deep breath and started reciting, just as though he were giving a military report—which, to some extent, he supposed he was. "I have not been an ordinary soldier since my first year in India."

Burwell interrupted. "But you were—you *are* in the army, are you not? Father did buy you a commission. All those letters—the latest ones from 'Major' Bodwyn, sent from France."

"That is true. But in India and then in the Peninsula I served with the Duke of Wellington—he was not a duke then, of course. I was a 'corresponding officer'—a spy if you will."

"We like to call it intelligence work," Fenton put in.

Burwell turned to this voice. "Fenton? You knew he was in England and did not tell me when I saw you at White's just a few nights ago?"

"Couldn't. Just hear him out."

"After Napoleon abdicated, the duke—Wellington, that is—asked me to help uncover spies that we knew to be passing to the new French government a remarkable amount of very accurate information—impeding negotiations in Paris and then at the Congress in Vienna."

"Why you? Why all this secrecy from your own family?"

Jake could tell that his brother was really trying to understand. "You know that languages and dialects have always come easily to me."

"I know you used to get all the best parts in the plays we did as youngsters."

"Yes. Well. The duke wanted someone to slip into England to work on the docks, for we thought the conduit must be with ships sailing regularly to and from France. We were right, up to a point."

"Oh, good Lord! Have I interfered in an official action of the government? Are you even now— If only you had contacted me . . ." his brother's voice trailed off as he looked from Jake to Fenton and back.

Fenton stepped in from where he had been standing since most of the chairs in the room were occupied. "The mission is over. With Lord Alfred Parker's invaluable aid, we dealt with it just last night. Major Lord Jacob Bodwyn is now free to be himself again."

"Whoever that might be," Retta muttered.

Jake felt his heart sinking as she seemed to be putting emotional distance between them.

Rebecca stood up and virtually screeched at Retta. "A lord? He is the son of a duke?" She emitted a harsh, mirthless laugh. "I cannot believe it. And you were teaching him how to become a gentleman? Oh, this is rich! Preposterous! Well, I won't have it! No wonder he fooled Lady Sefton and Lady Cowper!" She pointed a finger at Retta. "This means I won the bet after all—you did not train a common dockworker to become a gentleman. He *was* a gentleman all along! So I won. I will come by tomorrow to collect my new mare."

"No," Retta protested with what might have been a sob. "This cannot be happening."

There was a general buzz of conversation now. Gerald stepped forward from where he had been standing with Fenton and some others and said firmly, "Sit down, Rebecca, and watch your tongue. You are creating a scene for which you may be sorry later."

"You cannot talk to me like that in my own home. Lenninger," she wailed, but she did sit down.

Her husband patted her shoulder. "It's all right, my love, we will get this sorted out."

"But I won."

"No, Rebecca, you did not." Gerald's tone was calm and authoritative. "Think. *You* chose that particular man on the docks. The mistake was yours. The bet is simply nullified."

"He's right, Rebecca," Richard said from the back.

"Oh. Oh. Oh," she wailed. "You two always did take her side! And now you are doing it again! And now you have ruined my ball. I hate you. I hate all of you."

She started to run from the room, but Gerald grabbed her arm and pulled her away from the door.

"Oh, no you don't," he said. "You are not running away from this. It is as much your fault as anyone's. And you cannot run through that ballroom crying your eyes out and making the situation worse, bringing scandal on all of us."

Her husband came to put an arm around her and murmur soothing words to calm her. She allowed herself to be pampered into some semblance of control, but refused eye contact with either Gerald or Retta.

"She did not mean to say that," Lord Lenninger said to the room at large. "It is her condition you know. Come, now Rebecca. We must return to the ball—we must carry on. Melinda will help us. The three of us, along with Mama, will see that our guests are properly cared for. I'll ask the musicians to give us another waltz."

He and Rebecca, with Melinda right behind them, left the room and while those remaining in the room were still staring at each other silently, they heard the first strains of a waltz starting.

Finally, Retta stood up. "I have had enough of this ball. The rest of you may stay and put as good a face on it as you can manage. I am leaving."

"I shall come with you," Jake said.

"No. I never want to see you again."

"Oh, Retta," Lady Georgiana said, rushing to her side as Retta moved purposely toward the door.

"Rest assured, my lady, you absolutely *will* see me again," Jake called after her, his jaw clenched.

Chapter 21

Retta stood in silent fury and humiliation as she waited for the servant to find their cloaks for her and her aunt and uncle, neither of whom was willing to let her return home alone. Even when she at last entered the carriage and scooted to the far side of the seat she shared with Aunt Georgiana, she said nothing. She just wanted to hide. She wished the coachman had not bothered to light the lantern inside the vehicle. As the carriage rolled away from Lenninger House, Aunt Georgiana heaved a sigh and patted Retta's knee.

"Retta, my dear, I know you are feeling let down—"

"Let down? Let down, you say? What an understatement! I have never been so embarrassed in my entire life!" She stifled an angry sob. "I thought he cared for me and all the while—all these weeks and months—he—he must have been laughing at me. Laughing! And now Rebecca will spread it all about and the whole world will be laughing at me!"

"But, my dear," her aunt pursued gently, "you have never been one to care overmuch what others thought of you. You have always gone your own way and let the devil take the hindmost."

Barely able to keep from breaking into great shaking sobs, Retta said, "I do not ever remember anyone setting out so deliberately to humiliate me before. And that is exactly what Jake-whatever-his-name-is did!"

Uncle Alfred cleared his throat. "I think you are being a might harsh on the lad."

"Harsh? Uncle Alfred, have you any idea how really hard I worked at making those inane lessons worthwhile—and it was all for nothing. Nothing. And you! Just how long have you known about him? How long did you let me go on making an utter fool of myself?"

"Well, let me see . . . I think I have known who he was for about a month. But Retta, you must try to see reason. Jacob Bodwyn had a job to do, and, I must tell you, he did it at no small sacrifice to himself. At first he may well have seen the irony of a duke's son being taught how to be a gentleman, but at the time, that was merely a means to an end for him—the end, of course, being to stop those spies who would bring harm to England."

"What spies? Who were they?" Retta asked, her interest finally focusing on something other than her sense of hurt and loss.

"Yes, I have wondered the same thing," her aunt said.

Now it was Uncle Alfred's turn to heave a sigh. "You won't want to hear this, Georgiana," he began. He then filled them in on the entire story. Both women sat silent until he had finished.

Aunt Georgiana was the first to speak and there were shocked tears in her voice. "You are right, Alfred. That was not something I wanted to hear at all. Celeste? How she must have resented us all these years."

He wiped a hand over his face. "I find it difficult to understand either her role in the whole mess or Lindstrom's. I never would have dreamed he would betray his own country for a paltry piece of property in the Loire valley."

"Well, it was not merely property, was it?" Retta asked, feeling sorry for both her aunt and uncle. "It appears there was some prestige to go along with that. And Madame Laurent—she must have been sincere in wishing a better life for her son."

"I am certain she was," her aunt replied, and gave her brother a sad look as she added, "but they both betrayed long-standing friendships. That is hard to forgive."

Retta was spared having to reply to that, for the carriage had arrived at Blakemoor House and they all went immediately to their rooms. Retta supposed that her aunt and uncle would sleep as little that night as she would.

The next morning, she gave Jeffries strict orders that should Lord Jacob Bodwyn call, she was not at home. The following morning, she issued the same order and felt some bit of satisfaction when Jeffries reported both days that he *had* called. However, she was not best pleased in learning that her uncle, and then her aunt, too, had received him. And, truth to tell, that satisfaction was tempered by regret, but she could hardly back down, could she? When he failed to call on the third day and the day following, she began to feel panicky at the thought of never seeing him again.

She was angry and hurt that she had been played for a fool all these weeks and months, but when she let her guard down on her resentment, memories intruded and overwhelmed her: memories of sharing small jokes, the feel of his arms around her, the tenderness of his lovemaking. She avoided both the music room and the morning room, for they reminded her of him too much. She ignored her uncle's advice when he said at breakfast the second morning after the ball, "I think you should talk to him, Retta. Work this out." Her one consolation was that there was no danger of her losing Moonstar now. She cried into the soft warmth of the mare's neck. She cried far too often as some small thing ignited a memory. Her future looked bleak, but she could not bring herself to deal with it just yet.

* * * *

For Jake, the days following the Lenninger ball were some of the busiest, most emotional days of his life. He had gone home to Holbrook House that night with his brother and they had spent hours after Deirdre had retired just catching up with each other. He learned that his father and the other two brothers, as well as his sister Elizabeth and their families, would be arriving within the week for the season. Jake looked forward with eager anticipation to seeing all of them again.

The thing that would make that reunion complete would be if he could introduce his new wife to the lot of them. But that looked unlikely so long as Retta persisted in avoiding him. Deirdre had informed him that apparently Lady Henrietta was not only not receiving many visitors, but that she was not making any calls herself. He found that bit of news depressing; it hurt him to think that she was experiencing such anguish, but so long as she refused to see him, he could see no way of making amends.

The second time he called at Blakemoor House, he asked to see Lady Georgiana. She did not seem surprised at his request.

"I must admit, my lady, that I am embarrassed to be talking with you about Retta and me," he began. She had received him in the drawing room and invited him to join her for tea. She merely raised an eyebrow, and he felt like a bumbling schoolboy, but he plunged on. "I mean, I know you know about us—really know, that is—and the thing of it is that she simply must agree to marry me. I mean—"

"I know what you mean, dear boy," she said, letting him off the hook. "And I quite agree. My niece is impetuous and stubborn, as you must surely know by now, but rarely have I seen her be unfair. I know she cares for you, so I guess my best advice is to just give her time."

So he did. He gave her another three days, and then he accosted her in the park early one morning. It was now well into the third week of February. Winter was not ready to give way yet, and spring was just thinking of asserting itself. Some trees were sporting promises of flowers and leaves, but these had not yet materialized. The promise alone, though, raised the spirits of all London's inhabitants.

* * * *

Still depressed, Retta insisted on keeping to the schedule of her morning rides. Uncle Alfred agreed to accompany her this day and, as usual, he hung back when she insisted on taking Moonstar for a hard run. She was remembering that last ride with Jake as she returned to her uncle, to see him talking with another rider on a magnificent roan stallion. Jake. Her heart fluttered at the mere sight of him, but she felt distinctly shy about meeting him. Nevertheless, she was certainly not going to make a show of avoiding him. She would be just cool and contained.

"Hello, Retta," he greeted her.

"Lord Bodwyn," she said coolly, and refused to hold his gaze.

Uncle Alfred picked up the reins of his horse and said, "I think you two have a good deal to talk about." With that he urged his mount into motion.

"Uncle Alfred!" she called, but he ignored her.

She turned to Jake. "That was a rather sneaky trick," she said.

"I know. But desperate men seize what opportunities fall their way. And now, my Lady Henrietta, you *will* talk with me." He reached to grab her reins and led Moonstar to a nearby park bench, where he tied both horses and then reached to set her on her feet.

"I could scream, you know. *Someone* might hear me and come to my aid."

"Yes, you could," he said, "but I doubt you will. That is, I sincerely hope you will not do so." He grasped her elbow and sat down on the bench, pulling her down next to him.

"Well, say your piece and get on with it," she said, staring beyond his shoulder.

"Retta—" There was a note of impatience in his voice that she had never heard before. He put a gloved finger on her cheek and forced her to face him. Then he just kissed her. It was a very thorough and prolonged kiss, for she was unable to stop herself from responding with the same sort of longing that he showed.

"Woman, you are driving me crazy," he murmured. "Admit it: you missed me."

Chagrined now, she said quietly, "All right, I do admit it. But why didn't you tell me? Why didn't you trust me? Have you any idea at all of how much courage it took for me to ask you to—to—"

"Marry you? That is what you had in mind, is it not?"

Now she was embarrassed again. "Well, yes. That is what I had in mind, I think, though my suggesting it would have been most unorthodox." She turned slightly to look him squarely in the eye. "But really, I just wanted us to be together."

"And women—ladies—do not do the asking, do they?"

"Not usually."

"If you think about it really, really hard, you may remember that I was the first to mention marriage. But—all right, then, if that is what this is all about—" He moved to kneel on one knee at her feet. "My Lady Henrietta, will you do me the very great honor to become my wife?"

She laughed. "Oh, do get up. That ground is cold."

"Not 'til you answer me."

"Of course I will marry you." As he resumed his seat next to her, she added, "I rather fancied that fellow Jake Bolton, but I suppose you will do well enough."

"I happen to know that fellow, Bolton, loved you insanely, but I promise to love you just as much." He kissed her again, then raised his lips from hers just long enough to murmur, "Or more."

"And I promise to love you likewise, Major Lord Jacob Bodwyn. And I will, indeed, be happy to marry you."

"When?"

"Why, uh—"

"Today? Tomorrow?"

"Today? Tomorrow?" she echoed rather stupidly.

"Either one," he said. "But not much longer, please, Retta." He pulled a paper from inside his coat. "I have a special license right here."

"You were that sure of me?" she asked, feigning umbrage.

"I was that hopeful," he said, giving her a quick kiss.

"Day after tomorrow, then. Our families deserve some warning."

"Fine." He put the paper back in his pocket and drew out a small packet, which he placed in her gloved hand.

"What is this?"

"A birthday present. A day or so late, but it comes with birthday wishes and my heart as well."

She removed her gloves to unwrap it and found a small gold locket. She opened it to reveal tiny portraits of him and her. She looked up in wonder. "How— When—?"

"I picked it up three days before your sister's ball. Your aunt helped me get your portrait."

"Oh, Jake!" She threw her arms around his neck and kissed him. "I do love you so very much."

"Today, then?" he said hopefully.

"Day after tomorrow."

Epilogue

Major Lord Jacob Bodwyn and Lady Henrietta Parker were married ten days after her sister's ball. The ceremony took place in the drawing room of her father's London residence. They were attended by such family members as were then in town, and after as sumptuous a wedding breakfast as the Blakemoor retainers could provide on such short notice, the newlyweds retired to a suite in Grillon's hotel where they were known to be *very* late risers.

They were making plans to remove to Lord Jacob Bodwyn's extensive property in Derbyshire when, during the first week of March, England learned that Napoleon Bonaparte had finally made good on one of several attempts to escape his confinement on the island of Elba. He landed in the south of France and made his way north, gathering troops as he went.

This event, of course, interrupted the marriage of Lord Jacob and Lady Henrietta for what turned out to be Napoleon's famous "One Hundred Days" before his defeat in mid-June at a tiny Belgium village called Waterloo. This time, the allies were less generous in their treatment of the deposed dictator, and he was consigned to the much less opulent island of St. Helena where he was allowed a far more restricted entourage.

In the interim, the bride was invited to move into Holbrook House, which she did for a time where her new in-laws tried to assuage her worries over her husband's being in serious danger. They entertained her with stories of his childhood and youth and she became quite close to his sister Elizabeth and his sister-in-law, the Marchioness of Burwell. She warmed to his father who proved less austere than she had expected; in fact, he reminded her very much of her dear Uncle Alfred. During this time, too, she paid a prolonged visit to Cornwall to spend time with her friend Hero and with Harriet, who had also journeyed to Cornwall for their impromptu reunion.

Over four months after their wedding ceremony, Lord Jacob and Lady Henrietta were at last able to move to Derbyshire. They were accompanied by another set of newlyweds: Lady Henrietta's maid Annie was now the wife of Lord Jacob's valet, the newly promoted former footman Baker.

Privately, Jake and Retta felt that their marriage really began in early July when the major was finally able to return to his bride, but they could not make a public declaration to that effect. Since their eldest son had clearly been conceived in February, it was deemed a not very practical idea.

Meet the Author

Wilma Counts devotes her time largely to writing and reading. She loves to cook, but hates cleaning house. She has never lost her interest in literature, history, and international relations. She spends a fair amount of time yelling at the T.V. She is an active member of Lone Mountain Writers in Carson City, Nevada.

Readers can visit her website at www.wilmacounts.com.

Printed in the United States
by Baker & Taylor Publisher Services